AND FOR MY NEXT ACT...:
ALY'S RETURN

And for My Next Act....:

ALY'S RETURN

WHOEVER CONTROLS THE MUSIC,
CONTROLS THE WORLD.

GODDESS A. BROUETTE

And for My Next Act…: Aly's Return

Cover Design: Rena Violet Design
Editing: Enchanted Ink Publishing
Formatting: Rena Violet Design

ISBN: 978-1-7374147-8-0

Thank you for your support of the author's rights.

Printed in the United States of America

*For the feral eldest daughters, you're worthy of all the love
in the world.*

*And for the hispanic/latinx community that always embraced me,
thank you.*

Dear Reader,

When crafting these books I focus on letting my characters write their own story– no matter how flawed they might be. Due to this, I tend to write darker stories that some may find disturbing or uncomfortable. None of the relationships or scenarios in any of my books are meant to be romanticized or glorified. If this is not something you can handle, please do not proceed.

Aly's Return contains content that may be troubling to some readers, including, but not limited to, strong language, sexual themes, coping with abuse of all kinds, death, substance abuse, childhood trauma, robberies/attacks, and PTSD. Please be mindful of these and the heavy topics that will be discussed within And for My Next Act…: Aly's Return and other books in the Dark Fame Saga.

And for My Next Act…: Aly's Return is a Dark Hollywood STANDALONE and can be read completely without reading any of Arlissa's Stories. Additionally, a "fairytale" version of Aly's view of previous events is provided at the beginning of this book. However, since it takes place five years after the first two books, it does spoil the turnout of major events.

SPANISH DICTIONARY PAGE
WORDS USED IN ALY'S RETURN:

Sucia - Dirty

Adios - Bye

Amor - Love

Perfecto - Perfect

Ay dios mio - Oh my god

Si - Yes

Vamos - Let's go

Mija - My daughter or sweetheart/dear

Chancla - A flip flop/slipper

Abuelas - Grandmas

Mi reina - My princess

Bruja - Witch

Hermana - Sister

Cállate la boca - Shut up/shut your mouth

Mi casa, su casa - My house, your house

Mierda - Shit

Feliz Navidad - Merry Christmas

Mi cielo - My darling

Pendejo - A stupid person, an idiot

Que? - What?

ALY'S ALBUM TRACKLIST:

The Fame Vampire

intro (die for you)

angel/devil

castle

immortal ft. saint

no tears

eternally yours

fairytales

little less of us

never have i ever

the fame vampire

to the moon and back ft. taurus

haunted

outro (alone)

DELUXE

immortal (solo acoustic)

the fame vampire demo

un día

Once Upon a Time . . . *There was a peasant girl who wasn't allowed to speak or cry. Created out of lust and disaster, she embodied Catholic sin and impolite choices. Her mother cursed her pregnant belly with words of hate and disgust—performing acts to get rid of the child so sinister that if God himself saw, he would punish her with the fury of a thousand suns.*

The evil mother wanted nothing more than to be a queen herself, but like karma had intended, she spent her days and nights serving the village people and cursing the women who ate better than her, slept on better silk than her, and attracted wealthy men from all across the land. The birth of the bastard she hated so greatly could only be compared to the bloody delivery of Satan himself.

Her name was Lilith.

And from the moment she was born, the hate in the evil mother's heart only grew. She despised what she had created, never showing an ounce of affection toward Lilith and letting her belly go empty until her cries became unbearable. From a tender age, she learned to beg at strangers' feet for food, water, and a bath. Yet it was through the village that she was taught the way of the world. And as she lay in bed at night—weeping silently so that her mother wouldn't whip her for making too much noise—her heart yearned to be a part of the world she was told about at the top of the hill.

Every night she saw a great big castle outside her window. It loomed over her tiny village like it was mocking her. Or like it was beckoning her to come forth. But Lilith knew her childlike wonder could only take her so far.

"The king and queen live there," some would say.

"It'd take us three days on horseback to even lick the gold on the gates," others would chime in.

As she grew, she filled her head with paintings and writings about a world more dazzling than the one she experienced. A world where she'd never know famine and could meet princes at balls who would tell her that she was the most beautiful maiden in all the lands. But paintings and writings didn't quench the thirst bubbling deep inside of her.

She woke up one day and slipped away with the sounds of church bells while the choir's hymns that played outside her window held her like a warm hug. Beautiful rhythms filled the void like hot cement in her heart, and the voice her evil mother had tried so desperately to hide had been found.

By the time she was of menstrual age, the girl who never spoke began to whisper.

Naturally, she did grow up to be beautiful, and she told her only friend that one day she'd take on a soldier or, if she was lucky, a prince would rescue her from her rotting cottage. They'd live happily ever after in that castle on the hill where no one would ever know that they were once two girls from the village. And that day did come.

Lilith, who had spent hours on end singing in the forest, stumbled upon a manor hidden in the trees. The manor was haunting, with shadows looming over it, but its glamor called to her. Eagerly, she ran to fetch her friend, and upon her return an old witch greeted them and offered to make her wildest dreams come true.

"You have a beautiful voice, my darling. I often hear you in the woods. I tell you what, you'll never get another chance like this. No, no. You won't. And your face . . . You're as beautiful as the transition between autumn and winter," the witch whispered as her pointy fingernails grazed against Lilith's wounded flesh. "Your mother hurts you." She added, "I could make it so you never see her again."

"I want to live at the castle on the hilltop," Lilith demanded. "I want to be royal."

"Are you sure, my dear?"

"I don't know about this," her friend objected in a low tone, only to be ignored.

Lilith looked down at her ragged gown and tangled hair. Dirt lived under her fingernails, and bruises covered her arms. It was no way for a queen to live, and she would do whatever it took to claim what she knew in her heart was rightfully hers. What she had dreamed of her entire childhood.

And when the witch granted her wish, with a potion and a song, the last step was a contract for Lilith to sign.

"Remember, if you try to go back on our deal, you're mine," was all the witch said while Lilith eagerly signed the dotted line with cherry-wine blood from her palms.

Suddenly, darkness engulfed both girls, and the manor revealed itself as an old cottage made of rotten wood. She lay in the center of the forest with freshly combed hair braided neatly and a bright blue gown made of fabrics she had never touched before living in the village. Her friend lay next to her in bright yellow with curly brown hair down to her back. And like an invisible clock had struck twelve, two princes appeared. One hopped off of his horse and put out his hand. She couldn't believe it, no. She didn't believe it. However, when the castle gates creaked open for them, she knew her wish had come true.

Lilith quickly became The Princess. But she still craved to be The Queen.

She and her friend drank the finest wine and dined in the castle day in and day out. They slept on only the best silk and held polite conversations with the highest members of the court. Lilith played the finest of pianos and sang for her prince day and night. Yet she had been strummed, primed, and silenced once again. She lived a life similar to the one of roses, only grown to be admired and eventually plucked.

It wasn't her mother's arm that grabbed her this time, but instead, it was one from a man, whom she thought was the one of her dreams.

The girls became objects to vile and violent men who were untouchable. They had royal blood, something Lilith had lacked when she cut her flesh open to sign that contract.

She quickly learned that if she couldn't keep the prince's bed warm and provide him with an heir, she'd be deemed useless. The complex being that she had become was ground down to dust and reduced to a woman in a gown—put on display for her husband's and townspeople's entertainment. The freedom she craved from the village was an evil double-edged sword because there was no freedom in being royal at all. It was the same cage, except this one was made of diamonds.

"Something awful has happened," Lilith found herself whispering to the stars. "I feel as though my heart is turning more black than red with every day that I'm here. My emotions that were once so complex have been simplified to . . . rage."

On one faithless night, she was awoken by screams, and the town crier wasted not a second to tell the world that the eldest prince had been murdered. Everyone knew the girls were unhappy—rumors were traveling from the hill to the villages beneath them. Her friend had killed the beloved crown prince. And Lilith would be forced to watch her only friend hang for her crimes.

And so, Lilith did what she did best. She used her voice—she screamed and leaned on the other friends that she had made during her time in The Castle. She put on her finest jewels and gowns and ran amok in the village for all to hear and view. Lilith became a demon *in her own right, tormenting the town for blaming her for the actions of those she couldn't control until the prince dragged her by her hair into their quarters and demanded she learn about respect, image, and the value of silence. He then beat her until black and blue danced across her skin.*

She was once again shamed. A stain on the kingdom and everyone around her. The townspeople gawked when she walked by, and the servants began to ignore her requests. It wasn't long before she realized that her exile would soon come.

"Demon!"

"Blood sucker!"

"Murderer!

"You brought her into our kingdom!"

"Chaos follows where she goes!"

"Hang her! Hang the witch!"

She would not go quietly and not without the kingdom she knew belonged to her.

On her last night, Lilith waited until the prince had fallen asleep and prayed to the witch to save her. Despite the kingdom turning on her, she didn't want to lose all that it had given her. Desiring royalty was all she knew.

She could fix this if only she had more power.

After several hours, once her knees were sore, she chose to accept her fate. Lilith decided she would rather die than be a peasant girl ever again.

Near morning, in the midst of her dreams, a gust of wind sent a chill across her naked body. Her heart, which was once beating, had stilled, and she opened her eyes to see a figure looming over her. "What's happening to me?" was what she mouthed, but no words came out. The hooded figure placed a finger over her lips, and the blood in her veins began to go cold. Her gums ached, and her teeth moved—making room for two sets of fangs. Her nails grew, and every bruise on her body had vanished into thin air.

She screamed in agony, but not a sound came out.

"Kill him. Kill them all," a voice had whispered, yet the figure was gone.

It is said that Lilith committed mass murder that night, but it seemed impossible that such a small woman could take down a whole kingdom in such a gruesome manner. Blood dripped down the walls, and organs decorated the furniture. Body parts were found strewn across the courtyard, and teeth were thrown into the moat.

In the end, there was no king, queen, prince, or servants. There was only her, alone in the castle on the top of the hill.

Lilith became immortal. She wasn't just a vampire, she was a tortured god. Despite her power, she remained hidden in the shadows out of fear of being exiled again. Until one day, she was called to rise again.

—The Story of Lilith by Alejandra L. Garcia.

THE FIRST ACT

*I never believed in gods or divine entities. Not until
I sold my soul to the devil and became one.*

CHAPTER ONE

Blood dripped past my collarbone and dribbled like a stream between my breasts.

The belt was warmed on the stove for eons before my mother would wield it against me. Using it to hit the back of my neck, my head, my spine. But I didn't flinch; that just made it worse.

She screamed insults at me—*sucia*, worthless, lazy, stupid. It repeated until I was either covered in blood or tears. On the worst nights, it was both. On the best nights, I was awoken by a sweet melody that I could never trace. Time and time again, music saved me. Luckily, this was one of those nights.

I woke in a cold sweat, my heart thudding, disoriented. I placed a hand in the center of my chest, trying to calm myself. However, I knew the feeling of panic all too well.

Blinking into the pitch-black darkness, I made out the ivory furniture an interior decorator had insisted on seasons ago. From the vanity to the crystal chandelier, the shaggy rug, and the potted plants. A wave of irritation swept through me. I had chosen none of it, yet my credit card statement crowned me the proud owner.

Once I gathered my senses, I turned to my left, and the events of the night came rushing back to me through the lingering hints of my intoxication.

Deep, roaring snores reminded me that I hadn't arrived at The Castle alone. He was curled up and comfortable. Disgusting, really.

He came up to me—I think. No.

Memories of the house party appeared in flashes. It was only supposed to be a couple drinks. At least, that's what I remember telling my cousin when I agreed to join her for her co-star's birthday party.

Yet all I could remember thinking was, *I saw him on a billboard once, I think. No, I know. I could remember those green eyes anywhere.*

I had danced in circles until I *accidentally* bumped into the muscled man and watched as my friends shook their heads and laughed while I whined against him. He said his pleasantries, complimented my music, and tried to persuade me to leave right then and there. I giggled and fluttered my eyelashes like the damsel he wanted me to be, but little did he know I had chosen him first.

I slipped out of the bed and reached over to tap him on the shoulder. I tapped him again . . . And then again. And when that didn't work, I swatted him so hard that I tried to peek through the darkness to see if I left a handprint on his unclothed shoulder.

The large man jolted up with a start, clenching his muscles and balling up his fist before fully opening his eyes.

"What the fuck?"

Oh. An Egyptian accent? Almost forgot about that.

I went to retrieve my robe off of the vanity chair and tied it around my exposed body. No one slept in my fucking bed but me. Not since my divorce. So, every man who found himself here because I was too drunk to remember my boundaries over some dick? They got kicked out in the middle of the night.

"You can go now."

His half-asleep gaze darted to me, and he frowned. "Seriously?"

I jumped at him, rolling my eyes at the stupidity of the question. "Duh. Goodbye! Car services run through here without an issue. You should have no problem getting home."

"What happened to good mornings?" he asked in a stern voice as he gathered his clothes.

I deadpanned.

"You don't remember my name, do you?"

I shrugged.

The stranger scoffed, "Mena—Mena Sheik. Nice to meet you."

"Okay, well, thanks for reminding me." I walked over to my bedroom door and pointed to it. "*Adios*, Mena."

I didn't bother flicking on the lights as the man, who had to be carved out of stone and hand-delivered to my bed by God himself, cursed my name under his breath and walked into the hall. He knew better than to do it in front of my face, but I followed him down the stairs and whispered a false apology while watching him pout in my grandiose foyer.

God, he was fucking beautiful.

But the longer he lingered in my space, the more dread I felt.

He paused on the way to the black Jeep that had arrived to pick him up. The moonlight reflected off of his one-too-many rings and the acres of land that put miles between my nearest neighbor and me. Thank God there was no fucking paparazzi.

"Congrats on the Starlight nomination by the way. And the number one album." He snickered.

"Toodles!" I shouted as he crouched down to get into the vehicle.

But I couldn't hide it . . . I was smiling.

Fuck it, it was nice to hear.

The front door slammed shut behind me, causing a roaring thunder to travel throughout The Castle.

Just like that . . .

It was only me again.

The way it had to be.

There wasn't a single piece of furniture in The Castle that made the place look lived-in. The off-white couches were surrounded by a marble coffee table, a TV hung onto the wall, and there it was! Another fucking shag area rug.

It felt like a rental. But if I'm being honest, the only places I'd ever called home were the dreamhouses I created in Barbie Land. And, as I got older, the cathedrals I dreamt up in my mind. But never anywhere I'd actually rested my head—no. Never there.

On my way back up the stairs, I swiped an open bottle of cognac off the bar and tried to avoid the way my skin crawled every time I thought about the godforsaken nightmares that continued to wake me up despite the alcohol-fueled comas I put myself in.

My feet carried me to the bathroom, where the door was locked and the space was small enough to keep my eye on every square inch at once.

That control eased my beating heart—a learned tactic from childhood that always worked.

My journey to the bathroom was different now at twenty-five than it was when I was thirteen. The soles of my feet didn't sting with every step, and I didn't hold my breath before turning on the light and revealing my wounds to the mirror. Yet I felt as lonely now as I did then.

No amount of guys warming my bed would change that.

I finally did it, though. I finally got my number one album and my Starlight nomination for Song of the Year. It should have been Album of the Year—*The Fame Vampire* was a perfect work of art and a flawless representation of what it takes to win in the music industry.

I took the stories I had written in my head, documenting my past and rewriting it so that I was more than a fading pop star—I was a vampire queen who'd kill to keep her crown. A concept was created through my own romanticized history, and an album was birthed with visuals, scavenger hunts, and outfits that brought it all to life. *The Fame Vampire* was, without a doubt, album of the fucking year.

Whatever. I'd have to put that on my vision board for next year.

The Starlight Awards were presented by the most important names in music and had remained the most prestigious and notable award a musician could receive since the sixties. If an artist had a Starlight to their name, they weren't going anywhere.

That was a fact.

Nonetheless, after leaving a trail of PR terrors behind me—I did it. The last few years had felt like digging myself out of my own grave, but . . .

I did.

After being dropped from my fuck-ass ex-label and blackballed from radio, I tried to keep releasing and recording music. I tried to make my flesh as solid as concrete when the tabloids screamed in my face and the paparazzi did everything except trample me down right outside of my favorite Pilates studio.

Yet they still managed to crack my exterior.

Simultaneously, I became a puppet paid by the fans I had left to sing! Dance! Entertain!

The circumstances were minute to them—I had to keep producing their favorite product regardless of whatever the hell was going on behind closed doors.

Deep breaths, Alejandra.

So, if no one was going to listen to what I created . . .

Then I would take it away.

I took a year off. It was never my intention to be gone that long, but soon enough, not knowing how to feel turned into crying without warning. And when I could dream, I dreamt of someday remembering how to be happy. It was something I waited for, really. Being able to enjoy what I was made for once again and forevermore.

Like a real-life fairy godmother, my new manager, Nova, found me in a rental in Miami and told me she had a plan. All I had to do was put all my scars in the music and not be afraid to face them. The agony, the torture, the bullying, the losses—each of them had a place in the music. Despite what people were printing or typing—melodies pumped through my blood, and when I needed to, I spoke in poetry that could be emphasized by guitar strums. I was the embodiment of music.

So, *The Fame Vampire* was born.

I didn't bother turning on the lights in the bathroom when I entered. Instead, I took a deep breath and slid down the wall onto the ice-cold floor. The door remained cracked, and through the darkness, Solo entered the bathroom, her tiny paws padding on the floor.

She couldn't have been more than four pounds, and unlike everything else in The Castle, I could see her orange-and-black coat without straining my eyes—as if the kitten was glowing.

I put my bottle down and sprawled across the tiles to push the door shut and pull a throw blanket out from under the sink. It grounded me, reminded me that I was still here, and muffled the phantom banging I would hear when drifting off to sleep. I couldn't explain why my mother was haunting my sleeping state during the most prominent time in my career . . .

But she was.

And I didn't know how to get rid of her. I didn't know how to get rid of any of the monsters in my head other than writing fictional stories where I defeat them.

Crawling into the bathtub, I wrapped the blanket around me to distract from the frigid acrylic. Solo found herself in my lap, and I rubbed her small body until I was dozing off. The longer I was safely stored away, the more my brain calmed.

There was no longer anything to be afraid of; I was behind a door that locked.

CHAPTER TWO

"A LL RIGHT, DID WE get enough shots with the cigarette?" Nova asked the photographer, who seemed to be more into the camera than the subject of the photos: me.

She could sense my irritation before I did. Sometimes I wondered if she was tethered to me like she was with her actual daughters.

"Wonderful question," I muttered with the stick in between my teeth.

The sun was beginning to cook me through the French doors in my living room that doubled as our set today. The furniture had been moved out of the way to make room for a black backdrop and a single chair, which acted as my prop. The main attraction was the heavy brown fur coat I had on with nothing underneath. I was suffocating, but remained graceful and posed despite the sweat developing under my breast as my assistant hurried over to relight the flame of the cigarette without even being asked.

"Just one more . . ." the photographer mumbled as he crouched down to look through the lens.

Click! The flash bounced off of my sunglasses.

"There. That's the shot." He released his tight grip on the camera and took a deep breath before showing the photos to Nova, whispering about which one should be retouched and offered as one of the many deluxe vinyl editions of *The Fame Vampire*.

"Your robe," the set assistant whispered in a sweet tone as she helped me wiggle out of that heavy coat and into a plush purple robe before the entire room could catch their millionth glance of my bare body—the only items covering me were nude pasties and a black thong with a crystal heart on the back.

"Wrap set, guys!" the photographer yelled, his eyes still glued to the camera as his meaty fingers pressed the buttons with excitement. The crew members he brought along with him began to appear from different corners of my house. Some had gone outside to smoke. Others, like my team and friends, had found places to sit still and remain out of the way.

"I'll be taking this," Yessenia said as she snatched the lit cigarette from in between my teeth, pushing crew members out of the way in the process. "I told you, those are bad for you."

"Mmm, but they're so damn good," I said jokingly through a signature pout.

"Yeah, if you're trying to make sure you die before the rest of us," Yessenia muttered as she found a passerby to hand the cancer stick off to.

Savannah appeared in front of me as well. "I don't know, that's kind of on brand for her. The showstopper being the first out of the friend group to have a celebration of life in her honor. How else would she make sure we're all in attendance?"

I rolled my eyes and smirked. "Haven't you all heard? I'm immortal."

I parted through the blonde and the brunette, not even checking to see if they were following me up the grandiose staircase away from all the noise and chaos.

No one said a word as we passed a set of closed doors and entered the primary bedroom. I took a seat at my vanity, but not before taking a second glance to ensure that there was no trace of last night in sight.

Bed made? Check. Solo sleeping soundly against the pillows? Double check. Alcohol tucked away? Triple check.

I began to pull out my makeup remover and cotton pads, only catching the girls taking seats on my bed from the reflection in the mirror. Yessenia always sat down gently to avoid drawing attention to her weight. I thought she was beautiful, but she argued that, as her cousin, I was conditioned to adore her love handles, curves, and chubby cheeks. But I always told her to cut that shit out because she was on a hit TV show, and there were millions of people who had the same opinion as me. She was stunning and believed in herself more at nine than I did at nineteen.

Savannah inhaled and leaned against the upholstered bed frame, causing the top button of her matching purple lounge set to pop. I tried to ignore it, but it was nearly impossible.

Could anyone blame me? She was stunning beyond comparison.

The way her green eyes twinkled when she laughed and how her blonde hair fell perfectly past her shoulders—it wasn't a huge fucking shock that she kept a roof over her son's head by posing for high-end magazines and fashion campaigns. But I'm sure having an F1 driver as a baby daddy also helped.

Despite not being together, Jonah and Savannah were Hollywood's favorite family, complete with Stefan Elijah Allistar as the heir to whatever fortune Jonah's family had.

Was it normal to have a small crush on everyone you meet?

"Nervous about your first interview?" Savannah asked sincerely.

She wasn't the friend I asked for, but she was the one I needed.

I shook my head and began to wipe the red off of my lips with the soaking wet pad.

"I just want it to go right," I whispered weakly, casting my focus on my reflection.

"We'll be there . . . I swear, I cleared my schedule. Right, Yessie?"

Yessenia nodded even though her eyes were focused on her phone.

Savannah continued, "And Saint might be late like he is at this very moment but . . . We'll all be there. Nothing will go wrong. You aced your media training, right?"

"Mm-hmm. It went fine." I sucked my teeth. "I miss my cigarette."

Yessenia was now propped up on her elbow and staring a hole through the back of my head. "Aly. You made a great fucking album. A number one album at that. The entire summer was about you. This. An interview where you have the chance to tell your side of it is what was missing. You have a Starlight nomination, for Christ's sake."

My chest jolted in response to a burning shock coming from my lips. I had been rubbing the pad against the tender skin for so long it was beginning to get irritated.

"Yes. Song of the Year, but I'm against a bunch of newbies who shouldn't even touch the damn category." The bass in my voice caused a sudden silence, and they looked at me with worry in their eyes. I put my hands down onto the vanity, ignoring the red that had stained my fingertips. "Sorry . . ."

"It's always hard coming back," Savannah adds in a hushed whisper, obviously speaking from experience.

I swatted the air. "No, no. I'll be fine and it'll be fucking great, cool? Everyone's gonna love it—" A lump in my throat got pushed down. "And me. They'll love me. Or they'll twist everything I say and it'll make headlines for weeks." I shrugged. "Guess we'll see."

The women didn't say anything immediately, but I could tell by the looks on their faces and the avoidance of eye contact that they knew I was right.

I bit the inside of my lip, practically begging them to speak while I returned my attention to ripping off my fake lashes. "You guys are right. It's been fine for months. An interview shouldn't change that. I—I have you guys and Saint if he would fucking get here and—and I can handle it. Whatever comes at me . . . I can handle it."

"Is Taurus going to be there?" Yessenia whispered.

Right. How could I have forgotten?

My breath caught in my throat, but I swallowed it down. "Yup." I tossed my dark hair behind my shoulder. "I think I've gotten pretty good at pretending to be in love, don't ya think?"

"Ugh, at least he's not hard to pretend to like," Yessenia so politely reminded me. "If you ever want to get me anything for Christmas, him packaged at my front door works just fine."

Taurus Fucking Sawyer.

When my manager and publicist conjured up this *faux romance*, best believe I threw a damn fit. Me? Needing some fake relationship with a man who was more accomplished and idolized than me? It was a slap in the fucking face.

"Sure, Yessenia. If you want a cocky asshole who thinks everything he's ever released since he was twelve sounds like sex coming out of the stereo."

"Eh, not everything," Savannah chimed in. "He did do that kids' movie Jonah loves."

"The one that made billions of dollars," Yessenia *oh-so-helpfully* adds.

I huffed and spun my vanity seat around to face them. "When the contract ends, I will gladly let you two have at him. Until then, him and his stupid ass outfits are my problem because I, for one, can't afford to get dropped from another label."

So, for once in my life, I put a sock in it. And Aly and Taurus became a part of the plan. We debuted right before the summer and then I released "No Tears," strategically calling paparazzi to catch us in matching denim on Rodeo Drive, walking hand in hand.

From that day on, our love story was created, packaged, and sold.

"Honey, I'm home!" Saint's voice rang through the spacious halls, bouncing off of every dustless corner as he burst through my bedroom door. My eyes lit up, and so did everyone else's—especially Savannah's.

I watched the way her smile reached from ear to ear and how she completely turned her body on the bed to face him. I often wondered if she realized she was doing it—if she knew how obvious it was that she drooled over our best friend.

"Jesus, they're loud as shit down there, aren't they? Sorry I missed the shoot, *amor*." He kissed my forehead and went to do the same to the girls.

Saint was a tricky one with his perfectly sculpted body and thick Portuguese accent. Whenever anyone first laid eyes on him, they'd immediately notice he was gifted with three things—a beautiful face, moss-colored eyes that made you feel like you were the only one in the room, and a fire inside of him that no one dared to put out.

When we first met, he was smoking outside of a Prada event in a black dress with black fingernails to match. Some people snarled at him, others stopped to take pictures, but he looked so fucking good with his unbothered demeanor.

Like everyone else, I had heard of him. He was the child actor who moved to the United States and started a singing career, only to branch off into every other business known to man while his records flew off the shelves with little to no promotion.

I had only come outside because of how bored I was faking conversations while Nova networked. He asked if I wanted to take a hit and then lured me into a debate over Coke versus Pepsi. Even though the topic was nonsensical, I was hooked with every word that he was saying. Somehow the topic went from carbonated beverages to music, and the man who hadn't released a song in years told me he had a melody in his head that he knew I'd love. So, I took his word for it and "Immortal" was born, our first duet and the fourth track on my album.

He inspired me.

That's why I made him my best friend. A way of making him mine, I suppose.

"Look who finally showed up!" Yessenia exclaimed as her eyes darted between us. "How was the uh . . ."

Savannah interrupted, "Meeting for *Epifania*."

It was no surprise that Savannah, who was his first model for the fashion brand, remembered the name without hesitation.

The kiss on Savannah's head lingered before he took his seat next to her, naturally. "Perfect. I was in and I was out. But what'd I miss?"

"We were just talking about the interview with Kurt Cummings tomorrow. And ya know, how Taurus is gonna be there," Yessenia replied before anyone else could. Her cheeks always turned a bright pink whenever she talked about topics that excited her, even when we were kids.

"*Ay dios mio* . . ." I moaned before returning to aggressively wiping the eyeliner off of my lids.

"You got this." Saint cut through my obvious annoyance.

"Thanks."

"Just—be careful."

Everyone glared in his direction.

"Why—why would you say that?" Savannah asked, and the grin on her face told me she thought the caution was silly. And honestly, so did I.

"Yeah, what the hell?" I chimed in.

Yessenia only laughed, and Saint quickly joined her.

"Forgive me, I'm exhausted." He hid his smile with his palm before raising his head again. "I meant, have a great show. It'll be amazing. Even though . . . we still have yet to do our song live, but I'll let it go for now."

I rolled my eyes. "You mean those brutal-ass notes? Do you want me to embarrass myself and voice crack on stage?"

"Backtracks exist!" he teased as a roar of laughter erupted from my friends.

He was right, though. It was going to be amazing.

The plan was simple and had been since the start of my "gothic vampire era." Every time I stepped outside, my eyeliner was drawn on sharp and thick and my raven-colored hair would remain long and straight. I would be clothed in leather from head to toe on most days, and when I needed to make a statement, the fashion piece of choice would be daring and revealing. Perhaps something from an archive.

I had to become this unattainable thing that not even my die-hard fans could grasp.

That was the plan.

We managed to bypass the tension surrounding the interview and clink glasses filled to the brim with red wine once Nova let us know that the crew had vacated The Castle. I watched as they smiled and laughed, eating various cheeses and popping grapes in their mouths like candy that Savannah had scavenged from my kitchen. We talked about who was doing who and our nightlife plans after my interview.

Everything moved in slow motion, and for a moment, I got a taste of what my future looked like.

My chosen family cleared out within the next few hours to prepare for our respective responsibilities. And once the dust settled and the last goodbye was sung, The Castle became my prison again.

I quietly peeled the glass doors to my patio apart and slipped through the space. My bare feet met the cobblestone that had already been cooled by the moonlight. There was a breeze, but it wrapped me up like a hug from a friend rather than shoulder-checking me like an enemy.

After a few more silent steps past the low hedges and rose bushes, I made it to the pool and took a seat. The fabric of my robe gained in weight as my legs fluttered in the water. There wasn't a trace of anyone despite all that had taken place. Hell, if I was gone, there wouldn't even be a trace of me.

And maybe that was the point.

My phone buzzed in the fuzzy pocket. I pulled it out, and the text glowed on the screen.

Nova:

They want to pull 10% of your budget for Bianca Veer's rollout. They won't keep funding a full Starlight campaign unless they start seeing more return.

CHAPTER THREE

N OVA'S TEXT LIVED RENT-FREE in my mind through hair, makeup, and wardrobe the following day. It wasn't her fault, I knew that. And if I could rethink signing with Locke and Key, I would. Ever since they signed their South African pop princess, Bianca Veer, I had been fighting tooth and nail to remind them why they took me on in the first place.

She was golden brown, platinum blonde, and scandal-free. So, basically everything I wasn't.

And after a long pep talk, which mainly consisted of me bitching and moaning about being up against a newbie in the first fucking place, I knew Nova was right about one thing: I didn't have the luxury to be sad.

Kurt Cummings had asked me to come on his show, even though I always assumed I wasn't big enough for a Saturday slot on a late-night talk show—until now.

So, I kept my mouth shut as they tossed my hair into an eighties Hollywood updo and squeezed my small frame into compression tights and a leather off-the-shoulder mini dress. It was go time. And if I wanted to keep the rest of my budget, I had to remember that.

I stood behind a navy-blue curtain and took a few deep breaths. There was never a need to be nervous.

Not when you're the star.

"Please welcome to the stage, Aly."

The crowd cheered as the curtains pulled apart, and I immediately began walking along the stage, waving to the audience. I had my path memorized and didn't need to look anywhere except the cameras and the crowd. My dark-brown-painted lips puckered, and I used my last few steps before sitting down to blow the audience a few kisses.

I adjusted myself quickly on the cushioned chair next to his desk. There was a microphone, a view of San Francisco behind us, the audience in front of us, and my original vinyl propped up in front of him. I utilized my siren eyes and flashed him a sultry smile. "Kurt, hi."

The older man with salt-and-pepper hair chuckled. "Welcome to the show!"

The audience cheered along with him.

"Man, we've got to get into this album." He caressed the cover, which was white and red with a headshot of me, teased blonde hair, and the words *The Fame Vampire* written at the top. I wore a red strapless dress, but only the bust was visible, and an emerald choker to pay homage to the Mexican flag. My fake fangs and two markings on my neck told the story that I had written and placed in the album booklet, the story of Lilith. "I mean, what a comeback, seriously." He then pulled out the record, which had the image of an old gothic house on it. "I love this, by the way."

"Thank you. It was shot by a friend of mine, actually."

"Really?"

My energy was no match for his. Despite being well into his fifties, Kurt was known for energetic interviews while I always came off as a calmer presence until unraveled. At least, that's what the tabloids happened to say.

He set the record down on the desk. "You look amazing."

"You look amazing!" I exclaimed, pointing to his black suit and freshly trimmed scruff.

"Uh, we have to talk about this because last month you added a Starlight nomination to your credentials."

I forced a smile but kept my eye contact sweet and alluring. "It's insane, isn't it?"

"It's amazing. Song of the Year, and you know what? You deserve it. I heard your song on the radio for months. My kids love it, my partner loves it."

"Thank you. It blows my mind every day," I managed to chime in before he started talking again. "Like how are we here right now?" A question topped with a laugh so no one read too much into it.

"You're Aly, that's how."

"Stop. Stop."

"No, you are."

My cheeks flushed but I kept it together as I watched him pick up the album again.

"So, you did something very cool. Rumor has it that *The Fame Vampire* as a title and the title track came from a very interesting place. Let's talk about it."

"Yeah . . ." I had been trained on this, and I knew what to say. But what they approved wasn't exactly my truth. "You know—I think everyone knows I didn't intend to make an album. Like, when I dragged myself into that studio, it was not my goal at all. It was really funny, actually. But I was at an all-time low, and there were comments flooding my mentions on every single platform just saying the worst shit—can I?"

Shit.

"You're fine, you're fine."

"Okay, thank you. So, something I saw a lot . . . was 'oh no she's a fame vampire.' Or a bloodsucker, or something of that nature. And while I was processing everything that I was enduring, that phrase just stuck. But not in a way that hurt . . . I think. In a way where I was like okay, let me play with this idea. It became a truth I was willing to carry, a sandbox I wanted to play in. So, I cast everyone in that world. There were princes, servants, and . . . me."

He didn't lose eye contact with me for a single second, and with every syllable that left my mouth he nodded as if he understood.

"How did it feel to record from the perspective of someone who was essentially playing a character?"

"I was confused initially," I began. And the more I focused on his eyes, the easier it was to forget that there were cameras and a studio audience. "As you've heard, I'm sure, *The Fame Vampire* in itself is different from what I've done before. It's not the pop sound people were expecting, but I'm older now. I've experienced new things, and I think the blunt personal lyrics mixed with the imagistic undertone of the project was the only way to get that very dramatic but real point across. Once I understood what I was making and I was in the studio and working with the producers . . . It felt like I was telling the story in the right way."

Kurt folded his hands in front of him. "Were you nervous about how people would react?" His energy was calmer now, and for once, I felt like someone was actually listening.

I scoffed. "That, admittedly, was the scariest part. Before this summer, I had given the world so much space and time to decide what I'd come back like. To be fair, I did need that break, but the more time I was away, the more room I made for theories and questions." I could feel Nova wincing out of fear that my words would be misconstrued, but I didn't care. "Will I be skinnier? Thicker? Will my hair be red or cut short? Would I even still make music or launch a makeup brand? That . . . that's the scary part. Because when I was about to put "No Tears" out, I saw the theories, and most of them were wrong. So, I was like, wow . . . I'm going to disappoint everyone."

"But you didn't," he whispered.

My lips pursed, and I shook my head. "No. And that feels really good."

Kurt jumped up, and like someone had flipped a switch, his energy was back on ten, and my vinyl was once again in his hands. "Let's talk about the track list, then. I am specifically interested in the 'intro (die for you),' and the 'outro (alone).' What story are you trying to tell here?"

"Oh boy!" My heart skipped several beats, but I laughed until I could conjure up something to say under these studio lights. "This is my first truly vulnerable record. When I wrote the intro, I was in Miami at the time, which makes it the oldest song on the album." I felt my throat begin to close, but I couldn't let my nerves take the interview from me.

"I kept revisiting it, and it kept meaning different things to me until it became what it is now. I was ready to die for love and admiration."

Maybe I still was.

"Naturally, you still hear that nineteen-year-old girl who was just starting out until you get to the outro, and she's gone, but so is everyone else. And I think the outro wraps up perfectly where I was when I finished the album, too. I felt isolated, unheard, unwelcome. You kind of go through two extremes—from doing anything for love to wishing love never stepped foot on your doorstep ever again."

"Wow. Just wow. Amazing. So, I assume the relationship came after this feeling of isolation, then?"

I froze. My muscles clenched and my mouth became dry. Under the heat of the studio lights, I couldn't remember if I was supposed to be dating Taurus while the album was being created or not. The lies woven together to create the fake relationship and my actual reality had found themselves entangled in my brain.

I pursed my lips together and forced them to form a soft smile. "I don't think all my problems were fixed the day I got into a new relationship, and that's okay! He wasn't brought into my life to fix anything, but as time went on, I-I found that my heart was healing."

Kurt gushed at my save and so did the audience, but I knew what was coming next. Or at least I thought I did. "So, 'To the Moon and Back' featuring Taurus is quite the declaration."

I smiled . . . Hard. "It is. It is."

"He also helped produce, which you can hear from those signature thick piano layers . . . But the song itself sounds like a blend of both of you. Your music has an edginess that doesn't hide, but also a reggaeton influence, and somehow . . . Somehow you created a ballad. Now, I would ask you how that happened, but I actually have a surprise for you." His gaze shifted toward the curtain again, and I kept my pageant smile on, but on the inside, I was begging for it to be anyone other than Taurus who stepped through that curtain.

However, when the women in the crowd began cheering louder than anyone else and a six-foot-five shadow appeared, hovering over my figure, I was forced to look up at the man smiling down at me. If this were a cartoon, there would be steam coming out of my ears.

My moment.

My interview . . . And they called the bigger artist in.

Great.

I quickly reminded myself that Taurus was supposed to be my man and widened my smile as he bent down to kiss me on the forehead.

Taurus looked like success personified. He had golden-brown skin and kept his facial hair clean cut or minimal. His usual coils were braided straight back tonight, but the sides were still shaved off. And he had on a pair of sunglasses that looked like they were straight out of *The Matrix*, but they paired perfectly with the one . . . two . . . three silver chains he had on. It all came together with a cropped white dress shirt and black pants. God, he might have looked better than me.

I hated him.

"What is up?" he exclaimed as he threw himself down on the seat next to mine, not even hesitating to throw an arm over my shoulders.

I flinched but masked it with a hard swallow and a fake laugh big enough to throw me slightly forward.

"Hi," I whispered through gritted teeth, but hopefully, to everyone else, I looked like a happy girlfriend. "We were just talking about you."

Kurt was grinning from ear to ear now. "Taurus, I have had you on the show time and time again over the last . . . twelve years?"

"Fourteen, I think, something like that. Nothing too crazy," he responded casually with his deep voice that radiated through the studio with minimal effort.

"So, tell me. How did this song come to be?" He wasn't even asking me.

Only Taurus.

I had become a non-factor.

Taurus turned to me. "You wanna?"

Oh.

I sat up in my chair, fighting the emotions that were bubbling up inside of me. "It was the last song added to the album, actually."

Mostly because I didn't want to fucking do it. But I remembered the story we rehearsed and just spit it out. "Um, I was ready to make my first true love song. Like you said, a declaration. I wanted it to bring me—us—to tears. Like, I told him that was my goal, and we left it alone for a while before he came to me with a melody and a hook one night. So . . ."

Kurt motioned to Taurus, and he leaned forward in his oh-so-cool way, licking his lips and capturing all of the damn attention. "Being in the studio with her is an honor, man. Who's to say we don't have more coming for my album, though. Listen, that's a special song written by a special lady and I."

His album? Is that what this whole ambush was about? Promoting his album during my interview?

I swallowed my envy, my rage, and my disgust for the millionth time. I was on a Starlight campaign, and there wasn't a person on earth who was going to take this ramp-up from me.

Not him, not my label, not anyone.

CHAPTER FOUR

FORTY-FIVE MINUTES.

That was how much time we had to take my hair out of that godforsaken updo and straighten it. That was how much time we had to refresh my smoky eye and slap on my designer choker that resembled an animal collar, my skin-tight red mini dress, and the rings and earrings that were covered in dancing diamonds. In only forty-five minutes, professional photos were taken, everyone I knew was on their way to the venue, and my heart was still beating its way out of my chest.

My entire team had turned in for the night, but I had promised my friends I'd meet them at a club not too far from where the studio was. Saint had taken care of getting hotel rooms booked only a block away so that no one had to endure the hell that was an hour-long drive back to our respective houses and . . .

Maybe I needed another night out.

Another martini, and another blackout.

Yeah, that would fix it.

> I should just turn back around. I SWEAR I almost punched him in his face.

Yessenia:
> :////

Savannah:
> please come out, i doubt he'll even show

Saint:
> 'voice memo transcript' Sorry, my hands are busy but if you aren't here tonight I'm going to personally come get you myself

"Ready?" the driver whispered while staring through the rearview mirror. I could hear how busy the sidewalk was—crowded with paparazzi staking out the front entrance. Security was already standing tall outside of my door, waiting for the signal to open it and shield me from any fans who had stayed up too late.

I swallowed the anger that stilled in the back of my throat. I was a fucking superstar, and there wasn't time for tantrums when the cameras were on.

"*Si, vamos.*" I tapped the glass, and the vehicle door swung open. I was immediately greeted with camera flashes that were bright enough to temporarily make my nighttime surroundings look like they were in the daylight. I kept my gaze down when I crawled out of the backseat. Two security guards grabbed my hands, taking positions on either side to ensure no one got too close.

Within a blink of an eye, my long black fur coat was being peeled off of me and handed to someone else. I walked through the mouth of the venue that opened up to a large main floor. The floors and walls were painted silver, making the burgundy drapes and candlelit chandeliers stand out even more. There were two bars, one closest to me and the other several feet away. If I squinted, I could see a hallway that I could only assume led to more private rooms and bathrooms.

I looked around at the sea of people, but I didn't recognize most of them.

"Didn't get the all-black memo?" Saint appeared out of fucking nowhere and placed a drink in my hand.

I shrugged and brought the drink to my lips.

Strong and sweet.

"Oops?"

Saint chuckled and ushered me through the crowd.

"Aly!"

"Look who's here!"

"Wow, you look beautiful."

"I'm so happy to see you out again."

"Congratulations on the nomination, girl!"

I remained graceful despite the amount of people tugging on my shoulders and pulling on my arms. Saint managed to stop a few of them from pulling me into selfies I didn't ask for. But in the search for a second drink, we lost each other.

Fuck.

Eventually, I located the bar and gave up on the search for people I knew and found myself three cocktails down and using the stares from the shy men passing by to fuel my ego for the time being.

Then the rhythm of a song I couldn't say I had heard before enchanted me.

The vocals were familiar, but I couldn't put my finger on who it was, especially not in my hazy state.

A man, for sure.

His voice was soulful yet heavily auto-tuned to disguise its true potential and blended perfectly into the beat that was causing my hips to sway. A genuine smile grew on my face as I grabbed the hips of a pretty ginger who had danced her way next to me. We twirled and laughed through the chorus, and at some point I was handed another champagne glass. I drank it happily, soaking up the attention and realization that everyone was captivated by me.

And why wouldn't they be?

As quickly as the song had started, it ended and—

"It's good, isn't it?" The voice was deep and came from behind and above me like some sort of god had ripped the ceiling open and decided to speak to me. Irritated that someone was that close to my backside, I spun around and found myself stretching my neck to look up.

Fuck.

"It was yours, wasn't it?" I asked begrudgingly.

Taurus smiled. "That it was," he said, his voice sitting comfortably over the music.

"Then I regret dancing."

"Ouch. And here I thought we were well on our way to being partners in crime. I'm here for you."

"Oh, no, no, no." I placed my now empty cocktail glass on a tray as a server walked by, replacing it with a filled one. "You're here for you because you signed a contract and now we have what?"

"Seven or so more months of . . ." He leaned down to whisper in my ear, "Forced interaction."

My stomach fluttered, but I didn't make that part obvious.

Fucking annoying.

Cocky and annoying.

"You're annoying," I huffed before leaning in closer so that my hate for him wouldn't be misquoted as a "lovers' quarrel." "You crashed my fucking interview and now my night out?"

He rubbed the back of his neck, removing the sunglasses and revealing his intense brown eyes. "Crashed? I got a call from my manager, and I showed up. You didn't know?"

I shook my head.

"Damn. But we looked good up there, didn't we? We always do." Taurus smiled.

I almost did too.

I took a sip out of my glass and leaned into him some more. "Stay. Away. From. Me."

He shrugged, leaning so far in that I could hear his breathing. "Can't really do that, Superstar. To all these people, we're an item. So, wouldn't it be more odd if I wasn't by your side?"

Right.

He always had to be fucking right. And since this was the first time he was ever seeing me tipsy, drunk lips were starting to speak sober thoughts.

"Why did you even agree to this?"

Taurus bit his lip before whispering in my ear, "I admire you. And . . . if I could make music with someone as talented as you . . . Have a hand in the comeback? Hell yeah, I'm sold. It was a no-brainer."

I backed up, wanting to get a look at him to see if he was joking or high. There was no way he was sober and this . . .

Forthcoming.

"I—"

"Aly! Your video is playing!" I couldn't tell who had screamed it, but it caused Savannah to locate me pretty easily. Saint followed closely behind, and Yessenia had a hunk of a man's arm wrapped around her waist as she approached as well. And Taurus, well . . . He made his way to my side. We all faced the giant screen that I hadn't even noticed was playing music videos behind us.

A vintage car—one that the director owned himself, actually—appeared in the frame, and there I was . . . Seated in the driver's seat with my hair in a nineties glam updo, sunglasses sitting lazily on the bridge of my nose. I watched as the ten-foot version of me walked away from the car, a trail of gasoline following her. And as the rhythm of "No Tears" began to introduce itself, the vehicle exploded. Special effects, of course.

The scene switched to me on a stage in a strip club. The color scheme was dark with glimpses of orange, and I twirled on the pole in a Swarovski one-piece with heels that I distinctly remember tripping over more than ten times. Thirty-inch extensions were added to my hair, and when my low notes filled the room, everyone's eyes were glued to the screen.

It was the only video that didn't follow the theme of the fairy tale I had created. But wasn't fame and glamor a fairy tale in itself?

I don't know who you think I am

But you can get up out my face with that shit

Get up out my head with that shit
I'm not the girl you had before

The song addressed everything. The public ridicule, the blackballing, the divorce. I was twenty-three and had lost more than any one person had the capacity to handle. And when I sat there with my notes app open and a pain inside my heart, I really wanted to burn it all down.

I smell the perfume that I never wore
So I have no tears
Watch you walk out the door
Get up out my house with that shit

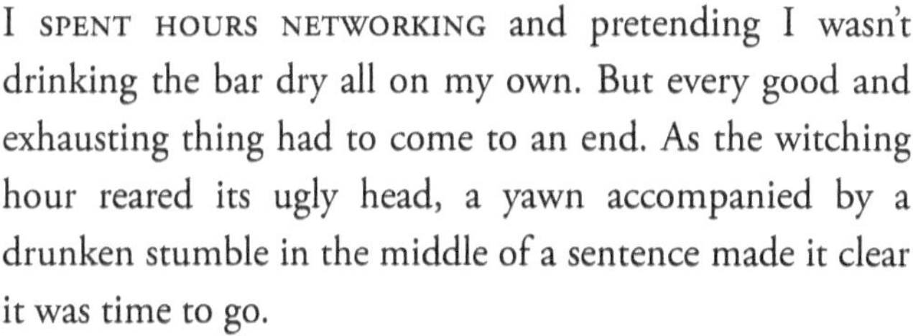

I spent hours networking and pretending I wasn't drinking the bar dry all on my own. But every good and exhausting thing had to come to an end. As the witching hour reared its ugly head, a yawn accompanied by a drunken stumble in the middle of a sentence made it clear it was time to go.

"Are you all right?" I didn't feel Taurus's hand on my arm, but when it registered, I lazily snatched my limb back.

"I'm fine," I slurred, glaring up at the man who I only saw have one or two drinks this entire time. "What are you still doing here, anyway?"

Taurus's face was decorated with amusement as he leaned against the bar, eyes not shifting from mine for a moment. Everything he did seemed like perfectly choreographed movements. There was no way I had met anyone like him before.

"Do you need a ride?"

I raised a brow, and then a small yet highly embarrassing burp slipped from my glossed lips. "You drove?"

All he did was laugh.

"Yeah, reminds me of what it was like to be normal." His sarcastic tone registered far before the words did.

I attempted to grab my phone off of the bar, missing the first time and scoring the second. "You don't know what it's like to be normal."

When my lowered lids opened enough to see the entrance, I knew the vultures on the other side would ensure that I couldn't make it far.

A deep sigh released from my lips, and I pivoted on my thin heels to face him. "Could you walk me to my car? My driver's waiting out there for me."

He didn't have to say the words *You need me more than I need you*, but I could smell it on him. It was in the way he didn't care to wipe that smug look off his face and—he enjoyed this. He enjoyed that for the rest of his life, I was a part of his story, and a contract forbade us from ever coming clean about how the entire thing was conjured up during a virtual meeting while I was knee-deep in vodka cranberries and cosplaying as a vampire queen who killed everyone who ever crossed her in my daydreams.

No, he didn't have to say it, but I could tell in the way he put his elbow out so I could loop my arm through his. We were a couple, right? At least it made sense to walk out with him.

Lost in thought, I didn't notice him turning us around and heading down the hallway.

I stopped in my tracks. "Where the hell are you taking me?"

He didn't pull me further with his large hands.

Shocking.

"I texted Nova to tell your driver to meet us out back. There's no way you're going out the front door like this."

I crossed my arms across my chest. "Wouldn't you want the photo op?"

"I don't care that much." The giant of a man started walking forward, and since everyone else I knew had cleared out by now, I had no choice but to follow.

"That's stupid. That's the whole reason you're here." I combated as the cold air smacked my body. I couldn't register how long it was before he was opening the car door and I was getting inside.

Alone.

"Or . . . I wanted to see the girl who stormed out of the studio earlier. Who . . . so happens to be my"—he mouthed the word *fake*—"girlfriend."

The door shut, and I was left with the lingering words like a ship pushed forward by the tide. It had been a long while since I was someone's girlfriend—or anyone's anything, really.

I didn't notice that I had been dozing off until I was being guided out of the car and to my hotel. I tripped over my own feet a few times. But I felt a false sense of security when I noticed there weren't any camera flashes. I didn't remember riding the elevator or even taking my key out. In fact, I couldn't put a face to whoever was leading me to begin with.

The cushion of the bed met my cheek.

When did I lie down?

I tried to pull myself up on the mattress, pawing at the blankets, but I couldn't grip them properly. A wave of exhaustion overwhelmed my body, and my limbs went numb. Thunder roared against the balcony doors.

I could barely process it while my eyes struggled to stay open. In between the heavy flutters, tree branches banging against the glass came across like something out of a nightmare.

"Hurry up!" someone whispered in a hushed tone.

Who's in my room?

I widened my eyes—or at least attempted to, but no matter how hard I tried to push through the three-ton weight that had become my body, I couldn't. I wanted to scream—feel something other than a desperate yearning to fall asleep.

"There's nothing in here," another voice stated in a much deeper, terrifying tone. Distorted noise was all I could hear after that.

When my eyes finally closed . . . I was fully in the dark. I couldn't differentiate between the shuffling or the voices. My heart wouldn't even beat against my chest—it only slowed as if everything was normal.

Maybe this was a dream . . .

Maybe if I leaned into it, I'd wake up in pajamas with Yessenia and Solo by my side.

A groan left my mouth. I couldn't hear it, but I felt the vibration in my throat.

My hearing returned. "I thought you said this would be a quick in and out."

"It is."

There was silence . . . Or a long lapse of time that I missed before I came to again. But this time when my eyes fluttered open, I could move my fingers. I tapped the blanket to be sure. Then a sensation traced up and down my exposed calves. It was followed by some murmuring that I couldn't make out.

They were still in my room.

The sensation went from light traces to a grasp around my ankle. Without thinking twice, I kicked back as hard as I could and spun around on my back. I crawled to the furthest end of the bed, finally coming face-to-face with the masked silhouettes wrecking my hotel room.

Drawers were pulled out of the dresser, my clothes were sprawled every which way, and the jewelry I wore for my interview was spilled in various places over the carpet.

Why hadn't they taken it?

The three strangers stood in shock for long enough to give me time to take in what I was faced with. My brain was covered in fog, but it wouldn't have helped anyway because they were covered from head to toe.

Their masks weren't ski masks, though. They were animal masks. Foxes? Their clothes were . . . black? Maybe navy blue?

I blinked several times, but my senses were still failing me. My head was filled with concrete as I tried to concentrate on how I could get myself out of this.

Suddenly, one of the men rushed over to me, grabbing and throwing my body on the floor in a manner that caused a stinging sensation to move all throughout. I winced but I couldn't keep my fucking head up.

I had to have been drugged.

Someone must have slipped me something.

My energy went in and out as my hands were tied behind my back using cables and my feet were the same. I couldn't scream . . . I couldn't make a noise louder than a whimper, but they stuffed my mouth with one of my socks anyway.

"No matter what, she's not going to be able to do anything. Look at her," I heard one say. But this one was a woman with a hint of a Latin accent. I could make out that much.

Another snickered.

I wanted to react.

I couldn't.

I could barely breathe, feel my heart in my chest, or the fire in my lungs.

Then everything went dark.

CHAPTER FIVE

A SOFT MELODY WAS WHAT awakened my body. Invisible strings peeled my eyelids open and . . .

I was lying in the tub, and what I thought was a lullaby eventually made itself known as the roaring of the AC unit above me. I moaned and kicked, noticing the daylight creeping in from the bathroom windows. My heart rammed against my rib cage, but at least I could feel it now. Once I became aware of that, my body ached in various places one by one. The bruising on my wrists and ankles where the cables were still placed, my waist where they had grabbed me, and my limbs that had been scrunched up in the porcelain bowl for possibly hours.

I searched for any more pain.

Any signs that something else . . .

That something much more terrifying had happened, but nothing.

It didn't take long for me to wiggle my way out of the wire cables. They were loosely tied, which I assumed was because they knew I was too out of it to be much of a threat.

I was set up.

Once freed, I ripped the sock out of my mouth and crawled out of the tub with the little energy I garnered despite previously being unconscious. Walking felt impossible. My legs were limp, and the only strength I had came from my upper body as I army crawled to the door. I used my free hand to pull it ajar and let out a bloodcurdling scream into the hall. "Help!"

Whatever I was drugged with left a lot to be desired. Despite my previous ability to get myself out of the room, I didn't have much left in me to remain awake. I was slipping in and out of my dream state where I was back in The Castle with a massacred village . . . And reality.

Where I was nothing but a wounded pop star.

At times, I knew I heard Nova's voice and felt her fingers laced between mine.

Maybe Yessenia's hand too.

At another point, I was lifted into a gurney and could only remember myself talking about the fox masks—over and over again.

The next time I came to, I was in a spacious hospital room with dimmed lights and a television hung high, playing an episode of a talk show I could barely make out. "I know, it's crazy. First, she fires her entire team, and then she has that outburst. You know what? I agree with the fans. That is the face of someone who has sold their soul. There's no other possible answer," one of the women said.

"You're awake . . ."

I looked to my left to see Nova, who clearly hadn't slept in . . . What day was it?

"I—hello to you too." I struggled to sit up against one of the teabags they had given me to pass as a pillow. "Jesus, I hope I don't look worse than you."

Nova attempted to run her hands through a tangled bob that had certainly seen some shit. "Glad you have enough energy to still be snarky."

The corners of my lips curled. "Well . . . Don't just stare at me. What did I miss and . . ." I wiggled the arm with the IV attached and winced at the discomfort. "When the hell can I get out of here?"

Nova's eyes saddened, and she scooted her plastic chair closer to my bedside. "Hey, hey."

She pressed a hand on my shoulder, and warmth traveled through my system. I wasn't sure what safety felt like with an older woman—or anyone, really—and I found myself blaming my mom for that.

But Nova was different.

She always had been and probably would remain the closest thing I'd ever get to a mother.

"You went on and on about a robbery and some men and fox masks? And then . . . you were in and out for almost two days. But there's good news, *mija*. They've already been caught, and there is nothing for you to be scared of. They didn't find anything of yours on them, though. But we're still looking, don't worry." Relief washed over me, but I wasn't granted a second to relish in it before she was talking again. "*Pero*, the extra good news is that after the news broke, 'No Tears' and the entire album have skyrocketed in streams and sales. If we move on it quickly and release the deluxe vinyls for preorder, we're looking at another week at number one with 'No Tears' guaranteed to head back up to the top ten."

I swallowed hard. My lips cracked, but before I could muster up the words, Yessenia burst through the door. "Oh my gosh, she's awake!"

Regardless of Yessenia's outburst, there was only one question that rang in my head. "This—this entire fucking thing is working in my favor?"

Nova leaned in closer to me.

"*Si*. That's just the world we live in," she whispered, trying to bring me back down to earth, I assumed. "But. I would rather us focus on you getting better and out of here. We'll talk about business later."

There wasn't an emotion on earth that could explain the cloudiness of my head and the fluttering of my heart.

"What are they saying?" I asked, as if my soul craved to know.

Nova hesitated but quickly realized that fighting me was useless. She pulled out her phone, scrolling for mere moments before reading, "This one is a post from *Pop Mania*: After what was reported to be a brutal robbery, Aly's fans are rallying behind her once again."

They loved me again.

Yessenia's voice crept up on me.

"We're all glad you're okay," she whispered in her soft baby-girl-esque tone.

"I-I need to get out of here." My fans needed to hear from me.

My cousin jumped to my other side, grabbing my searching hands so that I couldn't rip the IV out of my arm.

"I called your mom," she blurted out.

"Excuse me?" I shrieked. "You did what?"

She let me go and backed away while concern filled her features.

For the first time since I woke up, I wondered what I looked like. I felt the tenderness of my wrists and ankles and how sore my muscles were from being manhandled. My heart beat out of my chest, but it wasn't from the support of the general public or the anxiety of constantly having to lie about being in love again . . .

It was the fear of my mother.

The phantom hits from a *chancla* or the loud cumbia tunes on a late night coming from the living room while the expectation was for me to get up on my own for school in the morning.

It all came rushing back.

The tightening of my chest. The sudden caution of my tone.

Did I look like I had an attitude on my face? Could I provoke her with my body language? Sitting up too tall? Staring for too long?

"I thought . . . Look!" Yessenia finally began to explain. "You could have died. We had no idea who those men were, really. Or what they wanted yet—"

"And that was your fucking solution? To call my mom like I'm fifteen years old?"

"Okay, let's—" Nova tried to interrupt.

"No. Let her."

I sat up some more, wincing slightly as lightning struck my temples. "What was going through your head?"

"She's your mother and she—"

"No. I don't want to hear from you right now. Marabella is just the lady who grabbed me by my scalp and tried to drown me in the goddamn kitchen sink once upon a time. So, the next time you get any bright ideas—don't."

My head was pounding, but I still swallowed the lump in my throat. "Someone get the damn nurse."

CHAPTER SIX

TheY NEVER TOOK ANYTHING, but I had to tell everyone it was a robbery. Because if it wasn't . . . then what was it? I asked myself over and over again. However, the answer never came.

I couldn't access any other memories from that night other than those fucking fox masks. Their eyes were sinister behind them, like I was prey to the predator.

"Is right here okay?" the driver asked as he slowly drove around the giant fountain in the middle of the property and pulled up to the front door of The Castle. It felt . . .

Emptier.

But I guess it had been ever since my last relationship.

After my divorce, The Castle stopped feeling like a prized possession and started feeling more like a prison. I was Rapunzel and I had unknowingly locked myself away. So, I drank through that emptiness, listening to Aventura throwbacks and picking up a nasty smoking habit until it went away. I danced until I no longer loved him—screaming songs in a language he never bothered to learn. If he knew I was really here alone most nights without Taurus . . .

Would he care? Did anyone?

No.

In a perfect world, I'd be able to run back to Miami.

"Right here is fine," I responded in a somber tone.

When I looked up to see the blonde seated at my doorstep, my eyes ignited with hope and my lips tugged into a small smile before I forced them back to a frown. I called Savannah because she was the only one who wouldn't hover and would actually have something to say that was worth listening to. She shifted from one foot to the other on my porch, and the sun slowly setting in front of us caused her green eyes to glimmer. Her lush tresses were pulled into two French braids, and despite how exhausted I was, I still stared.

"Hey, babes," Savannah whispered while grabbing one of my bags from the driver's hands. I let her take it. I was too exhausted to hold them myself, despite there only being two.

I said nothing.

Instead, I unlocked my door and waited until the limousine drove off to push it open and let Savannah in. The lights flickered upon entry, and the sound of Solo's collar echoed through the immense space as she purred at my feet. I tried to focus on petting her, but all I could see now were a million entryways for a stranger to enter. There wasn't a gate high enough or a security system smart enough to keep me safe.

"Did you hear me?" Savannah asked in a soft tone.

I spun around. "Huh?"

Her hand was wrenched around the handle of my bag. "Where do you want this?"

"Oh." I dug in my purse for a cigarette and a lighter. The double C logo twinkled in the light. "Just leave it there," I grumbled, lighting the cigarette in between my long nails.

My pointer fingernail was broken off.

I ignored it and inhaled the smoke, lowering my shoulders soon after.

"Do you wanna swim?" The words slipped from between my lips, but inside I was screaming for someone to touch me gently.

Hug me.

Take care of me . . .

Like a mother would.

I was too damn old to crave something so nurturing . . .

So unconditional.

I spent my entire childhood watching parents show up to watch the most snobby kids perform their talents during winter showcases. They would sit there with smiles on their faces and video cameras in their hands. My mom never showed. Not when I got the lead in the school play or when I joined my school's dance company.

"Sure." Savannah's voice was calm yet concerned, and when I finally looked up at her, I could see the sympathy written all over her flushed cheeks.

Cheeks.

I wiped mine with my free hand. A single drop of salt water had escaped, and I hadn't even noticed.

Before I could toss my bag on the couch and open the sliding doors that led to the pool, my purse vibrated once . . .

And then twice.

I rolled my eyes and stuck the lit cigarette in between my teeth, letting the ashes fall on the squeaky-clean marble.

Unknown:

> I know you see me calling you, Alejandra! Yessenia told me what happened.

Blocked.

For years, the crushing weight that came from being accessible to her was lifted. Yet it was quickly replaced by the reality of the memories that were still coming back to me. The disgusting scratch of the comforter that my face was against for God only knows how long. The hollowness in my body that came from being so fucking alone. If I screamed, no one would have heard me. I pushed them far enough away to make sure of that.

My phone buzzed again.

Nova:

> Hope you got home safe, mija.

Nova:

> Spoke about the vinyl releases and they want to release another single ASAP and start pushing that along with the deluxe editions of TFV.

Nova:

> They really want the song and video with Taurus.

Nova:

> I'll confirm with him and we'll talk. The Starlight campaign is still happening!

I left my phone on the kitchen island and wiggled out of the disgusting jumpsuit that hid the bruises that were still present on my wrists and ankles. I watched as Savannah walked ahead, choosing to do her stripping outside and leaving her sweatpants and cropped hoodie on one of the many chairs.

I wondered if she had ever been through something so dark.

By the time I shook the thoughts out of my head, I was putting my cigarette out and standing at the edge of the pool in only a black panty set. The water rippled quietly, reacting to Savannah's upper body moving through it. My attention went from the crystal blue to the black acrylic painted on my toes and the bruises that sat where my anklets once did.

I stepped back, my feet carrying me to the deeper side of the pool—nowhere a woman under five-foot-seven should be. I put some distance between myself and the edge, stepping further and further back as I ripped my hair out of the elastic. When my strands fell down my back, I didn't care about fucking my extensions up or losing my breath. I didn't care about how Savannah could possibly be looking at me right now. I needed release.

I made soldier-like stomps to the deepest edge, zoning everything out except the water that was beckoning toward me. With a few steps left, I made the last-minute decision to jump.

In an instant, I was submerged in the liquid, too far down to reach the surface without swimming, but still too short to feel the bottom of the pool with the soles of my feet. I waded against the ripples, opening my eyes to see nothing but blue as chlorine filled my pupils.

For a moment, I felt safe.

My mouth opened, water choking me until it burned, and I let out a scream that only I could hear.

"DO YOU EVER JUST want to quit?" I blurted out, my voice hoarse from the amount of chlorine that had fought my lungs just an hour ago.

After my moment, Savannah suggested I bathe and get into something comfy instead of trying to drown myself. I agreed but proved useless when it came to actually finding something to wear. So, I sat on the floor of my walk-in closet, wrapped up in my towel, with soaking wet hair while she combed through my options.

"Every day," she finally responded before dropping the sleeve of my off-the-runway-and-never-worn coat. The smaller woman slid down next to me and adjusted her underwear straps on the way down. "But you can't."

I raised a brow. "Why not?"

"Who's going to fill the space when you're gone?"

I scoffed. "I'm not doing anything worth occupying space, trust me. Unless we're talking about *Pop Mania* headlines."

Savannah fake gasped and nudged my shoulder. "You are insane! Do you see how you created beauty out of literal fucking death? Seriously, open your eyes. Those blogs are eating because you're breathing. That's power right there." She fully turned to face me and yanked my hands so hard my towel almost slipped. "You are important, Alejandra. And if I need to remind you every day, I will. No matter how hard it gets or—"

My phone vibrated again.

I hissed before flipping it over.

Unknown:

Welcome to the show.

With trembling fingers, I quickly turned my phone back over. "If it's not work, it's my mother."

I tried to smile and pass it off as a joke, but my voice cracked, and my tears created blurry vision. Savannah pulled me into her embrace, and my tears began to drip onto her chest.

"When does it end? When does the fucking universe stop treating me like a punching bag?" I cried. "I didn't do anything wrong! And it's like I keep getting hit from every direction. I need a break!"

"You did nothing wrong," she whispered as she ran her fingers through my soaked hair. "It can't rain sevens all the time, babe. It just doesn't work like that."

I sniffled and peeled myself away from her, wiping my eyes and noticed she was wiping hers too. "Do you ever miss your mom?" The question was blunt enough to be considered rude, but she knew me better and quickly dismissed the tone.

"Yeah," she finally whispered, slowly nodding like it was the first time she had said it out loud. "I loved her, but she was sick. There was nothing teenage me could do."

I tucked some hair behind my ear. "Alcoholism counts as a sickness?"

I asked for my own knowledge. I never gave Marabella an excuse, and I damn sure wouldn't start because Savannah had a different outlook on her mom drinking herself to death.

I wanted to know, though. For no reason other than to make sure I didn't have the same disease.

Savannah nodded. "Addiction is a nasty thing. It takes away the people you love, and for a while I couldn't even look at a bottle of vodka without wanting to throw up . . . or cry." The woman rolled her eyes and smiled softly. "I couldn't blame her, though. She was so consumed with my dad that when he left, she stopped seeing color. I think the alcohol gave her rose-colored glasses, and I miss that version of her sometimes. But I knew after she died, I could never love someone like that."

"Someone like what?"

"Someone who loses themselves in other people."

I picked at a loose thread on my towel and let the words soak in before speaking. "What if that's what I want?"

"Then I want you to find it. Hell, you deserve someone who consumes themselves with you for once."

"And what if I can't have both? The romance of my dreams and the career of a lifetime . . . Because what? I can't forgive my mom? This has to be my karma."

She pursed her plump lips and shrugged. "I don't believe the two can't coexist, and I damn sure don't believe you haven't found it because of your mother. She's not here, and she can't touch you. Even after what Yessenia did." Savannah paused. "I think you've convinced yourself it's either or. Love . . . or power. But what if you could make sure you never heard from your mother again, and for once, it was love and power? What would you do then?"

I couldn't help but laugh.

"Rule the world," I finally answered.

CHAPTER SEVEN

A S DAYS PASSED WITHOUT me saying a word, the general public grew divided. More people began to theorize that I staged my attack because I needed to resort to gimmicks to sell a record despite my recent accolades. Others believed robbing a celebrity near the holidays required no further explanation. Both sides were still streaming my music.

Nonetheless, I was a ghost in the machine while my team sent out statements about respecting my silence and healing.

I hadn't been on social media much—mostly because I didn't care to see how anyone else was starting to celebrate the holidays. But I saw enough to notice that Taurus's page had gone dark.

A simple PR strategy to make people think we were in the same house . . . Same city, even. In their minds, his big arms were holding me close as he whispered into my hair that everything would be okay.

In reality, he could stay as far away from me as possible. I wasn't sure who drugged me or when it happened . . . But I was sure that he was the last person I was with.

It couldn't have been him . . . Right?

After my conversation with Savannah, my desire to be held and loved grew until my heart felt like it was bound to explode at any moment. I wanted to give Taurus the benefit of the doubt. I was corrupted by my need for something so unconditional that I'd write raw love songs about it until my fingers bled.

It was December, and I couldn't bet on Yessenia's place for Christmas festivities unless I returned her calls.

"Give Aly some room," everyone was saying to themselves to shield the fact that they hadn't even bothered to call. "She's healing."

Fuck that.

I was fine alone, and I was more than capable of creating my own holiday. Maybe I could go to Paris. Or I could start by decorating a tree.

I grabbed my phone off the vanity, but before I could call a car, a knock on my door made me jump out of my skin. No one texted. No one called. And the useless-ass security camera app wasn't loading.

The knocking graduated into violent banging.

"I'm fucking coming!" I screamed from the bottom of the grandiose staircase. My feet pitter-pattered against the cold marble until I reached the door and ripped it open with the fury of all my dead *abuelos*.

"What?" I ate my words and swallowed my tongue when I saw who it was.

"Alejandra." My mother stared at me like a lion with eyes on their next meal.

I spent years trying to erase how I saw her whenever I looked in the mirror, but all I saw now was myself in her dark eyes. They were wilder since the last time I saw her . . . More chaotic. Her cheeks were hollow from dramatic weight loss, and her plump lips were cracked and dry. What was once long, thick, and healthy black hair was now cut short and growing out of a dandruff-infested scalp.

I had so many nightmares about my mother that I considered every possibility of how she'd look when I saw her again. I imagined her reappearing strong like a Disney villain or frail and unable to construct a sentence because the heroin had rotted her brain. But I never considered her looking this sad . . . or dirty.

When I knew I was moving to LA, I told Marabella five minutes before I walked out the door. I didn't want to fight or scream . . . I only wanted to go.

With every shirt that I packed, I considered that I'd never see that bedroom again. With every dress I pulled from my closet, I knew my mother needed me.

It was strange, actually. The way she'd forget my existence for days on end or find new ways to beat me when I didn't behave as she deemed appropriate.

Yet she needed me.

I might have been the only person who ever truly saw her—a lost woman who was nothing more than a disgusting piece of shit who made me want to slit my wrists and bleed before I even hit puberty. So, despite her struggles, I wished her a slow fall to hell. She could roast like a marshmallow on an open fire too if Satan saw fit.

Because the mom I got damn sure wasn't the one I deserved.

I was so focused on her standing there that it took a moment before my vision dropped to the child holding her hand.

A literal fucking child.

Her long dark hair was frizzy and unkept, and she was covered from head to toe in cartoon-themed pajamas with smudges of dirt on the sleeves and pant legs. Her eyes met mine for no longer than a split second. They were the same as my mother's, except hers were filled with fear—not chaos.

"What—" I swallowed the terror in my throat. "How did you get my address? Who—"

"May we come in?"

I silently stepped to the side, but there weren't enough words in the world to calm the tidal wave in my stomach. She slipped past me, dragging the child behind her, who stumbled over her own two feet. She was holding on to a stuffed rabbit that was filthy and raggedy like it'd been thrown in the trash more than once. And knowing my mother?

If she was—

No.

I didn't have any siblings.

I shut the door and stomped behind her. "What are you doing here? Were the creepy texts not enough?" I finally asked while quickly scanning the living room to ensure there wasn't anything out of place for her to point out.

"I only texted you once," she clarified.

I furrowed my brow because I had definitely been receiving ominous texts from different numbers.

"No Christmas tree?" she asked.

Of course she found something.

"Um . . ." I chewed the inside of my cheek and shut the door behind them. "No. I've been on the road." *Liar.*

My mother pointed to the couch, and the child scurried quickly to sit down. She rested against the cushions as a look of relief swirled inside her pupils. I gulped. Even though I didn't know this child, she felt like kin to me. I could only imagine what she had been through if she was—but she wasn't. I was an only child.

"It would have been nice if you called me back, though." She wasn't even looking at me as she spit the words out with her thick Mexican accent. Instead, her focus was on the interior—the chandeliers and the elaborately detailed baseboards.

"Hm." Marabella turned up her nose to my face as if she knew. As if she could see the ghosts in the walls as well as I could. Her focus shifted to my face, and our eyes met once again. She looked lifeless. "You've done well for yourself."

She was pacing now, her dirty trainers smudging mud and whatever the fuck else all over the polished gray. "I read about it all, you know. All of the things you didn't bother to call your mother about. Your marriage, and then divorce. Found out about that through a coworker, by the way. But boy was it entertaining when the talk of the office was the girl who you dragged out here. But! At least you could write a song about it. Isn't that what you do? Or is someone hired to do it?"

"I've written almost everything I've put out," I said through gritted teeth.

I swore the swords that pierced my heart all those moons ago were removed when I left that house in search of a better life. Yet I was standing there with fresh wounds caused by her hateful tone.

"I'm sure," Marabella said sarcastically, a disgusting smirk completing the sentence. "But you know what I noticed the more I read articles about my eldest? You're your mother's daughter, *mi reina.*"

I was functioning on autopilot. Her presence was enough to bring upon the heaviest of rain clouds. I hadn't felt this small since the robbery—a feeling I was growing accustomed to once again. And maybe it was the only constant I'd ever have. My mortgages never paid for sanctuaries.

I never had anywhere to run.

"You never wanted anything to do with me, Marabella," I still managed to say despite how dry my mouth was.

She stepped closer. I stepped back.

"You've convinced yourself of that? I am your mother. That couldn't be further from the truth. Okay, okay." She put her hands up and walked across the open space while sunlight beamed through the glass doors behind her. "I loved you."

Even after all this time, the past tense felt like another sword was cutting through my already bleeding organ.

"Then you loved me the wrong way. Especially since this is the first time you're saying it, and it's in past tense."

She sighed. "We fought. All parents fight with their kids, Alejandra."

"No. You hit me."

"I was provoked."

"How can a six-year-old provoke you?" I yelled in response, wiping away a tear that escaped from my welling eyes. My hands were trembling.

Marabella didn't reply. Instead, she observed me like a project she had been working on from afar. Deep in Carson City, she had her hands in my life without even trying. Molding me—ruining me—knowing I wouldn't ever be able to live a life without her handprints branded on my skin.

Solo brushed up against my ankle, and I picked her up—just in case. I was finally rich. I had a nice house. I had a cat. I had fans. I had friends. I had my music. I was only trying to live. I didn't need this. I didn't grow up to be sad again. "You have to go. I will call the cops—I swear. I don't—I don't know how you got through the damn gate, but when I find out who was on call today I will have their ass—"

She commanded the room by raising her hand and causing the crowd in my head to silence. "I am here because you need family right now."

I shut my mouth. My nightmares . . . They had to have been warning me of her return. But what could I have done to prevent it?

"Oh, look at you . . ." She circled me like a shark in the deep blue oceans, and then her cold hands touched my face and sent a shiver down my spine. "You're exactly what I looked like at your age. You have the same amount of rage in your eyes too." She glanced over to the child on the couch. "Like she will one day."

"I'm nothing like you."

"Well, you're the furthest thing from a kind girl, aren't you? Cold. A mastermind at using your past as a canvas and painting with the blood. I did what I had to do, *mi reina*. And I succeeded. I made you strong enough for this world. So now, I need you to do something for me."

"No."

"Yes. And I've seen proof. And it's okay. Why are you so scared of being your mother's daughter?"

"Because I would never want to be someone who doesn't know what it feels like to love someone other than themselves," I spat out despite the shaky hands that were covered by Solo's body.

"So why do you live alone if that's not who you've already become?"

"Being alone is my choice. It's called self-care. Look it up." I forced out another lie and paired it with a not-so-convincing eye roll.

Instantaneous pain introduced itself to my cheek because the taller woman had lifted her hand and struck me across the face. The child gasping was the only noise I could hear through the loud ringing in my ears. I held onto Solo tightly, and her nails dug into my skin like an anchor, keeping me from drifting beyond the shoreline. When I finally managed to see past the flashes of red, the only eyes I saw were the child's.

A stranger to me. But I saw her sorrow as if it was my own. I understood her furrowed brow and the screams captured in her lungs—a feeling I knew all too well. She wasn't allowed to scream, tell Marabella to stop, or express her fear. It all remained bottled up and sealed away. She couldn't survive on her own, so she was unable to escape the scorned woman who had become a *bruja*.

"Watch your tone," she finally ordered.

I took another step back, swallowing the lump in my throat as the pain faded away.

She had made her way over to the child, rubbing the top of her head gently before ripping the elastic that was caught under the tumbleweed of hair somewhere.

"Ow," she whined, but as soon as it slipped out, she covered her mouth.

"So she's . . ." I kept my distance, so much so that I was backed up against the bar.

"*Tu hermana.*" Marabella's lips curled into a weak smile.

I tapped my tongue on the roof of my mouth, hoping to get some moisture but failing desperately. My blood had run cold, and my heart had slowed its beating.

My trembling hands stilled.

My sister?

She ripped her fingernails through the child's unkempt hair, whose eyebrows furrowed and nose scrunched in a desperate attempt not to verbally react to the pain Marabella was causing her tender scalp. I didn't know this child, and I felt nothing about her being my sister. Yet I wanted to take her hand. Let her know that one day . . . she won't ever feel this way again. And eventually, our mother—like most monsters—would go away as she got older. And if they ever reappeared, they'd already have one foot in the grave. We may have been tormented by the memories and phantom pains, but at least when it was over, it wasn't the real thing.

It would never be the real thing again.

"Hello?" Her snapping knocked me out of the trance and brought me back to the situation before me, my eyes locked with the little girl's.

"Back in dreamland, huh?"

"No," I muttered.

"We lost the house, you know. But!" She threw her hands up in surrender. "I guess none of that matters to you right now. I had enough going on, and still I came to make sure you were okay. The *superstar* wouldn't even answer my calls, though."

"Your sister lives an hour away, and I'm sure she answered your calls." I pulled out a barstool and took a seat, growing accustomed to the fact there was no escaping her until she was ready to leave on her own.

"I haven't spoken to that almond-pushing bitch in years."

I scoffed and placed my elbow on the bar. "Being obsessed with Atkins diets is a sin now?"

She glared at me, but I could tell that slap took the last of the energy required to reprimand me. "My sweet girl Josefina deserves a home."

Josefina.

I watched as she squeezed her rabbit while specks of dirt covered the redness of her cheeks. "This isn't a home."

"Quit your melodramatics. It has a roof and central heat, does it not?"

I forced down the lump in my throat, taking more effort than usual because of my lack of saliva.

"Right." My eyes welled up again, but there was no fucking way she'd see another tear fall. "You know, for a split second I thought you were here because you cared." I spoke quietly. "Not because finding out what happened to me put a damn bat signal in the sky for you to come running and try and stay with me."

Despite her history and how she never faltered when it came to ruining my day—or my face—I still expected her to at least attempt to hold me. But no.

"We have nowhere to go," she spat, "and if I'm being quite honest, I stopped here because I do care. I wanted to see your face even as scrunched up as it looks now." The words stung like venom, but she was pleading now. "Fine. Don't believe me. But look at her! She's hungry. She's tired." She was pointing to Josefina now. "My little girl sleeps like a sweet lamb when she's comfortable . . . Like you did when I'd peek into your room on those worst nights. You never once looked like you had a bad day when you were sleeping . . ."

She was close to me now, the back of her hand hovering over my cheek. Marabella's bony hand dropped back to her side, and I allowed my breath to flow once again.

"Think of her. You don't need to give me anything, unless it's out of the kindness of your heart. But she is only a child. Her life has barely begun. Her light still shines, don't you see it?"

I stared past the dark-haired creature that had crawled straight out of my nightmares. I tried to ignore how her talons were digging so deeply into my shoulders. I wanted to say no, stand on my truth of her being the worst thing to ever happen to me . . .

But Josefina was innocent.

I hadn't figured out what that meant yet, but I knew it gave me more empathy and less restraint all at once.

"I—I'll have to think about it. You can both stay one night. But only one, Marabella. I'm so fucking serious, or I will call and have someone drag you out of here, okay?" I sighed deeply, disappointment and a whole other clusterfuck of emotions dancing around my aura.

"That's fine. We won't touch anything." My mother picked up a single worn duffel bag. "Show me where we can drop our things."

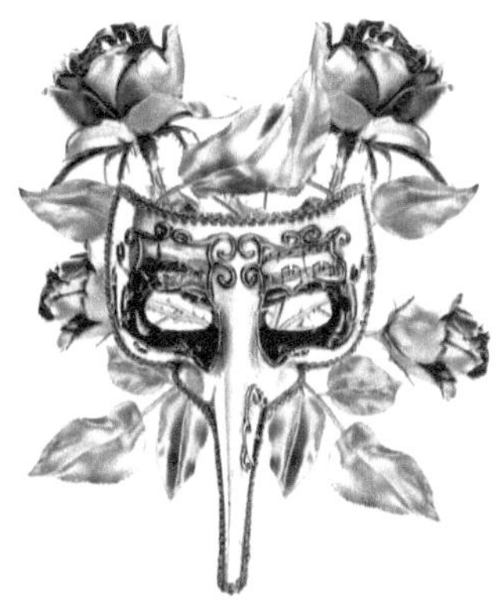

CHAPTER EIGHT

“I WANTED TO SAY thank you so much for the unwavering support . . . It's . . . ?”

“Um, let's say something like—you're eternally grateful, the support has carried you through one of the toughest times of your life, yaddi-yaddi-yah and . . . This hasn't stopped the era,” my publicist suggested on the other end of the phone.

I barely caught her exact words since my mind was on my mother's unwanted and sudden appearance.

“Okay . . .” I whispered under my breath, typing whatever I recalled as fast as I could onto a picture of the sky that I had taken last summer.

A notification dropped down from the top of my screen.

Unknown:
Stay tuned.

“Stupid fucking spam text,” I mumbled.

“Huh?” the woman on the other end of the line asked.

I shook my head and swiped the text away. "Nothing, I sent you the post to check and just . . . Post it. I can't be bothered to stay logged in. But I'll talk to you later. I'm about to get out of the car."

"Okay, love. Call me if you need anything else."

She hung up before I could answer, but I didn't mind. I was more focused on looking out of the window, The Castle appearing brick by brick as the car drove up the hill. It was haunting, almost. Immense, lonely, and unsafe. My mother being there only made it ten times worse. I had been gone for three or so hours, and it was barely noon, but . . . What was she doing? Had she touched anything? Why would I leave Solo in there with her?

I took a few things with me before I left to meet with Nova. My wallet of course, any spare keys I had, all of my identification, and the few baby photos that I stole when I moved out of her home. Had she even noticed?

"Miss Garcia." The driver was already out of the car with the door open for me. December gloom painted the sky as clouds covered the sun from shining. I nodded politely, using one hand to grab onto his and ripping off my sunglasses with my free one.

"Have a good rest of your day," I muttered as I walked up to the front door and searched for my keys in my purse. My long black heels dug into the welcome mat—the silence was eerie.

Relax. You're being fucking insane.

After swallowing my nerves—or faking like I had, I pushed the now unlocked door open and was greeted by an empty living room.

"Hello?" I called out but got no answer in return.

Nothing was out of the ordinary as I walked through the entrance, shutting the door slowly behind me. My nap blanket was still folded on the couch, and the barstools were still neatly tucked under the bar.

"Hellllo?" I sang, a slight attitude in my tone. I kept my purse close to me just in case, passing that damn mile-long staircase and flicking every light on that I had passed to illuminate the space. The door to my basement, aka in-castle studio, at the far end of the first floor was still shut. But there was no way anyone could have been down there fucking with equipment because I took that key with me too. My nails traced against the back of the couch as I walked around my house with a little more urgency.

Had she already left?

Maybe I should look into getting my damn security camera app fixed.

Once I reached the bar, I gave it a quick scan, only to realize that none of my alcohol had been touched either. I heard the pitter-patter of Solo coming down the steps, and before I located her, she was pawing at my ankles. I looked down, squinting to notice that her normal orange fur had some sort of brown paste spread onto her toes.

I picked her up.

"What the fuck . . ." I muttered to myself as I rubbed the cat's paws on my shirt—washing machines existed for a reason. "Lord, let this be chocolate and I may consider walking in a church."

I turned more lights on before moving on from the bar to my open kitchen space. When I looked up past the island, I noticed that the fridge wasn't completely closed, but before I could even make it over there, there was a piece of ripped notepad paper with some writing on it and an uncapped pen not too far away.

I picked it up and recognizedthe handwriting immediately.

Marabella always had beautiful handwriting. It was something I was always jealous of as a kid. On our good days, I remembered begging her to teach me how to write so delicately and not as violently as I did. My teachers would always say I wrote like I had been waiting ages for someone to ask me that one question. Or like I had somewhere else to be and just needed to get the words on paper.

No one will tell you this, so I will. You're just as fucked up, greedy, destructive, demented, and corrupted as me. Next time you look in the mirror or you sing those songs that I planted inside of you . . . See me. Instead of turning your nose up, SEE ME. But let's hope, for Josefina's sake, you are also like your father.

You can afford her. So I hope you take care of her.

I swallowed the pain in my throat.

My father.

I learned how to love the sound of the guitar and marimba because of him . . . And then he vanished. He left me with a woman who would only hand me poisoned flowers on Valentine's Day if given the option.

Tears welled up in my eyes as old wounds continued to reopen, but then I heard shuffling coming from the dining room. I never went in there, and it was easy to forget about since I had to turn the corner behind the kitchen to get to it. I would often walk past the opening and sit outside to eat instead, where it felt less lonely than being surrounded by seven other chairs.

I turned the corner only to be hit with a strong scent of chocolate and looked down to see a trail of spilled syrup going from the doorway to the underside of the table. I crouched slightly, and the culprit was shivering with chocolate syrup covering her hands and face. I let Solo go, but she ran to rub against the child hunched over under the table. She was as unkempt as I left her this morning.

But let's hope, for Josefina's sake, you are also like your father.

I pushed the ball of spit down my throat, my heart racing as the weight of responsibility suddenly sat on my shoulders. *You've got to be kidding me.*

No. No. No.

This couldn't be my life right now.

Not now.

Not ever!

You can afford her.

Maybe a local foster home would take her in—or even a church. She finally looked up at me, ripping me from my train of thought and reminding me that I had to deal with her now.

The electrical shocks, the attempted drownings, the starvation . . . That had been my reality for as long as I could remember. On the best of days, she had forgotten I was there and directed her anger at her new husband. They'd fight it out, and while it was traumatizing as fuck, it was better than being the target.

"Can you . . ." I checked the attitude in my tone, softening it to something she wouldn't be afraid of. "Can you come out?"

Josefina took a break from licking the syrup on her fingers. I didn't even want to think about where the hell that bottle ended up.

I put my hand out. *"Por favor?"*

Her eyes were big and brown, like a baby doll. Without fear present, they sparkled like starlight. But it didn't matter. I didn't create a life for a child—I created a life for me. God dammit, I deserved a life for me.

After everything I had been through and every drop I poured out of my cup into everyone else's—why did I have to give again? Where was my relief?

Josefina placed one sticky and freshly licked hand into my palm. I winced and gagged but managed to pull her out with my eyes closed.

"Okay . . . Great," I whispered, catching Solo's judgmental eyes in the corner. "What are you looking at?"

Josefina looked up at me, and I swore she cracked a smile, but it disappeared as quickly as it came. Before I could figure out what to do next, my phone vibrated.

No, it had been vibrating all along. I kept a hold on Josefina with one now syrup-coated hand and used the other to scroll through the hundreds of notifications that had flooded my social media apps.

Pop Sonic Posted: Aly reassures her loyal fanbase that it's not over yet, thanking them for their streams and support over the years.

@greyandra4ever: im so glad she's okay omg :((

@liafuturistic: mother is mothering iktr

@lifeinc0lor: i kind of want her to rest but im so glad we're still continuing the era

@barbiedoll777 replied to @lifeincOlor: hasn't she been resting for the last few years? Bitch better be UP.

@alygarciasource: STREAMING PARTY TONIGHT AT 7, LETS GET ANOTHER WEEK AT #1

They were . . . quite literally eating out of the palm of my hand. My phone buzzed again, causing me to quickly exit the app and open my texts instead.

Nova:

> Taurus is down to film the video, especially since No Tears is still going so fucking strong. Is your mom still there?

Taurus:

> Can we talk before we shoot this video? I'm heading to NY in a few days, but I'm free before that tho.

I typed a quick reply to Nova and ignored Taurus's text for the time being. If anything was going to make my mood worse, it was mister pretentious himself. And . . . I still couldn't prove that it wasn't him who did it, yet. What would he gain from it?

The memory smacked against my brain once again. However, I remembered something I hadn't before. A tattoo, on one of their wrists as they tied me up. A symbol? I couldn't make it out. I forced my eyes closed, but the haziness didn't clear any further.

My arm was tugged on.

Shit, I had forgotten about her that quickly.

"Okay . . . Let me call someone who might actually know what the f—french to do with you," I mumbled to myself before dialing the only numbers I knew by heart.

Once I could get her somewhere else, I could get back to work. I'd get my Starlight award and then some.

Another minor setback wouldn't stop me.

CHAPTER NINE

"SHAMPOO PLEASE . . ." SAVANNAH'S VOICE hummed throughout the guest bathroom. I used the excuse that I didn't want the child upstairs yet so I didn't overwhelm her. But in actuality, she was fucking filthy, and dealing with her in the bathroom downstairs was a lot easier to swallow for me than the one in my room—or the other one down the hall . . . Or the half-bath at the very end of the second floor of The Castle. But how many bathrooms I had was beside the point.

I passed Savannah the shampoo as she used her free hand to keep trying to wash the matted tangles out of Josefina's hair in the sink. Crystal-clear water from the faucet turned muddy, and the bubbly suds went from white to a brown paste. Savannah looked like she wanted to cry, and honestly, if she didn't, I would think she was broken. She had a motherly instinct instilled in her that definitely skipped me.

I didn't know much about kids, but when we tried to put her in the tub and she fussed, I remembered all the times I watched Savannah with her son Stefan.

So, when she refused to let us put her in the bath or dress her in the pajamas Savannah brought for her to wear, I tried to force the love and forgiveness I had for Stefan onto the girl—the child who was supposed to be my sister. Yet I felt nothing. She wasn't someone I'd jump in front of a bullet for.

What the fuck did that mean?

"She's five!" A strong Portuguese accent pulled me from my train of thought. Saint was pacing around the living room doing God knows what while Yessenia was outside talking to her mom. And hopefully begging her to take her fucking niece.

I deserved that much.

"Huh?" I asked, poking my head out of the bathroom to find him digging in the duffel bag that I hadn't even noticed was still here.

He had a slip of paper in his hand, waving it like a white flag. "Birth certificate."

The taller man walked over to me with an accomplished smile. That smile had been nonexistent when he found out he was partying while I was being held hostage. I told them all not to blame themselves.

How could any of us have known?

More than ever, I needed all of them here and smiling . . . That was what would help me. Even Yessenia.

"There were also some clothes in here. They're all dirty and . . ." He shuffled through the bag some more. He tended to lose his words whenever he got too hyper-focused on one thing. "They have holes, so I'd toss this whole bag, not gonna lie to you."

I raised a brow. "Nothing else in there but nasty-ass clothes and a birth certificate?"

He nodded.

I ran my hands through my loosened hair, wanting a bottle of wine thrown at my own head. "That was the plan all along . . ."

Saint raised a thick brow.

"To leave her. When Marabella stopped by . . . She had the bag, but if this was all that was in it . . ."

"Where do you think she would have gone?"

"Mexico." I rolled my eyes and leaned against the wall, motioning for him to give me the paper. Once it was in my grasp, I held it up. "We were never close, you know."

"Shocker." Sarcasm dripped from his lips as he joined me against the wall.

I nudged him. "*Cállate la boca.*"

We joined in light laughter until my gaze dropped to the worn paper in my hands. The corners were browning, and the four lines from how long it had been folded were deep enough to rip it clean apart. But I could still see everything that mattered.

"There were times when I was so disgusted by her. I blamed her for everything. My dad leaving, there being no food in the fridge half the damn time. I saw her in two ways: a drug addict or an abuser." I watched his eyes fill with sadness—I felt bad for talking about it so casually. "I don't know . . . I just wonder how Josefina sees her."

Josefina Cruz.

One parent signature was my mom, Marabella Cruz, but the section for an additional parent was empty.

Go figure.

There was no chance I was taking her to her father, anyway. Any man who watched how Marabella behaved didn't deserve to have their child back. And for all I knew, that was who she was running off to spend her last days with.

"I think all she sees right now is an opportunity to leave all that shit behind her." Saint finally spoke up. "I'm not one to give familial advice, but . . . Those times when your mom didn't feed you or didn't come home, what'd you wish for?"

I shrugged. "Anyone else."

"And what'd you get?"

"Me."

He leaned in closer and pushed my hair behind my ear. "And what does she have now?"

"Me," I whispered.

"Mission accomplished!" Savannah poked her head out the doorway, causing me to pivot on my heels and face her. She gently pushed Josefina in front of her, a towel wrapped around her head, as they walked into the hall. "I'm not saying I'm a wizard or anything . . . But I would be one hell of a girl mom."

Saint lifted his chin at her and winked. "I'll get right on that."

The words *get a room* entered my thoughts but never left my lips. Even as they exchanged more flirty comments, my focus remained on the child. This was the first time I was seeing her face without anything distracting me from it. She was beautiful. Her cheeks were plump and painted hydrangea pink. Her button nose was perfect for pinching, and the little curls that snuck out of the towel on her head only made her more precious. She pursed her lips and frowned repeatedly, like she was trying to learn how to smile . . .

Like she was still so damn scared to.

Two dimples appeared briefly, as deep as mine.

"Thanks," I said simply and turned on my heels to head in the opposite direction.

I didn't stay around to watch how they probably stared at me, because if I did, I'd have to address the tugging in my chest and the tears that were blurring my vision.

THE SMELL OF *ARROZ con pollo* filled the kitchen. All of my recipes were made from scratch, a skill I'd picked up from the internet and Yessenia's mom.

Growing up on an all-cereal diet wasn't a great introduction to cooking authentic Mexican food. While I struggled to convince my mom to go grocery shopping, my cousins were cooking by the time they were eight. So, I tried to make the time to learn, and eventually, it became therapeutic.

I wasn't sure what Josefina ate, and since she wasn't comfortable enough to talk yet, I had no way of finding out.

She had me.

"Dinner's done!" I sang, taking the plate I already made for myself and plopping down on an empty seat on the couch. Saint was deep into his phone on the furthest end, Savannah camped out on the floor, Yessenia took the chair not too far from us, and Josefina was sitting in an identical chair toying with that dirty rabbit that I was too exhausted to even try to wash.

Yessenia cleared her throat. "Are you gonna . . . ?"

I looked up from my plate, already stabbing the food with the fork. "What?"

"You have to make her plate."

My vision shifted from Yessenia to Josefina. "Right . . ."

Saint chuckled. "Are we sure we want to leave her alone with you? I got an extra room."

I flashed my middle finger at him as I put my plate on the coffee table. "I'm sorry, do you want her?"

"Maybe we shouldn't joke like that with . . . you know," Savannah interrupted, her eyes widening repeatedly in Josefina's direction.

"Right."

Per Savannah shouting from the couch, I cut the chicken into small pieces and made sure not to give her too much rice. I had some fruit punch in my fridge and put it in one of my million unused water bottles because . . .

Why on earth would I have had any damn sippy cups?

After I set the plate and cup in front of Josefina, she stared at it as if she was starving—yet she didn't touch it until everyone else in the room had gotten up to make their own plates.

When I sat back down, I chose a seat next to Yessenia. Despite my annoyance at her actions, I didn't have any anger left in me to spare. We ate and laughed while a children's television show took all of Josefina's attention. I almost forgot she was there—that was how still she was.

"There's a party at Wave if anyone wants to go. I've been working on getting this fucking invite for months. But I got it, and I can bring guests." Saint spoke into the group.

Yessenia sat up, tossing her hair to the side. "When?"

Saint took a piece of food out of his teeth with one hand, holding his phone in his face with the other. "Tomorrow night."

Savannah, who was now seated on the floor in between his legs, looked up at him. "Who will be there?"

He glanced down at her with a bright smile. "Me."

"We should go," I interrupted.

"What about Josie?" Yessenia whispered.

"Josie?"

"Well, I thought we could give her a nickname."

"Oh." I hesitated. "I can get my assistant to watch her. But if I'm stepping out, I'm sure I'll be forced to bring you-know-who with me."

Saint pulled a toothpick from who knows where. "Mmmm . . . See if he can stay back. The Espósito kids will be there."

"Who?" I was on my own phone now and casually scrolling through my feed of fan pages, friends, and idols.

"Who?" they said in tandem, clearly mocking me.

I looked up from my phone, the bitter taste of a few hate comments lingering on my tongue as I clicked it against the roof of my mouth. "Am I missing something?"

Yessenia leaned over the arm of the chair, wild eyes lighting up like I opened Pandora's box. "You don't know the Espósitos?"

"Timeless Music," Savannah said absentmindedly. Finally, someone who was speaking my language. "You know, Taurus's label."

Timeless Music was one of the labels that gave me an offer before I met Nova and signed with Locke and Key.

Timeless had a reputation.

One that they had held with an iron fist for decades. There were rumors about them—something about it being one big successful cover-up for the mafia. None of that mattered at the end of the day because Timeless bred superstars, but so did Locke and Key. They were basically neck and neck in terms of stats, but Timeless's artists had an edginess about them. Taurus was labeled as a revolutionary for the way he blended genres before hitting puberty. They had the most grandiose production for their tours, and their rappers were probably the grittiest—and the best. They were the trendsetters. Even their pop stars pushed boundaries. But that was all I knew about them.

And honestly, if it wasn't for Nova, I would have picked them.

"I know Timeless," I whispered, disguising the audit I had just done in my head.

"Then you know the Espósitos," Saint corrected, with his phone still shoved in his face.

"Nope."

Yessenia sighed, relaxing in her chair again. "Antonio Espósito is the CEO, like his father before him and his father before him and his—"

"Get to the point."

She doesn't say anything to protest my attitude—probably a smart decision. "Antonio has four kids. Two with his first wife: Andrés—he's the oldest—and Camila. She's a year younger, but they call them 'the Twins' anyway. He's also got two with baby mommas we don't know. I think one was Dominican, though. And the other was from Venezuela? Anyway, Romeo and Julian."

I turned to Saint, ignoring how lost he was in playing with Savannah's hair. "Why don't I know these people?"

"They're ghosts," he said absentmindedly.

"Ghosts?"

Savannah looked up. "They have social media pages, but they all only post like once a year. And for nepo-babies . . . that's really strange. Especially considering how well known they are. Actually, I think after Julian transitioned, they just had enough with unsolicited opinions, but that was years ago."

I raised a brow, trying not to make it too obvious that I was searching them up as we spoke. Their names . . . They may have rung a bell, but I couldn't remember a single scenario where anyone like that had stood out. Maybe the responses to Julian, but I stayed away from cruel tabloids since I'd had several written about myself. It was possible in the whirlwind of media attacks and personal losses that I missed something.

Or someone.

"How the hell are they still relevant, then?"

Yessenia clicked her tongue. "They're them. Like I said, Timeless is a family business. Whether it's actually a huge mafia cover-up or not, they're still a force in the industry. I met Camila once on set."

"So . . . one is an actor?" I pried, but my phone screen showed that I was clearly correct. I had short blurbs of the family pulled up for a later date.

"Yup, and Romeo doesn't do shit, but he's gorgeous, so he's been in front of a camera more times than not," Saint chimed in, and I swore he was drooling.

"Julian's a painter, last I checked. And a really good one too," Savannah mumbled, scrolling on her phone while she tried not to purr at her hair still being toyed with.

"And . . . the oldest?" His picture was the largest on my screen. Thank God no one else could see because he was gorgeous. His hair was in a buzz cut, but there were older pictures where he would dye it or even braid it. He had tattoos covering his arms, neck, stomach, back, and hands of various images—but the one that stuck out the most was the image of a woman with her eyes closed on the side of his neck. He had light facial hair, thick brows with slashes in them, and tan skin as if he was always perfectly sun-kissed—no doubt the Puerto Rican genes shining through. But his eyes were dark and soulless, and if I didn't know any better, I'd say they were black.

"He's going to take over the company," Yessenia answered. "I don't know what he does besides that. But everyone knows—Timeless Music's eldest always takes over the company."

Savannah stood and began grabbing her things. Shit, the sun was setting. "Unless they die."

Saint nodded, hovering closely behind her. They made no attempt in concealing that they were leaving together. "Happened with Antonio."

I stood. "He had an older brother?" I glanced down at Josefina, who was still sucked into the TV that was basically muted at this point.

"Luis Jr., yeah. The original oldest. Died from pneumonia. Antonio got the company instead, and the rest is history."

Yessenia also rose. "To be fair, the record label has been skyrocketing under Antonio."

"Mm-hmm," Savannah agreed. "Too bad death runs in the family."

"Don't be superstitious," Saint teased before turning to me. "So you're going?"

"Yeah," I said without hesitation. "I'll be there."

I needed that Starlight award, and a solid campaign always included brushing against the right shoulders.

Before leaving, Saint mentioned that he'd send our names to his contact and told us to make sure we replied when they texted because, no matter who you were, they checked the guest list at the door.

My phone buzzed once I shut the door behind them, and an unknown number popped up. I clicked on the message, and a black image with a block of text appeared.

You are invited to an Elite gathering at Wave this Saturday. No guests allowed. Make sure you fully read and understand the rules below. Failure to commit to this simple task will remove you from consideration of any future events. Please show the code sent after this message at the door where phones and any other electronic devices will be confiscated. Thank you and see you soon.

Rules

1. Guests of any Elite gathering will have their devices confiscated at the door.

2. NDAs should be signed up to 24 hours prior to arrival. Failure to do so will result in your invitation being revoked.

a. Per the NDA, discussion of Elite gatherings of any kind, before or after, will not be tolerated. Practicing discretion is strongly advised.

3. Lastly, and most importantly, do not engage in anything that you cannot handle. Staff are not responsible for you or your well-being, and by entering our gatherings you are waiving your right to take legal action to any degree.

The symbol on the bottom sent chills down my spine and turned my blood cold. It was a lot clearer now that I was staring at it sober. An eye. I gulped.

How could I be so stupid?

The tattoo on the man's hand . . . It was an eye.

My phone buzzed again.

> **You received one encrypted document from Unknown!**

The NDA.

My hands trembled as the feeling of being completely powerless crept back up without mercy. I had to know.

What if those people were involved? And if the siblings would be there . . . What if Timeless was involved? And Taurus—

My phone buzzed again.

Taurus
> Free or not?

I pushed his text up and, while I could still stomach the thought, tapped the email and opened the document, quickly agreeing to every piece of legal jargon that I refused to read and sending it back. I was going to be at that party, and most importantly, I was going to figure out what the fuck happened to me in that room.

CHAPTER TEN

I STAYED UP ALL NIGHT researching what that symbol could have been and if it was connected to Timeless. Articles materialized about the Espósito siblings, Taurus, and theories dating back to the early 1800s.

There couldn't be any truth to it.

An industry where political figures drank baby blood and actors sacrificed their parents for fame wasn't the industry I had been in for the last six years.

Despite my fear of another nightmare, I spent all night filling my head with bogus articles until I drifted off to sleep on the loveseat. Fascinated by the TV, Josefina stayed up as long as she could too, until she passed out on the couch.

I was awoken by my phone buzzing one too many times, thanks to Nova going on and on about the scheduling for the music video. Everything came back to me like bolts of lightning, and I spent the morning licking my wounds and making sure my assistant could babysit.

Before I could give Nova any answers about the video, I had to talk to Taurus. Then I'd go to the "gathering" and, hopefully, by the end of the night, I would have gotten to the bottom of it all.

At eleven a.m., when I caught Josefina's wandering eyes in the living room—a space she hadn't left yet—I remembered that children need breakfast. I plopped a bowl of dry Cinnamon Toast Crunch in front of her, and she devoured it like it was the first time she had ever tasted it. I wouldn't be surprised if that were the case, actually.

While she was occupied once again with TV, snacks, and Solo, I took a long shower with the faith that she wouldn't move. And forty-five minutes later, when I crept back downstairs with wet toes, hair, and a robe—she had moved. Except it was simply to the floor to play with my kitten a little longer. The scene was endearing. I watched from behind one of the large pillars as Solo let her rub her back and scratch behind her ears. They didn't fear each other, and it seemed like they understood each other— more than I could ever understand her.

My sister.

I shook off the thought and texted my assistant to get here quickly—I had an hour and a half before my driver would arrive to take me to Taurus's. I sat crisscross-applesauce in my walk-in closet, mentally scanning the infinite amount of clothing options. Eventually, I settled on a sheer black top, an oversized leather jacket, jeans, a pair of sunglasses, a pointed heel, and slicked my hair in a bun to go for something more . . .

Timeless.

The doorbell rang, but before I could react to it, an unfamiliar shriek almost ruined my sharp wing liner. I took a deep breath, putting the eyeliner down and thanking whoever was up there that I was done anyway. The screaming continued and so did the doorbell—

"What the hell?" I screamed from the top of the stairs as I stomped down as fast as I could. Once I made it to the bottom of the staircase, the screaming stopped, but I didn't have a clear view of Josefina anymore. The clicking of my heels against the marble intensified as I made my way to the center of the living room, hoping the couches were just blocking her. But what I found was a trembling child who had curled into a ball and was whimpering.

"You've got to be kidding me . . ." I said under my breath, bending down to reach out to her. "Josefina."

She didn't look at me and winced at the sight of my hand. The doorbell rang again, causing another scream to pierce my ears.

"Okay . . . Okay. I'll just go, um, get it." I tried to wipe the annoyance out of my voice but fuck—what was going on with her?

I slapped my hands on my knees before getting up— she jumped again.

"Fucking fantastic," I muttered to myself.

My assistant came in with a cheery attitude, and I quickly explained to her the discretion of the situation. No one was to know that there was a child in The Castle, and if there were ever a time to honor the NDA I made her sign, it would be the current moment.

I slammed the door and hoped that she'd have a smooth time with Josefina because I needed one thing to go right.

Just one.

The ride to Taurus's house went by faster than I could fathom. I swallowed every vile thought I had about him while I still had a few seconds until my next performance.

If the paparazzi were camped out, then this would be my first public sighting since the robbery. It was simple:

I had to be the loving girlfriend who wanted to see her boyfriend.

Not the desperate girl on a mission to figure out why every path led back to him.

We pulled into a cute neighborhood of modest yet expensive homes. They all had flat roofs and more windows than I could count, with orange lighting illuminating their porches. Some were gray, some were black, but they were perfectly landscaped all the same.

My car pulled into a driveway, and where I expected a lavish mansion with far too much space—or even a glass house—I found an unassuming white house with a two-door garage and details that screamed wealth from the solid black roofing to the cobblestone and neatly trimmed bushes. It was obvious that he had paid a lot for this. But it was also obvious that he didn't need much room. It was nothing like The Castle.

When I made it to the glass door with black framing, I was only able to hold up my fist before it swung open.

Click!

A camera flash from behind one of the trees broke my focus. I jumped back a little.

Breathe. Smile.

"You're early," he said in his normal low register, a shining smile appearing as he looked down at me.

He was shirtless.

Great.

I tried to ignore his chest in my face. It glistened like he was working out only moments before. In fact, since his hair was braided back, I could see the sweat beads that had formed on his forehead. His etched abs and broad shoulders gave him an athletic build that was virtually God-like thanks to being six foot five.

"By like five minutes. I didn't expect you to live, like, down the road," I whispered, unsure how close the paparazzi had gotten.

Taurus stepped to the side, and it was then that I noticed the gray sweatpants. Thank God for my sunglasses. "*Mi casa, su casa.*"

I sighed exasperatedly and counted my lucky stars that he didn't fucking touch me. I slid past him, but the home that welcomed me in was enough to make my jaw drop. He had skylights in his living room and disappearing walls that brought the outside in. I hadn't noticed from the front how much property he had out back, but it looked like acres and acres of gorgeous land. The sun was high in the sky and illuminated the room without having to turn on a single light.

When I looked up, there were beams on the ceiling, and when I looked down, white oak on the floors. A fireplace was lit not too far from me, and all the furniture that I could see was black or white. The house was big enough to say, "I have an award shelf somewhere in here," yet small enough to make sense for one person—like I thought outside. In corners, I caught a glimpse of framed pictures of him and family members or friends—a personal touch.

The door slammed.

"You speak Spanish?" I asked in hopes that he wouldn't notice how silent I had become.

"Had to take it in tenth grade," Taurus answered simply before stuffing his hands in his pockets and making his way to the center of the living room.

"On your tour bus," I mentioned.

He only laughed. "You can sit anywhere if you'd like. Unless you're in a rush."

I raised a brow as I took a few steps closer to the couch but opted not to sit. "No, no rush."

He leaned against one of the ivory accent chairs, but I didn't care to act like I was watching him. I crossed my arms over my chest in hopes to fill the silence with action.

His rebuttal was simply clearing his throat. "Do you want water or anything?"

It was so painfully awkward, and a mature person would admit that this was their own doing, but I wasn't there yet in terms of self-growth. Maybe a small part of me wanted to fix this, get to know him, and get comfortable. However, a much larger part of me despised him and, more recently, feared him. The green monster in the pit of my stomach had fully taken control because every time I saw him, I had to remember the girls in middle school wishing they were dating him.

Me included, ironically.

"No. Not unless I can prove it's not spiked or something," I spat out finally—yet his reaction wasn't what I expected.

Instead of laughing or admitting that I had caught him in the act, his eyes softened. He looked at me with sympathy, and his thick brows furrowed out of concern. It made my mouth feel dirty, and my insides twisted in a tight knot.

"Look," Taurus started before he glided across the floors to the kitchen island I had moved to to put more distance between us. He crouched on the other side for a second, then came back up with an unopened case of bottled water in one hand.

It took everything out of me not to gawk at the way his biceps flexed and his veins popped from holding the weight of those bottles with one hand.

"Unopened, just got it delivered this morning. No pressure, though." His voice was soft, replicating the sweet tone I had become accustomed to from listening to his tracks.

"Sure, I'll have one," I caved. Plus, I was getting really tired of the cottonmouth I had developed while being in his presence.

In an instant, he placed the case on the island and ripped open the plastic to pull out a bottle. And unfortunately? It was the only thing filling the awkward silence between us. I found myself needing to say something. It was either that or risk him noticing that I was staring at him between breaths. I might have hated him, and I definitely didn't trust him, but I had eyes like every other person in this fucked up world . . .

And damn, he looked good under the natural light.

"Thank you," I whispered when I grabbed the bottle out of his hands.

He opened one himself. "So, I did want to talk about . . . the last few weeks."

I raised a brow. "To apologize?"

Taurus chuckled. "I guess we could start there. But I was going to ask how you've been first. You know—"

I cut him off before he could say the words. "I'd prefer the apology, and then maybe I'll tell you how I'm doing if I feel like it." I took another few sips and wiped the red lipstick off the rim.

"I'm sorry for crashing your interview." His tone was sincere, but he didn't stop there. "You didn't deserve that. But I swear on my life, I thought you knew that was the plan."

It wasn't his fault, and I knew that. But I couldn't afford to be mad at Nova or my fans for wanting this from me. If romance was how I had to sell music, I had the entire summer and fall to get over it—I knew that, but it didn't make it sting any less. "Whatever. Just make sure you're at the video shoot."

"Surprised you even want me there, stingy."

I rolled my eyes. "Gotta give the people what they want, right?"

He showed me a toothy grin. "I don't know. I think it'd be cool if you got in costume and tried to be the both of us."

"Shut up."

It seemed like the more irritated I became, the more he chuckled. "Now why do I have to shut up?"

"Because you don't know what it's like."

"What what's like?"

"To want so badly to be a part of something that keeps shutting every door in your fucking face. Or putting you in jeopardy." It slipped out before I could catch it, but I was falling through the cracks.

He scoffed and placed the bottle down so that he could grip the edges of the island. "First youngest solo artist to have seven number-one US albums. Two diamond singles, multi-platinum albums. Most-streamed song on all streaming platforms to this day. Eight number-one hits on the Hot 100. Most social media followers by a male musician, not that that one matters as much."

"Your point?"

He shrugged and put his hands up. "And all they see to this day is this: an adopted black kid with a deaf Asian father and a black mother and sister who were picked up off a farm and brought to LA to sing and dance. So, I think I know what it's like to want to be somewhere you're not welcome."

I swallowed my shame and toyed with the water bottle cap to hide how fucking insensitive I must have sounded. "Right. Sorry."

"It's easy to forget." His tone softened again. "I get it. But I live it so . . . If anyone gets that fucked feeling in your head right now, it's me."

"Hm." I bit the inside of my cheek. I couldn't accuse him of anything after that, so I had to go another route. Maybe I could get something else out of him. "Can I ask you something?"

"Shoot." Taurus crossed his arms over his chest and leaned against the counter.

"The rumors." I paused and decided to just own sounding like a crazy person for the time being if I was off base. "About Timeless. Like the mafia and all that." I watched as his eyes grew distant. "Okay, look. I was being silly and reading my timeline, and I came across this insane theory that like—there's this society secretly holding Timeless up. And I was like . . . Oh my God, you're their biggest artist, so you would definitely know if something was up, right?"

The man stalled but quickly forced a laugh out. "What? Man. You know you can't read anything from those 'celebrities are Satan' freaks."

"I'm serious!" I forced out a laugh to match his lightheartedness. "It creeped me out."

He rubbed his nape aggressively. "Nah, nah. I don't know shit about all that."

"Not even like an eye symbol or something?"

He frowned and blinked nervously. "How long were you reading through this?"

I shrugged coyly. "Long enough for your name to pop up."

"Hm." He brushed his bottom lip with his thumb and gave me a long look. "The more you know."

Sweat beads continued to form on his head, and he twisted the water bottle cap over and over again. He was hiding something.

Taurus continued in between an exaggerated deep breath. "But aye, look, I didn't just ask you here to talk."

I scrunched up my face. "Excuse me?"

He stood up straight and walked around the island to meet me, once again showcasing his height and physical dominance over my smaller frame. His dark eyes stared down at me. My panic had reached the ceiling, but my feet remained planted on the hardwood.

What the fuck is going on?

"Can I admit something?"

"If you insist," I shot out quickly, the racing beat of my heart pulsating under my top.

"I've been dying to hear you play something since we recorded those last tracks. And you've never seen my actual studio. You know, where the magic happens."

"Oh."

"You down?"

"I-I guess," I answered, still unsure of what I was signing up for. Despite my best judgment, I couldn't ignore the invisible string pulling me toward him.

"Come on." He brushed past me and motioned me to follow.

I followed a safe distance behind him.

We walked past a frameless glass enclosure and through the hallway where globe chandeliers hovered over our heads. Taurus made a quick turn to the white oak and glass staircase, and when he walked up to the second floor, my heart continued its rampage. At least I had the sunlight to illuminate everything around me, but . . .

Oh.

The barn door at the top of the stairs was wide open, and I was welcomed by a home studio that was more luxurious than mine, but it also had a completely different vibe than the rest of the house. With everything else being black, white, or a pale blue—this room exploded with color.

The overhead lights were dim, but I could see the red and yellow lamps scattered around the space. His studio didn't have a giant computer in the back, but instead, more instruments than I could physically count. If he could play all of these, I would fucking kill myself on the spot.

When we first recorded "To the Moon and Back," it was a pretty quick studio session. If it were up to me, we would have done the entire track via voice memos and Pro Tools. Taurus didn't work like that, though. In fact, in every feature he did, he ensured that they worked together in person.

As the reigning Prince of Pop, he had every right to make demands like that. It was one of the first quirks of his I learned about. Regardless, the session didn't last long. I had stayed for maybe an hour to watch him work on his verse and left as soon as it was ready to be mixed and mastered.

There was an electric guitar placed in the center of the burnt-orange carpet next to a small keyboard. An acoustic guitar to my left and another to my right. Then three more electric guitars in different corners. Two of which were signed. The sound panels were a wine red and plastered all over the walls—there were even two on the ceiling. Under one of the panels was a small window that allowed visitors to see into the recording studio, and not too far from that was the door that led into it. I peeked through the window and saw a mic and headphones—everything I needed to tell me that this was the real fucking deal. In the furthest corner of the room, a gorgeous coffee-colored drum glowed under the orange lighting. I traced my long black nail across the cymbal on my way to take a seat at the piano.

"When was the last time you were in the studio?" Taurus asked as he leaned against one of the only clear spots on the wall.

"What do you mean?" I asked rather defensively.

"You look . . . amazed, that's all. So, I'm assuming it's been a minute."

I bit the inside of my cheek. "I've just never been in one like this."

Which was true. Every other studio I'd been in, including my own, the computer had done a lot of the heavy lifting.

Taurus picked at a loose thread on his sweats and took a seat on the carpet. I looked down at him but kept my squinting glare to a minimum. He reached for the keyboard closest to his feet and touched each ivory key with care. There were a few seconds in between them, as if he was carefully considering where to go next.

Fm. Silence and careful consideration. *C#.* Another brief pause. *Eb.* A longer silence. *Fm.*

He went on like that for a while, piecing together each key and the sound it made to correlate with whatever was going on in his head. He was able to memorize his previous steps like it was being recorded, and after several seconds passed, the hesitation left his fingers. He followed the same key path and nodded his head along with the sound traveling through the room. There was a sweet sense of pride in the way he moved his fingers and how he did so in such a sensual way.

It was effortless and almost intimate.

The more into the music he became, the more mesmerized I became.

It had been a long time since I was impressed by someone who wasn't the woman I saw in the mirror every day. He was a natural. Music always came easy for me, and I think it did for him too.

"New Edition?" I blurted out.

Taurus looked up and immediately smiled with his eyes. "Good ear."

I got up from the stool and walked over to where he was sitting. I considered sitting next to him, but the keyboard between us would keep everything professional. Most importantly, it would keep me safe.

The music stopped. "You wanna try?"

"Oh, don't let me get in between whatever you two had going on."

He tilted his chin up in my direction. "Come on, it'd be an honor to hear you play."

A "fine" was all I could muster as I slid the keyboard closer to me. Electricity radiated off of it as it beckoned my fingers closer. I pressed one key and then several others quickly after. The rhythm came out of nowhere—nothing I had ever heard before. It was both aggressive and vulnerable without a single lyric assigned to it. I pursed my lips and continued to play. At certain parts, it became clunky. I stumbled over my own fingers more times than I liked, but the general essence of it—it was something that would serve as the soundtrack to my nightmares for weeks to come.

I forgot he was there until I looked up and abruptly stopped playing. His dimples were deep, and there was no confusion or distaste on his face . . .

Only that stupid toothy grin again.

"I think we've got a strong start."

I scoffed. "A start? That was fucking good!"

His smile didn't fade as he took the keyboard back, replaying the melody that I had debuted except—elevated. A change of key here, a different tone there.

I fucking hated him.

"I meant what I said, by the way." He spoke over the melody.

"What?"

"It's an honor."

My cheeks heated, and I finally removed my sunglasses. I folded the black frames neatly and let them rest on my lap. "I almost forgot what live music sounded like," I admitted.

His eyes studied me like they studied the keyboard mere moments ago. "You haven't performed anything live from the album yet, right?"

I shook my head.

"When was the last live show you went to?"

"Well." I tried to find a way to say this without sounding like a fraud to the male pop star of our generation. "I was poor and then . . . I've been busy as shit. So, I've never seen a live show other than my own, and like . . . performances at award shows. Do those count?"

Taurus's eyes widened, but he quickly wiped any sign of shock off his face in favor of keeping me comfortable.

"Barely," he finally answered. "I'll have to see about that."

"See what?"

His gaze dropped back to the keyboard. "Just trust me."

How could I explain why I couldn't without accusing him?

Although, that wasn't the scariest thought roaming through my head while I stared at him. It was the realization that I was playing with fire.

CHAPTER ELEVEN

"I SAID, SHOW YOUR CODE." The refrigerator of a man standing in front of the closed door spoke sternly. My stomach ached at the sight of his bulging muscles and clenched jaw. He wasn't dressed like a typical bouncer, though. No, he had a full suit on with red-and-gold accenting. Like a knight protecting his castle, he stood firm and denied anyone who didn't have the right to enter.

The party was at Wave. But when Saint, Savannah, Yessenia, and I had escaped the paparazzi and entered the establishment, no one asked for my phone or proof of the signed NDA. We walked into the club, and the music blared while smoke erupted from the ceiling every time the bass dropped. I began to wonder if I had gotten pranked, but when Saint led us to the back, I noticed there was more to this place than I was previously aware of.

As we walked down a long corridor, my phone buzzed. I immediately muted all my notifications—my assistants updates about Josefina would be the fucking death of me.

When I went back to The Castle to get dressed after bolting out of Taurus's place, she was perfectly fine. I slipped into a red dress that hugged my curves, and flat-ironed my hair until it was bone straight and tucked it behind my ear. To finish the outfit, I selected a pair of mile-high stilettos and my signature black sunglasses, of course.

"QR code."

We were getting closer in line, and I may have been the only one trembling. The corridor was dark and gothic. It was a complete 180 from the disco vibes that Wave had captured.

Timeless artists I vaguely recognized were standing both in front of and behind me—but there was a mix of others I had never seen a day in my life.

I rubbed my phone screen, and the invite glowed with the symbol mocking me at the bottom. Every time I looked at it, a red-hot flash traveled through my body, sending me into a panic that I had to fight to swallow.

It was the same as the nightmares. It struck a familiar fear in my heart as my mother did, as failure did.

In a desperate attempt to feel stable, I grabbed Saint's hand. Maybe with him holding on to me, I could stop seeing double vision. I could sense Yessenia and Savannah burning holes in the back of my head instead of focusing their attention back to the front of the line.

Yessenia opted to wear a black leather skirt and a top that could barely hold her triple Ds in. She complemented it with a high ponytail and side bang that made her look like a real-life Bratz doll. Savannah, on the other hand, wand-curled her hair and wore a jeweled bra with a matching skirt and knee-high pink boots.

Naturally, everyone within a five-foot radius was stopping her to tell her how hot she looked.

I commended Saint on not showing a hint of jealousy, but to be fair, he was giving out compliments of his own to strangers who passed. He opted for some jeans and a black tank top. For a man with muscles that looked like they burst out of every shirt and a perfectly sculpted face—he could do the bare minimum like that.

"QR code."

I had to let go of Saint's hand since he was handing them his phone. The device was scanned, bagged, and tagged before being confiscated. He didn't flinch or object, which meant neither could I.

Saint walked in with his chin up and his shoulders relaxed. When they opened the door for him, I could barely see what was going on inside. I squinted through my dark lenses, but where my sight failed me, my ears caught the intensity of the bass bouncing off the walls. Then the door slammed behind him.

"QR code."

My breath quickened, and I shifted my weight from one foot to the other until I stumbled back and let Savannah go in front of me, pretending to search my purse for something.

Yessenia tugged my arm and whispered, "Are you okay?"

I snatched my arm out of her grip.

"I'm fine. I just didn't have it pulled up fast enough." I kept my vision straight and unlocked my phone so I could hand it off despite my fear. She didn't say another word, and before I knew it, Savannah waltzed into the mystery space as well.

"QR code."

Every part of me wanted to say never mind. Maybe I could outrun the trauma clouding my brain and stiffening my muscles. What if the damn blind gossip pages caught wind that I ran away from a secret event?

Fuck no.

The thought alone made me want to vomit. I handed over my phone.

Scanned. Bagged. Tagged. Gone.

He placed a stamp on my hand. The eye symbol stained my skin with the number 3-4-1 printed neatly in the middle.

"Don't lose that," he commanded before opening the door just enough for me to slip in.

I quickly slid through the space as if the opening was timed, and when I looked up, a new world was presented to me.

Instead of disco or EDM, the DJ was spinning rap and R&B mixes. The dim purple lighting was the only reason I could really see anything. I stepped away from the entrance and walked off to the side, holding on to the railing that separated me from the dance floor down below.

I looked down into the pit where people were dancing and grinding against each other, smoke machines going off every now and then.

My eyes scanned to my left, and just like any other club, there were sections that people rented out. However, these sections were flooded with men in suits and skimpy girls laced over them like winter scarves. To my right was the bar. I let out a sigh of relief when I noticed Saint and Savannah and immediately started to make my way over.

Wait. Yessenia.

I turned back toward the entrance, giving her a few seconds before I went off without her. I couldn't prove it, but the hairs standing on the back of my neck told me that I was being watched.

In a matter of moments, the door swung open, and Yessenia faltered into the new space. I made my way over to her.

"You get in okay?" I asked over the music, looking at my cousin, who had her arms wrapped tight around her wider waist.

The look of confusion quickly left her features. "*Sí.* Just—what did he get us into?"

I blew out my cheeks. "Good fucking question."

She reached out toward me. "Hey. Really quick, can we talk?"

I was on a mission. Not that she knew that, but my patience was growing thin with talks. "Um—yeah. What's up?"

"I didn't know all of that. You know that right? About Marabella. And neither did mami."

"I'm sure," I said nonchalantly. My mother was a narcissist, and it was easier to blame her than someone who I knew had nothing but pure intentions.

"Look, I'll talk to Mami about taking Josefina off your hands. I'm sure she'd like something to do since retiring."

"Really?" I tried to hide the excitement in my voice.

"I'll try but . . ." Yessenia's lips formed a straight line as she stared at me, looking deep into my eyes like I was something to pity. "People aren't the problem, Alejandra. And I know you've convinced yourself of that but . . . One day, I hope you'd at least consider trying with her."

She slid past me, not brave enough to hang around for my rebuttal to her unsolicited advice.

Whatever.

As long as she talked to her mom, I had nothing to complain about.

I was about to follow her to the bar when a voice loud enough to catch my attention echoed from behind me.

"Yeah, yeah, yeah! Just go pull my car around, cool? Cool." The words belonged to a curly-haired man who was clearly off his ass. When I squinted and focused on his mustache, tan skin, and diamond chain with a blinding eye pendant, I swore it was Romeo Espósito.

Two men built like towers walked on either side of him and escorted the stumbling prince down another corridor. I waited for ten seconds, whirled around on my heels, and started walking to where they had vanished to. However, the further away I got from the entrance point to the dance floor downstairs, the less light became available to me.

I walked deeper into the halls, and an overwhelming sense of isolation began to swallow me whole. I went from being able to hear loud music to only hums and whispers behind each closed door I passed.

I took a left turn and ended up down another corridor. Faint footsteps echoed behind me. I quickly turned around, but no one was there. I sped up through the darkness that seemed never-ending. The fear in the air was thick, and a lump in my throat bobbled as I tried to keep myself together.

"Aw, shit. My new favorite toy has delivered herself right to me."

CHAPTER TWELVE

I ONLY MANAGED TO TAKE three steps before being wrenched back by a ruthless grip on my arm.

Everything moved in slow motion.

My hair whipped behind me when I spun around on my heels to face whoever had grabbed me. I yelped, but all sound quickly dissipated from my lungs when I realized I was only looking at a figure covered by clouds of black.

My eyes hadn't adjusted to the darkness, but I managed to make out a man as tall as Taurus but as heavyset as a beast. If I could squint through the dark enough, then I could also see a sliver of light reflecting on his bald head.

There was as much space behind me as in front of me. If I wanted to run, I'd have to pick a direction and hope he didn't know the layout or that he wouldn't grab me first. I lifted my chin and stuck out my chest, choosing to go the difficult route.

"What the fuck did you just say to me?" I called out to the stranger who surprisingly let me pull my arm away.

It throbbed, but I didn't have the luxury of worrying about that right now.

He inched closer—I stepped back. There was a small ceiling light that the predator moved directly under, illuminating the disgusting and slimy man that the voice belonged to.

"I said," he hummed, his thin lips curving into a smirk. "My new favorite toy. You don't remember me, do you?" The stranger smirked. "Looks like Alice finally found Wonderland."

I stomped. "I was looking for the bathroom. Now, excuse you."

He chuckled and placed a hand on his chin, showcasing a tattooed eye symbol on his wrist.

The same symbol that could place him in my hotel room.

The cops were sure they got the guys, but none of the three men they arrested had those tattoos—or was a woman.

"I can show you where it is." He stepped closer again, pointing behind him to the open door he must have come out of.

"I'd rather rip my own eyes out. Now, move." My accent grew thicker alongside my irritation, and I rolled my eyes, attempting to push past him, but I didn't make it far. Almost instantly, I was yanked back by a merciless grip on my shoulder and I hit the brick wall—hard enough to ensure I got the point, but not so hard that it left any lasting effects.

"I said—"

"Hey!" another voice roared from the end of the corridor that I hadn't explored yet. Except this voice didn't sound American—at least, not completely.

He had a Puerto Rican accent.

"What—what the fuck you got going on over here?"

The large man backed off of me, but his musk lingered. My legs trembled, but I refused to let my knees buckle.

"Saw miss thing here wandering the halls. I was just wondering where she was going, sir."

"Mmm . . ." the other man muttered.

It was then that he stepped into the small light, only allowing me to see half of him. He was shorter than the beast—only by a few inches, though. My gaze dropped to his right arm, which was partially covered by a loosely fitted white dress shirt that he had rolled up to his elbow. He was covered in tattoos. Or at least his right side was. A scorpion on his hand, some smaller miscellaneous symbols on his knuckles, giant pieces on his forearm that I couldn't make out—angel wings, maybe?

When I looked up, I noticed the tattoos extended to his neck and then caught a glimpse of the two slits in his eyebrows. If I hadn't known any better, I'd say I found Andrés Espósito.

"What do you want me to do with her, boss?"

Boss? Andrés wasn't old enough to be anyone's boss.

"Go."

"Go?"

"Now."

The men spoke as if I wasn't even standing there. Without hesitation, the beast walked back to the door he came out of and shut it behind him. I was left with my back against a wall. My heart was in my throat, and my stomach was in my ass—and Andrés? He was on his fucking phone.

I used the silence as a sign and decided it was better to not stick around. I slowly straightened my stance and took a few steps back up the hall while he was busy typing.

"Not you," he calmly ordered, sending a thunderstorm through my system.

I dug my heel into the floor and cursed silently to myself before turning to face him. "Um, thank you for that just a second ago. Appreciate it. But I gotta go. These are obviously not the bathrooms."

He stuck his phone back in his pocket and turned around to walk further down the hall. "This way."

I weighed my options once again. I could run back out into the area where the people I actually knew were. Unfortunately, though, I had a sneaking suspicion I wouldn't make it far in the damn house of horrors with henchmen behind hidden doors.

Or I could do what he said and meet the same fate as if I tried to run.

None of my questions would be answered if I ran.

"Where are we going?" I huffed while trekking behind him.

He said nothing.

"Hello! I'm talking to you." I stopped in my tracks after passing one too many closed doors. "I'm not fucking moving until you tell me where I'm going."

Silence.

"So, what? You're just gonna lead me to your super scary dungeon without a damn hello? You don't even know me. I could be a psycho killer or something." I forced the words out, but the truth was that the pit in my stomach was gnawing at me to run while I still could.

In the center of the darkness, all I heard was a deep and annoyed sigh. "Alejandra Garcia. Twenty-five years old and signed to Locke and Key. Not the choice I would have made, but you're still up with the big three—so good for you. Divorced, and if you're looking to remarry, let me know."

I heard him smirk.

"Your ex-best friend caused quite the frenzy, but you going missing for a year and then coming back in the hands of Taurus Sawyer to go against your bubblegum pop roots was probably the most interesting stunt a popstar has pulled in decades. Your dad is nowhere to be found. So your only available parent kept around a circus of men who only made matters worse. Any idiot who listened to a song past your singles or, more specifically, your leaked tracks could put that together. But never mind that. You made the mistake of meeting your hero, who ended up being your first manager. Lucky for you, you didn't get molested by them—well, by her, at least. I'm not sure what other idols you might have, and the men in this industry are . . . touchy. Details, details, details. You were robbed, and that blew up as well. And I assume by now it's being used to boost sales. Which led you to me. So, now that we've proven I know you. Let me show you my *super scary dungeon*."

My chest burned, and my sunglasses felt so heavy on my face that I ripped them off and stuck them in my purse.

No.

I had to keep my wits about me, and I couldn't allow myself to be fazed by information that was publicly available on my fan pages. "You're wrong about one thing."

"Doubt it." He was closer to me now, but I never saw his silhouette move. I could smell his cologne—it was musky and sweet all at once, like roasting marshmallows on the campfire.

"I didn't come back in the hands of anyone but my damn self, thank you very much."

"I stand corrected."

Andrés pulled open a door that revealed a room with some actual fucking lights. Thank you, Jesus!

On the other hand, it allowed me to finally see him in his entirety, and the Getty Images didn't do him justice. His sharp jaw was covered in stubble, and when he licked his plump lips, I almost lost my focus. His hair was shaved down, so at least that was accurate, but the two nose rings layered on top of each other were definitely newer. His dress shirt was untucked with the first three buttons undone and rolled up to show that his body was nothing more than a canvas for permanent artwork.

The door remained open for me, so I slipped past him and into the room.

I surveyed my surroundings to find that I was standing in an office. A desk, cream walls, a laptop, and a waste basket. There wasn't a single window, only a vent that blew out cold air. The right wall was lined with TV screens playing security footage of both this area and the real Wave.

He was sitting in this room watching me.

I gulped and faced him. "What do you want?"

Andrés grinned and walked past me, grabbing a bottle of liquor from under his desk and pouring it into a shot glass. "I could ask you the same question."

"Who was that guy?" I managed to find a second to tug at the unforgiving fabric of my dress and pull it down. "He smelled like a damn dive bar."

He chuckled, taking the shot like it was water. "You won't have to worry about him. Although, it is nice to meet you, Alejandra."

"Aly."

"Well, *Aly*. You have never stepped foot in one of our gatherings before, and when you decided to . . . You're very far away from the people you came with. So, how can I help you?" He leaned against his desk and crossed his ankles as he analyzed me. His eyes were dark and chaotic like enormous tidal waves craving destruction. But through them, there was amusement detailed in his half smile.

Andrés knew more than he was letting on.

"I got lost. I said that like thirty times. And you found me last I checked," I blurted out.

Andrés laughed again before heading to the other side of his desk and toying with his computer. "You lie like you sing—effortlessly and well," he said more to himself than to me. "You're looking for something."

I crossed my arms over my chest. "Okay. So tell me what I'm lying about since you know everything."

"You want to figure out why you've been marked."

"Marked?" I spat out.

"*Correcto*." He turned his computer in my direction to showcase some sort of profile with my ID photo blown up in the top left. "You've been in the system for a year already."

I bit my bottom lip just enough to avoid eating my lipstick. "The system?"

He only nodded and carelessly turned the screen back to him. "The recruitment system." He motioned to the computer. "Everything with the Elite Order has a process, a set of rules, and the system is a part of that."

"Why are you telling me this?" I blurted out nervously. I watched enough movies to know once you learned the villain's plan, then you were pretty much dead. But what I couldn't quite figure out was if this was the part of my fairy tale where I had met a warlock . . . or another prince with keys to a new kingdom.

Andrés considered answering and instead continued his original train of thought. "According to the notes in your file . . ." His eyes quickly scanned the screen. "They almost passed on you. Didn't seem worth the fight to give a struggling pop star well on her way to becoming a has-been the upper hand. Honestly, it would have made this a lot easier for me if they did, but it's not too late to pull you out of the running."

I came across something called the Elite Order in my research the other night. It was talked about in books, essays, and blind items.

The diamond symbol Timeless artists would make with their hands, sacrificial references in music—it all came back to the Elite Order. They were said to be a secret society full of powerful people, and no matter who we elected as president or how well-versed we became in cybersecurity, they always had the upper hand. I didn't believe a single bit of it.

Not until now.

"Too late for what?" I asked, hoping that he didn't notice my brain had momentarily left the conversation.

"One question at a time," he said sourly. "Where was I? Oh, *si*. You almost got passed on. Then the summer came, and even though you were blackballed from events, radio, all that shit, you caught our attention." Andrés's vision remained on the screen as his right hand controlled the mouse. His left hand found itself hovering over the tattoo of that lady on his neck. "You were then marked, and the process began."

I said nothing.

He spun the computer around again, but this time on the screen were pictures of Solo, Saint, Savannah, Nova, Yessenia, Taurus, and my mother.

No Josefina.

For some reason that brought breath back into my lungs. At least he didn't know everything. "*A Series of Unfortunate Events* is what my grandfather named it. The first step after getting a recommendation is the, uh . . . Let's call it an audit. Surveillance, a deep dive on you, your friends, boring, boring technical shit."

"That's not a deep dive. That's a felony."

"To you," he corrected before turning the screen around again. "Then there's your first trial to see if you fold under pressure. Pressure makes diamonds, and well, diamonds are timeless."

"My robbery . . ." I whispered more to myself than to him.

"She's getting it." He clapped his hands together before walking back around to the front of the desk and leaning against it. "The Elite Order has been around longer than you and I. We work in fractions. My father oversees the music industry and—"

"The mafia," I guessed from my research and the rumors my friends had filled me in on.

"Bingo!" he exclaimed with a sinister grin.

I picked at my cuticles and kept a tall chest. "So what part of the process is this?"

"Let's call this a detour. Officially, you haven't gotten there yet."

"Gotten where?"

"The initiation. If you pass that, you move on to the sacrifice. Now let's say you do all of that—then you get anything you could ever want. You become the people you idolize in the blink of an eye. Or you fail and don't even sell-out your own funeral."

He paused and let his gaze sweep over my figure. It was like he could tell that my belly was growing hot as it filled with fear.

"But I pulled you to the side to offer you a way to skip all of that and still get everything you dreamed of. You take on a role next to me. Skip all of the technical shit and the embarrassment," Andrés deadpanned.

"Like a prostitute?"

"Like a bride."

I scoffed. "I'm not for sale."

He couldn't help but laugh. "I'm giving you a way out. If it makes you feel any better, it's a mutual ass-saving, and honestly, you don't know what you're getting into without my help."

I scrunched my face up and stepped back until I hit the wall behind me. "You just told me that I'm being recruited by the boogeyman, and my robbery was a fucking hoax. And now you want to help me out of a situation I didn't even know I was in, with a marriage of all fucking things?"

He casually ran a finger past the diamonds on one of his chains. "I'm presenting you with an option. A role much more fitting for you. Members are broken and reduced to soldiers. I could make you a queen."

"You can't make me what I already am," I corrected.

I had to admit it was triggering, and the tightness in my chest confirmed that. A man who had my files and photos of my friends and family on a computer screen wanted to own me for reasons that I wouldn't understand until I agreed. My skin crawled, and my muscles ached.

"Only a person willing to drown won't grab the life jacket." He hummed. "It's either me or them, Aly. At least with me, all my cards are on the table."

Andrés stood tall, and my entire body froze. I held on to my purse so tightly that if I squeezed any harder, it would have burst open.

"If everything you're saying is true, then what can one man do for me that an entire society of people can't?"

"I have something they don't. The Midas Touch."

"Just because you've painted it golden doesn't mean it's not a cage."

He stalled and so did I.

The entire world went quiet.

"You're already in a cage, *mi amor*."

"So, if I don't agree, then you'll throw me to the wolves? The wolves being . . . Your people or whatever," I finally said.

"*Correcto*."

"I'll take my chances with the wolves," I countered, not hesitating to make my way out of that room and back into the dark hall. I didn't stop for a reply or to see if he was following me. After a few cautious steps, I ran at full speed until I could hear the music again.

I didn't even search for the others before bolting for the door and collecting my phone. My heart was racing, and my lips were quivering, but now that I was back in the real world . . . there was no room to crumble or look panicked.

I had to stay alert—remain posed and photo-ready for any recording phones or flashing cameras. I hid in a stall in the bathroom of the main club, turning my phone on to call my driver. When I did, a text alert caught my attention.

You are invited to the First Initiation. No guests are allowed. The address, date, and time will be sent to your device upon confirmation of attendance. Please reply YES or NO to communicate your commitment after thoroughly reading the rules.

The Rules

1. Guests of any the Elite Order initiation will have their devices confiscated at the door.

2. NDAs should be signed up to 72 hours prior to arriving at an initiation. Failure to do so will result in consequences that are not limited to your invitation being revoked.

a. Per the NDA, discussion of the Elite Order gatherings of any kind, before or after, will not be tolerated. Practicing discretion is strongly advised.

b. These NDAs differ from previous ones you may have signed. You are not to share any information about these initiations, including receiving an invitation, to anyone, regardless if they attend other events.

3. Lastly, and most importantly, your word is your bond. Once you say yes, we expect you to comply with the full extent of the initiation. Failure is one matter, forfeiting is punishable by death.

CHAPTER THIRTEEN

L USH GRASS TICKLED THE soles of my feet, and the sun beamed overhead. A warm glow of a spring day, gifted to me by a bright blue sky, engulfed my being. When I looked down, I was dressed in a pale pink sundress, and my nails were painted lilac purple. The trees and bushes surrounding me grew a variety of fruits, but my attention diverted to the wild vines of guayas that were ready to be picked. I walked over to the sweet green fruit and bit into the shell until it cracked. I sucked on the orange pulp and let the juices trickle down my chin and onto my dress. I ate another and another until my mouth became bitter from the aftertaste.

I couldn't bring myself to want to leave this vibrant paradise.

I wiped my hands on my dress and looked over to see a child playing in the distance. One—no, two. People continued to materialize that I hadn't recognized.

Then a house on a farm.

A majestic white horse walked past me.

Follow it?

Not before grabbing a bunch of guayas and holding them close to my chest. I skipped through the grass and chased after the animal who was leading me to the house. I picked off another fruit and cracked the shell, sucking on the pulp like before.

My gaze fell to my fingers and saw that the clear juice had turned blood red. It was sticky, thick, and all over my fingers and face like honey.

I stopped in my tracks, and blood dripped from my mouth and off the tips of my fingers. Every drop that hit the ground caused a blade of grass to go from green to brown. The horse trotted off into the distance, and the sky turned from blue to a striking midnight black. A cold crescent moon replaced what was once a warm sun. Violent rain fell onto my skin and burned through it like acid.

Then she appeared.

I dropped my fruit and placed a hand over my eyebrows to shield my eyes from the rainfall.

The woman stood tall several feet away from me with a strong silhouette and a blurred face. She wore an Elizabethan-era black dress with an obsidian-encrusted crown to match.

I raised a hand, she raised a hand.

I screamed, she screamed.

Where I conveyed genuine emotions, her copies were only lifeless imitations.

"Look at me!"

"Look at me!" she screamed back.

I woke up soaked in enough sweat to swim in. The echoes of my dreamscape screams replayed in my head, and I tried to shake them out as my eyes readjusted to the darkness of my bedroom.

"Last time I drink to try and fall asleep," I lied to myself before scanning the room to see that the pillows and blankets had been kicked to the floor and the fitted sheet had come off. I got up and stepped over the pillows to grab my phone off the vanity. It glowed in response: 4:45 a.m.

A haunting feeling lingered over me, but it wasn't from Andrés or what he had told me. No, it was from my own inner demons.

I sat at my vanity chair and typed his name in the search bar.

I had met a lot of men in my life. Men with accents, men with tattoos, men with a similar stature.

What I had never met before was a man who made me quake.

Men were a means to an end at their best and idiots at their worst. Easy to conquer with the right smile and touch—and even easier to throw away once you were done.

They practically begged for me to dig my heels into their balls and drain them of whatever power the patriarchy created for them.

My exes also promised that they'd make me golden, but once the mask slipped, they were always dreadfully boring, lacked any kind of spice, and their only personality came from mimicking the men they idolized.

Or me.

I always had a catalog of them at my disposal. Beautiful idiots who couldn't tell smart from wise. They happily signed NDAs in hopes to become my number one and sent gifts to my door for no reason at all.

None ever made me feel as panicked as Andrés, though. Or even as flustered as Taurus.

I scrolled through the news tab, but as always, the press was useless.

Antonio Espósito's 4 Kids: All About the Bachelor's Children

Andrés Espósito's Father Backs Anti-AI in Music: "Protect Our Musicians"

I typed "The Elite Order" in my search bar once again.

My phone took longer than usual to load. So long that I got up to check the router, and eventually, the screen read, "Error. Please make sure you've spelled all words correctly."

My blood ran cold.

I tried various versions of the name, and nothing I had accessed before was available. Andrés had pictures of me, my friends, and my family and had been watching me. He wanted me to be able to access the information I found before, and now it was gone in a matter of hours.

I wasn't safe, and no one I knew was either.

Josefina.

I quickly got up on my feet and bolted down the steps. When my toes reached the icy tiles of the first floor, I searched for her in the wide space.

There she was. Sleeping soundly on the couch under a blanket two times her size. I breathed a sigh of relief and walked over to her.

Josefina stirred, and her eyes fluttered open shortly after. A quiet mutter slipped from her lips, and she sat up, rubbing her eyes and holding on tightly to that dirty bunny.

Okay, Alejandra, I thought, *now or never.*

I made my way from the back of the couch to the front, crouching down in front of her. "Hey . . . kid." I swallowed hard and tried my best to imagine that she was Savannah's son . . . or a fan . . . or a colleague's child. Not my sister, who I, whether I liked it or not, was responsible for until I could offload her onto someone more worthy of taking care of a child.

Someone who had experience or enough room in their life to cater to a kid. Like my aunt.

I swore I saw her brown eyes twinkle at me, like she saw something in me that I hadn't quite caught yet.

"I'll find you a good home, I promise. It'll be safe, too." I dropped to my knees so that I was more at eye level with the child. "As for now . . . we need to take a bath." The word alone caused her to jump.

I tried again. "You can take your bunny with you if you want. Maybe you both can get clean."

Her eyes were studying mine with more wisdom than I would ever expect from a child. Her chocolate swirls that filled the white space in her eyes analyzed me in a way that made me feel . . . seen.

"Josefina," I said softly.

A soft jab hit my cheek, and I blinked several times— *did she fucking poke me?* Josefina giggled, but it only got louder when she poked my lips right after.

Ew. Ew. Ew.

I rose to my feet, and the sound of her rhythmic tickled spirit filled the empty living room. "Okay . . . Josie. Can I call you that?"

She ignored me and held her bunny tight while she roared with laughter. I did a few quick turns around my house for something—anything that would get her attention and get her in the damn bathroom.

Solo slept soundly under one of the barstools by the kitchen island. I hiked up my pajama pants and scooped the growing kitten off the floor before stomping back to my place in front of a calmer Josie. She still had a nasty case of the giggles, and for a moment, I was looking in a mirror.

Pure childhood joy.

Something she felt safe enough to experience because of me.

For the first time in years, I enjoyed my own reflection.

I shook the thoughts out of my head and shoved the cat in her face. "Solo wants you to take a bath."

Josefina cocked her head to the side like I had grown a tail and three extra arms. She remained quiet. Solo, still sleepy, dangled in my hands.

I sighed and gently put my kitten down before staring the spawn in her eyes. I wanted her to know I was serious, but not so serious that I triggered her the way people carelessly triggered me.

"You like chocolate, don't you?"

Josefina perked up, more intrigued now than she was before.

"I make a killer chocolate tres leches."

Her interest flickered again.

"I will make you one even though it's the middle of the night, but—"

She was already up and even took the initiative to grab my hand before I could grab hers.

I started to walk with her.

"We don't have bedtimes here or even rules, really," I continued as I led her up the stairs that didn't feel so daunting tonight—turning on lights as we went. "And today . . . I'll let you in my room." I pushed the door open to my bedroom and watched as her eyes sparkled at the sight of all the furniture and the space, which undoubtedly exceeded anything she had ever seen before. She wasn't old enough to understand the awards on the shelf in the far-right corner, but I could tell she felt the energy of my bedroom.

It was everything I had ever dreamed of when I was her age.

I pushed open the door to my bathroom, and a gust of wind welcomed us in.

My sacred place had opened its arms to her.

I had sat in every corner sobbing from a nightmare at one point or another. It was my isolation chamber where I didn't have to explain to anyone why there was a blanket under the sink or an emergency bottle of vodka.

That was what made isolation such a tempting treat.

No one had the opportunity to ask why I let my hair get so long. No one was there to notice when I binged TV all night and slept all day. There was no one there to watch me rot on the couch, on the floor, in bed, or by the pool.

I could exist freely.

I could be as bloated as I wanted and never think twice about a breakout. I could get drunk and lose time as often as I wanted. It wasn't a desirable way of living, but it got me through the worst times of my life.

Isolation was the only home I ever had. And with all that time spent hiding, there had to be a piece of me forever lost within the walls of The Castle.

The water had been running, and if it weren't for Josefina's arms wailing around and her bunny slapping my ass, I wouldn't have noticed.

"Oh," I uttered while scrambling to turn off the water and sprinkle in some very expensive bubble bath. "Okay . . ." I pointed at the tub, which was filled with warm water and smelled of lavender. "You're going to get in there."

Before I could finish my sentence, she was already trembling in the furthest corner of the room.

I walked over to her and placed a hand on her cheek. She wanted to fight it, but quickly succumbed to my touch. I didn't want to hurt her, and she knew that.

I recognized the way she shook and tried to cover her throat. She must have remembered the way water filled her lungs, the fight to keep her eyes open until they burned so badly she had to close them. I never understood why my mother tried to drown me. Or why I used to find a safe haven in bathtubs until my robbery.

Now?

The idea of being in one felt fucking suffocating.

There was nowhere left for girls like us to turn to.

"Hey . . ." I looked at the bunny she clung onto for dear life. "My bunny . . . Can I call you that?"

She nodded. "*Si.*"

"Um . . ." I gulped, wondering what would truly put an end to the trembling and get her in the bath. "There's nothing scary about baths, okay?"

She didn't budge.

"You may have seen a monster before, but no monsters live here or can visit you. This is a . . . castle!"

She eased up, turning fully to face me once again.

"There's a man outside guarding The Castle, and I'm inside . . . making sure you're safe. You are like a pretty princess. And my job is to take care of you… I'll take care of you." I placed a hand on my chest. "Me. Your sister."

There was no clear way to tell that she understood what I said. Or that I even did. But she let me help her undress and refused to let go of the bunny throughout the entire process. In fact, he had to go in with her. I had no complaints because the bunny smelled like shit too.

To combat the silence, I played her some of the songs from my first EP and album. She seemed to move more to the *Spanglish* ones and absolutely hated anything that featured a rapper.

I leaned against the wall to pet Solo while scrolling on my phone, and she played with her soaking-wet bunny and the soap dish. When it was all said and done, the sun had risen fully, and I was able to dry her off before putting her in a shirt that fit like a nightgown on her. My bed was right there, and having her sleep on the couch felt . . . monstrous at this point.

So, I gathered the blankets and pillows off the floor and remade the bed because princesses should never sleep in anything less. I then tucked her in and watched as she drifted back to sleep.

But as she lay there, next to her, I wondered, *How could someone sleep after a life like that?*

I still hadn't figured that part out.

CHAPTER FOURTEEN

I REREAD THE INITIATION TEXT over and over for days to come. Reminders counting down to the event from unknown numbers came in at least twice a day.

An initiation and a sacrifice (whatever that meant) were all I had to give up to have everything I could ever dream of. It sounded easy enough.

I wanted to be a household name. I deserved to be immortalized. So why hadn't I confirmed yet?

The constant battle in my head was growing to be exhausting. Maybe that was why I agreed to go with Taurus to a concert despite my first big performance and second interview of the era coming up.

Late Nights with Nila. Hosted by one of the most legendary ex-acts in the game.

Nila Arora started her career on prime-time television. She was America's sweetheart. She had played the role of the wholesome daughter of a wealthy businessman, and she played it perfectly until the show ended, and she ventured into music.

That transition didn't go over so well.

She pioneered the first "good girl gone bad" rebrand my generation had ever seen. Looking back, there was nothing odd about a twenty-year-old woman wanting to show some skin and hump a hot guy in a music video. But parents both in America and India burned her merch and forbade their children from supporting her any further.

Despite the backlash, she made a shitload of money, got married three times, did a couple of movies, had kids, and still made time for two very public breakdowns.

Her second rebrand came three years later when she launched a cookware line, started wearing pastels, married her wife, and came back to TV with *Late Nights with Nila*.

Nila was the pop industry, especially for women of color.

If I fucked up, missed a step or a note—she'd know. So why did I agree to go to a concert right before instead of rehearsing? Unearned confidence, I guess.

Electric performances and undeniable stage presence were what she was known for, and retired or not, a true artist never loses their touch.

It took a lot of begging, but when I got back to The Castle, I was able to convince Yessenia to take Josefina for the night so that I could see Innamorati in concert and hopefully get some inspiration prior to my Nila debut.

When the car pulled up to the back gate, a woman who was too busy talking into her earpiece ushered me into the stadium.

The energy was indescribable.

The swelling of the drums filled my ears, and the growing excitement of the audience caused goosebumps to appear on my exposed chest as I was practically galloping to keep up with the woman's speed.

My body was dressed in leather pants, a black bralette, and vintage Celine knee-high boots. The look was brought together by an oversized leather jacket and some silver chains and rings.

I was led backstage where I swore I saw the band tuning up their guitars and getting ready to go on. I wanted to stop and say hi, but apparently time was unforgiving.

The woman motioned me to walk faster as she opened a door and started sprinting up the stairs. I was practically chasing her, and the continuous crescendo of energy caused by the drums wasn't helping my anxiety.

Finally, we reached the sky box.

She pulled open the big steel door, threw me in, and shut it behind me so that she could run back to whatever she was doing.

"Jesus," I muttered under my breath as I adjusted my jacket.

"Welcome in." The cheeriness in Taurus's voice almost earned him a response, but when I looked around, I was standing in a glass box above the arena where the fans couldn't see me.

"I—"

Whatever snarky comment that was going to slip out of my mouth was cut off by a more up-tempo energy from the riffs of a guitar that contrasted the drums warming up the crowd mere moments ago.

The roar of a chant filled the arena shortly after. "Enjoy the sound! Join us in the crowd! Enjoy the sound! Join us in the crowd! Enjoy the sound! Join us in the crowd!"

The lights dimmed until it was pitch black.

They continued to chant.

Red stage lights erupted around the space, and fog machines went off from various directions.

"Enjoy the sound! Join us in the crowd! Enjoy the sound! Join us in the crowd! Enjoy the sound! Join us in the crowd!"

The lead singer, a lanky man with a blonde buzz cut, came out in nothing but a kilt and black platform boots. He lifted his hands up once he got to the center stage and grabbed the microphone off the stand.

The chanting came to a sudden halt.

The entire arena was at his command.

Their guitarist came next. She was much shorter, but her presence was immense. She had half of her hair colored blonde and the other half blue, brought together by a fringe bang. She wore see-through flare pants and a top to match, not even looking at the guitar as she strummed it to all hell.

The bassist came next, and from my fangirling, I knew that he was the twin brother of the drummer. Both of them had long blond hair, so that was pretty obvious.

"Stand up, stand up! Gather around, gather around! You're about to feel something you've never felt before," the lead finally sang, and the entire crowd exploded with shrieks. From a distance, I was sure I saw someone faint.

"Looks like a daydream, feels like a nightmare. I don't recognize who I've become."

The members gave the lead his space as he worked the crowd. He embodied every lyric and was either really good at acting or was definitely off his face.

They were all so mesmerizing. They didn't need extensive choreography or a million dancers, and the crowd worked with them as if they were at rehearsals, too.

My phone buzzed, and I broke out of my trance to quickly look down at it.

> **Reminder! You have one AutoSign document that has not been fulfilled.**

"You can't go back, you drank the blood and haven't paid your debts. It's too late, you're one of us now!" he continued to sing.

I slowly dropped my phone and stared back through the glass. The drums had halted, and the only one playing now was the bassist.

When he lifted his hands to clap, so did everyone else.

They were in charge in a way that I had never experienced.

"All right, I'm going to need all of you pretty motherfuckers to do one thing for me, all right?"

Everyone cheered.

"If you've seen us live before, you know we like to start this shit off right. So, when this beat drops, we're going to fuck this shit up, got it?"

Everyone screamed.

"I want to see mosh pits. I want to see head banging. I want you to fuck this shit up, do you hear me?" he screamed even louder, and they did as well.

Sure enough, when the drummer clapped his sticks together over his head, the music swelled and everyone went crazy. People were knocking each other over, and like it was perfectly planned, a giant mosh pit formed where they ran in circles and punched strangers until they bled. Those who were glued to their seats raised their phone lights and illuminated the arena like a million fireflies.

My eyes shot down to my phone. I couldn't bear the thought of Taurus staring at me in such a hypnotized state. I reopened the invite and the NDA that went with it.

I had two options—plain and simple.

Reply yes or no.

I wanted this. I wanted to fill an arena on my own and captivate people without lifting a finger.

I could have it all. I just had to say yes.

Fuck what Andrés said—I had the opportunity to be bigger than I ever imagined.

"It's amazing, isn't it?" Taurus spoke in a low, alluring tone. He was hovering behind me, but I couldn't look up. His hand found itself on my shoulder, and a shiver slithered down my spine. "It's what we all want, ain't it? To have fans screaming your name like wolves howling at the moon. It's an exhilarating fucking feeling. Shit, addictive too."

"Says you," I muttered.

He only laughed.

My finger hovered over my phone screen where a simple "YES" had already been typed. I pressed send, and another message populated.

> Thank you for confirming, Alejandra Lilith Garcia, born August 8, 1998. If this is not you, reply with STOP. If this is you, reply YES.

> Yes.

> Thank you. Your attendance to the First Initiation has been confirmed. The event will take place at 1384 Park Avenue, December 21st.

Tomorrow?

"You can't go back, you drank the blood and haven't paid your debts. It's too late, you're one of us now! But wait, there's no way out!" the crowd sang along.

> Our records indicate that you have not filled out your NDA. Would you like to expedite your signature for a processing fee of $99? Reply YES or NO. Caution: Replying NO will terminate your invitation.

"I want this for you. You gotta experience it, man," Taurus continued.

I broke my focus from my phone and finally looked up at him. "Can I ask you something?"

"Shoot."

"When it really got hard for you . . . What would you have given to be where you're at now?"

He looked to the ceiling to debate his answer before looking back down at me. "Shit, everything."

"Me too." I looked back down at my phone and typed "yes" before I could chicken out.

> You have two hours from delivery to electronically sign and send it back along with your payment.

CHAPTER FIFTEEN

I SPENT THE NEXT TWENTY-FOUR hours doing everything besides losing my mind.

I often stared out the window and wondered what was more possible: snow in Los Angeles or Andrés's warning holding some truth to it.

Was I actually handing myself over to the wolves in exchange for a ten-pound award? Possibly.

I had to try nonetheless.

My future depended on me.

The address given placed me on the property of an actual castle. Not to be confused with the mansion I laid my head at but instead a fortress with an unforgiving darkness looming over it. Gray stones of various sizes stuck together to complement the pointed arches and stained glass windows with diamond-shaped panes. Ancient statues of cherubs with clipped wings surrounded the fountain out front and pointed toward flying buttresses that could only be from the Gothic Revival of the 1800s. Even in darkness, I could tell that the property was well taken care of, but as I got closer, I noticed foliage growing around the front-facing gable roofs—a stylistic choice, no doubt.

A gust of wind caused me to shudder, and crows cawed like they were warning me to go back to The Castle while I still could.

The instructions were plain and simple. Once I said yes, I had to see it through.

A guard stood tall at the entrance and followed my entire journey to the door. He wore a well-fitted suit with no identifying markers. It was black from top to bottom, but what struck fear in my heart and caused me to lose my breath was the raven mask he wore. It was made of some sort of metal and was painted black with gold outlining. There were no distinctive facial features visible.

Only green eyes that felt . . . hollow. No.

Evil.

I gulped, holding out my phone with the invitation, assuming that was how I would be granted access. He ignored my phone and gave me a questioning look.

I immediately wondered if it was the jeans, hoodie, and jacket I chose to wear that was throwing him off. A dress code was never sent, so I went with something practical. Sneakers so I could run, but designer ones so I looked like I knew how to spend my money.

The large stranger lifted his hand, and I flinched, but the device he was holding released a red light that scanned my face and body from top to bottom. When it beeped, he steadily pulled the colossal brown doors open, revealing a foyer like something I had only seen in movies.

Golden lighting introduced me to bustling individuals in identical raven masks and black robes, a few of which were stopping every so often to gawk at me in the entryway and whisper amongst themselves.

Obsidian-colored statues of knights and animals were placed in various corners, and a large vase of roses was planted a few feet in front of me before the *Titanic*-esque staircase. It was then that I stepped inside without question.

There was no time or space to look hesitant.

I caught sight of a few fox masks sprinkled within the ravens. They were also obviously a heavy material and painted black with the same gold detailing.

First one, then two, then dozens in red robes.

My body froze.

Those were the same masks that stared me down and tied my legs and hands together.

The door slammed shut behind me, and the roar that echoed through the house shocked me back to reality. I swallowed the lump in my throat and attempted to take a few more steps inside, only to be halted by a tight grip on my shoulder. "Robe."

I raised a brow but quickly fixed my face and nodded as a smaller woman, also in a raven mask, dressed me in a boysenberry-colored robe that swallowed me whole.

"Stay put," the smaller woman commanded. I knew better than to disobey in unfamiliar territory, so I kept my hands at my sides and did just that. The woman walked into a room where the door was left ajar, but it was so dark in there I couldn't tell what the room actually had in it. Before my eyes could adjust, she appeared from the darkness with a different mask in her hand. Nothing like the ones I had seen so far.

A mouse.

As she reached above me and snapped the strap against my head . . . only one thing was clear.

They were the predators, and I was the prey.

She pushed me forward, and I heard her begin the same process with the person who came behind me. I wanted to look and see who else was entering, but my gut was screaming to keep looking forward.

A guard protected the striking staircase with black railing and vibrant red carpeting. He was dressed in a black robe and his raven mask like everyone else who clearly belonged here. He waved me to the left like an impatient TSA agent.

I turned and made my way down the corridor and ran into a crowd of people. They scattered up and down the hallway but were all facing the same direction. It was obvious as I passed the stained glass and baroque artwork that there were people who knew each other and figured that much out. On the other hand, there were others like me, who were looking like lost puppies through their masks and depended on the ushering of the men posted at every corner to direct us.

The scattered group had expanded to clusters of us crowded in a long corridor. Chandeliers illuminated the space ahead, and anticipation rose as the whispers around me slowly died off. I looked around, wondering if there was a signal that I had missed.

Nothing.

Instead, I focused my attention forward, remembering to keep my chin up despite the weight of the mask. My neck strained to keep my head up, and every so often, I had to force my hands down whenever they rose to take it off or at least loosen the strap.

Through the small windows for my eyes, I could see a pair of large doors being swung open without warning by two ravens.

What was revealed was more than I could have imagined on my own.

Everyone began to hesitantly tiptoe through the opening and welcome themselves to an awe-inspiring space. It was as large as a palace ballroom, dripped in gold, and detailed with blood-red accents. There were four seats.

No.

Thrones, that were placed on a stage so tall we couldn't touch them if we stood on each other's shoulders. The doors slammed behind us, and while some people jumped, I kept a steady gaze ahead.

Four cloaked figures walked gracefully onto the stage. They weren't wearing black or red, though. They were dressed in royal blue from head to toe. Their cloaks had hoodies that hid their hair and gloves that matched the robes, and unlike the ravens, their masks were eagles with golden beaks.

When they sat down, the ravens positioned in each corner of the grand room ushered us to as well. I plopped my ass right on the floor while my heart tried to warn me to get the hell out of there. I ignored it and chose to occupy my nerves by picking at my cuticles until they bled.

"Welcome, Council." A man bowed to them, stepping off to the side of the stage.

They simply nodded back in goosebump-inducing unison. It was at that moment that I noticed the triangle behind them. It had an eye in the middle, and if I didn't know any better, I would say it was looking right at me.

"To be here is a luxury." The tallest eagle on the far right spoke so calmly, yet it bounced off the walls like bass on good speakers. "To be here is an honor." He sounded older, like someone's reminiscing grandfather would. "To know the Elite Order to the extent that you already have is a dream much greater than what you've managed to conjure up yourselves. And that—" He paused and lifted a finger like a professor mid-lecture. "That is why we are still here and opening our world to you. The new world needs minds that are expansive and teachable so we can continue to mold it in our image."

"Each and every one of you is powerful in your own way. It's why you were invited." The next eagle spoke, and this one was obviously a woman with a slight European accent. "You all have your own natural talent and influence, yes. But to survive our initiation, you have to let go of everything you've learned and instead follow the true you. Letting your instincts guide you is what this organization was built on many . . . many moons ago. And together we will craft a world that is ours to harvest and feed from whenever and however we see fit."

The next one sat up, commanding the space almost immediately. "To do that, we need strong people. Dedicated people. This isn't about scratching an itch or feeding an appetite. This isn't about securing your spot in the Songwriters Hall of Fame or a billion-dollar movie deal. No, no. It's much bigger than that. Because those are frivolous goals created by us to seek out people like you. What it's really about is becoming immortal."

He took a breath, letting the words seep into my skin like rain falling from the sky. "First, you must prove you're worthy of serving the cause. That will be your first task. Don't say I didn't warn you."

The last one sat in silence, having nothing to offer, but if I squinted, I could see their eyes darting back and forth from corner to corner. They were analyzing every person in the crowd. We were being hunted.

The raven who stepped off to the side returned, standing close to the thrones but not in front of them. "We will be handing out numbers. They will fall between one and four."

Four more ravens walked to different spots around the floor, boxing us in.

The man on the stage pointed. "One. Two. Three. Four. Once you get your number, you will gather with your group. Then you will wait for your initiation to begin. Good luck."

CHAPTER SIXTEEN

Two.

The number was engraved on what had to be a small golden plaque. It wasn't any bigger than my hand, but I swore at the top right corner of it, there were specks of dry blood.

A glob of vomit bobbled up and down my throat.

Two women had gone not too long ago, and it took them about fifteen minutes before they were wailing and being escorted out by two large ravens. Group one had only one person escorted out so far, but they were more frozen than sad. Group three hadn't had anyone return yet, but no one had really gone in so far. And group four, well . . . The same person had been in there for quite a while. No one else had been called yet.

It was clear that whatever number you had determined the trial you had to go through. We were handed our numbers with precision and intention.

Absolutely nothing was random.

An aggressive tug on my arm forced me away from my group, and without preparation or even a prayer to a god I didn't believe in . . . it was my turn. My knees were buckling and my feet felt like they were covered in cement.

I swallowed.

The golden walls turned gray as I was escorted away, and my chest squeezed like a blood pressure cuff was wrapped around it. My heart roared when I was met with another fucking hallway. Except this one was filled with tapestries and framed artwork that depicted bloody battles of gods I only knew from middle school classes.

I read the engravings at the bottom of the frames: Demeter hung by grape vines, Dionysus drowning in a sea of blood, Icarus on fire, Aphrodite with a sword through her heart. An unsettling rhythm pulsated from my chest, and if I were insane—which I very well could have been—I'd remember the tempo and make a song out of it.

The doors we walked past were exactly what I'd expected. No matter the haunting undertone of the palace, everything was kept sparkling. They were freshly polished, and even in the dim lighting, the paintings were clearly well-kept. We stopped at a shut door, and I was pushed directly in front of it before the raven escorting me walked away.

I could run right now.

To the right of me was the ballroom, and there was no way I was getting far if I ran that way.

To the left of me was a damn mystery.

The black door was pulled open before I had a chance to sort my own thoughts out. I looked up to see an eagle mask looking down at me. I couldn't tell which one of the council members was standing before me, but the intensity of their silver eyes was almost enough to knock me off my feet.

Why would they go through the trouble of wearing contacts?

"Proceed." The woman manifested a sweetness to her voice like a lioness on the prowl.

I slipped through the space she opened for me and felt the weight of my purple fabric dragging against her blue robe as I passed her.

The room was as dark as the hall, but besides another door at the other end, there was only a table, two chairs, a bottle of labelless deep red wine, and one glass.

"Remove your mask, Alejandra." A soft click signaled that the door was now locked. And no amount of sarcasm could cure my cottonmouth or halt my trembling hands.

I couldn't hide my fear without my mask. I couldn't focus on the pain of holding it up instead of my racing thoughts.

I ignored my shaky hands as best I could and reached for the strap at the back of my head to pull the mouse face off, placing it gently down on the ground.

I was sure my makeup was smudged from all of the sweating I had been doing, but there was nothing I could do about that. I couldn't see her face, but I swore I heard her smirk.

"Have a seat."

I obeyed, taking the seat facing her so that she couldn't surprise me.

"Why that seat?"

I swallowed the lump in my throat. "I picked it randomly."

She pulled out the other chair left and gracefully sat down, the waves of blue flowing behind her. "Let's not start on lies, songbird."

The stranger poured the wine and didn't stop until it was almost to the brim. "That's rule number one. Rule number two is that you finish this glass." She pushed it toward me, and I stared at it.

Mierda.

I was the self-proclaimed town drunk up in the hills. I've chugged more wine than what she was offering on my couch while binging cartoons.

I could do this.

"I know everything about you, Alejandra," she continued. If she had access to half the information Andrés did, I didn't doubt that. "I know your wildest dreams." Her gloved finger traced against my jawline. My entire body shivered, but I kept my face stone cold. "I know your past, your present, and if you pass . . . I'll know your future. Drink."

I lifted the glass to my lips without obvious hesitancy. It took all of my strength, but I did it.

The wine was sweet and went down smooth. It was like nothing I had ever had before, could have been some old-age rich shit they kept hidden in a cellar.

After swallowing, I took the silence as a chance to speak. "So what is left for me to do?"

"Tell me the things I don't know."

I opened my mouth and closed it before opening it again. "You already know everything about me."

Her eyes twinkled. "Some demons don't live on paper."

"What about my future?"

She was silent, but I swore from her eyes that she was smiling. There was something so eerily familiar about the woman hovering over me. It caused a gnawing in my gut and a whisper in my mind that screamed, *"I know her!"*

"You crave a legacy that even you can't escape. An impact that will forever be imprinted on the world and especially . . . like one of your less-spoken dreams: Mexico. In our future for you, you make your mother's homeland proud in a way she never could. In a way that won't make you feel so empty."

"I already feel hollow," I said through gritted teeth. My heartbeat slowed, and I took that as a sign to keep drinking the wine.

"That brings me to my second point." Her sultry tone mixed with the European accent was an intoxicating cocktail.

So intoxicating that I didn't notice my fingers going numb.

"If you fail, I see a different future. I see you being reduced to nothing. You will live the remainder of your life submerged in a dream that you'll never touch until it rots you from the inside out. A tragic story of a dazzling starlet who overdosed in a hotel bathroom that her bank statements would later show she couldn't afford anyway. That would be your final statement to the world."

The longer she spoke, the more her accent slipped through the cracks. The European one wasn't real.

Silence filled the room, and she stared at me until she was ready to speak again. "Are you ready?"

I began to feel dizzy and no longer in control of my own body. I was numb, and fear had suddenly been replaced with a need to be touched. After blinking several times, I was able to focus my vision once again. I couldn't be weak.

I couldn't fail.

"Yes."

The woman rose from her seat, and before I knew it, my robe was sliding off of my body, and the purple was spilled onto the floor.

I leaned into her touch.

It felt warm, safe, and secure.

My eyes fell closed regardless of how badly I fought to keep them open.

"Tell me . . ." she whispered in my ear, the beak from her mask rustling through my hair. Her breath created a cold chill down my chest.

My jacket and hoodie had also been removed.

I was losing time.

I was losing track of everything.

"What is your deepest desire?"

My mouth parted, but nothing came out.

"What would you give up your soul for, Alejandra?"

"I—" My head fell back, and I succumbed to her embrace. "Everything."

"More."

"Um . . ." My brain momentarily stalled like I had forgotten the English language. "I wa—want a Starlight Award. A lot of them . . . I want to be adored to the point where my fans are feared."

"More. Bigger."

"I want a legacy."

She ran her hands through my hair, I thought.

There was no confirming it since I couldn't feel the nerves in my scalp anymore.

"You think too small." The whisper traveled through the air like a threat. "That's why you need me, love. A real mentor to tell you what to do, what to wear, and when and who to speak to. I want you to be my favorite project."

I fell forward onto the table.

She had let go of me.

"Your initiation will now begin."

"Help . . ." I muttered against the steel. "Please."

I couldn't move or even see my own fingers.

"No."

A door creaked. It had to have been the one behind me.

"Your first task is to gain control of your mind and body. I don't want a fragile soul. I want one willing to fight for her life. How can you live forever if you can't protect yourself?"

"What did you do to me?" I whined once my eyes filled with tears.

The effects of the drug had an eerie similarity to the one that kept me still in that hotel room. I was teetering the line of being in and out of consciousness. Every finger twitched.

"I will give you everything you could ever dream of. You will be someone in this industry to fear. The Starlights and diamond records are accomplishments that won't make the first six pages of my resume when I'm done with you. Your worst day will be someone else's biggest dream. But first, you have to get up."

I gripped the ends of the cold table in front of me, squeezing my thumb underneath to push myself up.

Everything had gone numb.

My muscles tensed, and lifting my head felt like lifting a semi-truck on my shoulder blades. I blinked several times, and tears streamed down my cheeks, but eventually, I stood.

I managed to step around my robe and noticed my pants and sneakers were across the room. I was in my underwear.

I didn't recall them being removed.

"Good girl. Now walk to me." Her voice sounded distant, but I followed it like a siren's song. I stumbled through the door, holding on to the frame to keep my balance, only to be met with a steamy heat.

"I am the only being who can give you what you ask for. No more giving up on yourself, Alejandra. No more being surrounded by people who don't know what true success really is."

My hair dampened instantly and stuck to my back and nape.

I had lost sight of her.

My stomach fluttered like a butterfly trapped in a cage. She had sunk her razor-sharp teeth into me, yet I only desired to be close to her.

I focused on what was before me. Even through blurry vision, I could tell that the room was hauntingly large. A few inches away from my feet were columns of stones with steam bouncing off each one. In the far-left corner was a glass booth with only a sink and a bucket.

"Aren't you tired of letting yourself down?" Her voice echoed through the room.

Where was she?

Wake up, Alejandra. It's a dream. It has to be, I thought over and over again.

The door slammed shut, and I jumped out of my skin, almost losing balance and falling face-first into the rows of stones. The temperature radiating off them hit my face with an unforgiving heat. Then I was pulled up.

"Strength is our greatest asset. And strength comes from the Order." Her soft hands sent a shockwave through my system when they gripped my shoulders, and I wanted to kick myself because it calmed me. "Hence the term . . . strength in numbers. The ones before you have done the hard work and claimed the world as you know it. Those who control the media control the world. And you have been given an opportunity that some people would die for. So it's only right that you die for it first. Your soul is tainted. You've been wounded almost daily since birth, my songbird. But to repair it, I have to uncover it. Do you understand?"

All I could do was listen. My body became so heavy that leaning against her provided my only sense of relief.

"This is my favorite room by far. The fire and ice room. It's warm here . . . You feel it, don't you?"

I nodded lazily.

"But in that box over there, it's sub-zero temperatures. It might sound scary now, but you'll need to cool down."

She let my body go, and with all my strength, I kept myself upright. Her steps echoed, but I had lost her once again.

I focused on the rocks instead. There were three, maybe four rows of them. Or ten?

I couldn't focus. They kept multiplying, and eventually, the length of the stones varied every time I blinked.

"Crawl to me."

I dropped to my knees like a desperate sinner at the cross, and without a sliver of doubt, I put my hands in front of me to position myself on all fours. I placed my first hand on the stone and immediately jumped back. It shocked all the feeling back into my system when I looked down and saw an open blister on my palms.

"I said crawl!" she demanded, her voice roaring from the other end of the room.

I tried to remind myself to keep hiding my fear, but I couldn't navigate what muscles in my face were activated. I took a deep breath and closed my eyes before putting my hand back on the stone.

I winced at the pain but added my next hand, then my knee, my other knee, and moved up so that the balls of my feet could join. My entire body felt like it was on fire, and all I could think about was Marabella.

As I moved step by step, wincing every time I touched a new stone, I remembered the times she held my hand over our gas stove. I remembered the way the heat radiated from the flames and teased my skin.

Except this time, I was actually burning.

Once I could smell flesh, I opened my eyes, peeling my charred skin off of every rock. I had to be almost done.

I had to be.

I looked up to find that I was only halfway.

I continued to crawl as tears flooded my eyes and fell onto the stones, mixing with whatever blood and skin I had left behind me and turning into steam.

There was nothing I could do except keep going. And when I couldn't see that Starlight Award in my mind anymore or my adoring fans begging for me to keep doing this—not for me, but for them—I saw myself. I saw her from ages four to twenty-four. I watched her wish on stars until she could push past the closed doors. And when that visual had run its course, I bumped into something soft, and my wounded hands touched a cold . . . floor.

I made it.

I quickly peeled the rest of my body off the stones and launched myself as far away from the pit as possible. I held my limbs against the wall like a wounded dog, naked and afraid. I couldn't recall when she took my bra or underwear off—it had to have been when I entered the room.

My remaining energy was spent feeling the way my hands, knees, and feet stung with a vengeance.

"I—I—"

"Don't say it." She was kneeling before me, cupping my chin with her hand as I looked into those silver contacts. "Do not forfeit yourself when you're already so close."

I squeezed my lips into a tight line.

"You did great, my child."

Her approval satisfied me. It didn't cure the way my fingertips begged for treatment, but it stilled my beating heart for a moment.

"Now for my favorite part." She lifted me by my arms—or at least the shell of me that still had some fight in her left.

I blinked again after limping for several painful steps.

I was in the box.

The sudden change in temperature jolted me awake, but my eyes barely opened. The sweat beads building on my chest, back, and arms froze. I shivered uncontrollably while my teeth chattered so loud they sounded like they were about to break into pieces.

"Wha—what are . . ." I slurred. I could no longer form a cohesive thought.

I couldn't hear her reply once my gaze fixated on the sink that was not only filled with water, but ice.

My throat worked up and down with a swallow. I hadn't noticed before, but I stopped breathing.

I was already preparing to drown.

"I—I—" I tasted the salt from the water that had dripped from my eyes and onto my lips. "Ca—" A gloved hand covered my mouth.

"Sh . . . my little songbird. You see this feeling?" Her fingers danced along my exposed skin, leaving goosebumps behind. "You're dying. Physically, emotionally, and mentally. But now . . ." Her hand wrapped around my neck, and I felt weightless. My hair, my breasts, my hands . . . Nothing held weight anymore. I barely understood how I was still standing.

"I'm going to show you how easy it is to give life as it is to take it away."

I couldn't process a word before my head was dunked into the freezing-cold water. I screamed, but no sound came out. Bubbles surrounded my wide-open eyes. Once the water started to burn my lungs, I was pulled out by my hair.

"Question one. What is your greatest fear?"

My teeth continued to chatter. "I—" I said through a shaky breath. There was no use in lying. "I-I d-don't want to be forgotten."

"Good answer."

My head was dunked back in the freezing cold. I closed my eyes and saw my mother—I saw her hands, I heard her snicker. I heard her words and felt the way she forcefully maneuvered my body. I felt the hate every time she touched me and never failed to catch the disgust in her eyes when she remembered I existed.

I was a mistake.

I felt the air again, and my vision was forced to the ceiling. "Who means the most to you? Who would you die for?"

The fire in my lungs made it impossible to form a thought.

"Who means the most to you?" she repeated.

She dunked my head again.

I suffocated for a few seconds before she allowed me air. The strands of my hair had turned to icicles that slapped my shoulders and face every time I was swung back up. She asked and kept asking, but I had nothing to say. The answer was no one.

No one was more important than who I could become.

After the fifth dunk, I felt myself fading. There was no way I was going to stay conscious . . . I couldn't.

The final time I was pulled up, I used whatever energy I had left to utter the only words remaining. "No one."

"Excuse me?" She released her grip on my neck.

"No—no one. I have no one." I fell back into her arms, and she let me.

The last thing I saw before my eyes closed were my pale blue hands. My heart slowed to struggling beats like I had been asking it to all night because she was right . . . I was dying.

But I fucking won.

I WAS IN AND out of consciousness until my eyes fluttered open one last time, and I was back in the first room.

Fuck yes, temperature control.

I looked down to see my robe had been put back on, but the rest of my clothes were neatly folded on the table. I wanted to get up, but I couldn't. I still felt so dizzy, but whatever I was drugged with was numbing a majority of the pain.

The door swung open, and I slowly raised my head as far as my soaking-wet hair would allow. The council woman was gone.

She had to be.

The person who entered was masked as a raven. They were pretty stocky. I could tell that much from the way the robe hugged their figure.

My eyes begged to close.

Fear crept up like an old friend. I crawled the best I could to the corner of the room, but I wasn't quick enough. "Please . . . Please. Did I make it?" I pleaded as the large raven picked me up and tossed me over their shoulder like a sack of potatoes.

"Please . . ." I whispered. "She didn't tell me I failed."

"Shut the hell up for a second." The frustrated voice sounded familiar, but I couldn't put my finger on it.

"Who—" My body begged and screamed for a break. "Who . . ."

I dozed off for what felt like a moment, but when I opened my eyes again, we were in a different hallway. "Where are you taking me?"

"Stop. Fucking. Talking."

I knew this man.

I remembered what I was told. I couldn't win anything if I wasn't in control of my own body. For all I knew, whatever was happening could have been another part of my trial. So, instead of talking, I put all my energy into keeping my eyes open.

I watched every turn he made and noted every heavy step he took. It felt useless since I got lost and shut my eyes more than once, but I tracked our movements as best I could.

"What the hell are you doing?" A woman's voice sent a fight-or-flight reaction through my system.

I knew that voice.

A thick Puerto Rican accent that I heard the first time I was drugged and held against my will. I was able to get a quick glance at her before he whipped around to face her. I caught long red hair—no blonde? A black robe too.

No mask.

We had to have been in an area where they no longer needed them. Did that mean I made it? Could I see the other members now?

Focus, Aly. You've seen her before . . . Where?

"What does it look like I'm doing?" His accent finally registered, too.

With my eyes closed, it dawned on me. That girl was Camila Espósito.

Which meant—

"I don't think kidnapping is a part of the initiation," a random voice chimed in.

"Fuck off," my captor said.

It didn't take more than a second for the dots to connect in my head.

Andrés.

I swore I stopped breathing, but I couldn't make it obvious. I couldn't react because he very well could be trying to kill me right now.

"So this is it? This is your choice?" she asked.

I needed to sleep.

No. I had to stay awake regardless of whether my eyes were closed or not. I had to.

"She's perfect," he responded.

"Not one I would have chosen."

"I don't know, I see the appeal," another voice chimed in, more nonchalant than the others.

"Whatever gets the job done. I don't give a fuck who he picks."

I had to have been missing pieces of the conversation. I heard steps. Frantic ones that were getting closer to us. I was fading. I couldn't hold on much longer.

"Let me see her!"

I knew that voice.

Saint?

CHAPTER SEVENTEEN

I T HAD TO HAVE been a nightmare.

The anguish, the agony.

The shock that ran through my body when the temperature switched from hot to freezing cold.

My frozen strands of hair were acting as whips against my neckline and upper back. It was a nightmare, right?

No.

Saint's voice echoed loudly through my head as I gathered my senses. My palms ached, and my knees screamed for relief as the blanket I was under weighed heavily on them. The sun aggressively beat on my forehead. I could feel its warmth from the welcoming rays.

That didn't make sense. I could never feel the sun from my bed.

Wait—where the fuck was I?

I jumped up, and my eyes flew open. I was swollen and dizzy, but that was the least of my concerns.

Before me was a room that definitely wasn't fucking mine. Black was painted on all four walls complemented by red LED lights running along every crease and corner. I whipped my head to the left, seeing a giant window wall that showcased acres of land, rocks, and a beautiful body of water far off in the distance.

I could smell the sea salt from inside.

I ripped the midnight-colored comforter off to reveal a gray T-shirt, which covered me down to my knees. Both joints were fully wrapped in beige bandages that were already starting to darken in the center, and my hands were given a similar treatment. Someone had taken me, cleaned me up, changed me, and even dried my hair.

"Good, you're up."

My line of sight followed the voice to the bedroom door. Sure enough, Andrés stood casually, leaning against the frame with a smirk on his face.

"Where am I?" I whispered angrily, feeling too sick to fight, but I couldn't let him know that. "And where's my shit?"

He stepped forward, and his hand hovered over the doorknob. He didn't close it, though. He just let it drop back to his side.

Fuck me not being able to drive. I couldn't get out of here without a ride, even if I wanted to. I had to play it safe and smart.

I had to get to The Castle for my interview.

For Solo.

For Josefina.

"Your phone and clothes are in the drawer next to you," he said calmly, inching toward me with every breath.

I took his word for it. There was no way I'd lose sight of him for even a second to check that drawer. Andrés's demeanor was oddly welcoming despite his attempt to look as threatening as possible in his tank top that showed all his muscles and the bandana that covered his hair. However, the diamond pyramid chain with a bird coming out of it on his neck caused my breathing to accelerate.

My fear had nothing to do with him as a man and everything to do with the society whose branding he wore so proudly. I had seen the triangles and the eye symbols before. I always assumed it was from a designer I had yet to work with.

The truth was much more sinister, and I wished I had never uncovered it.

The conspiracy junkies and has-beens were right. There were people pulling the strings right under our noses, and for the first time ever, I was almost in on the joke.

"Why am I here?" I asked in a low tone. Only a second passed before the realization of what he took me from introduced itself into my brain.

If I didn't complete the initiation, they'd take everything from me.

I bubbled with rage and spoke again. "What did you do?"

Andrés took a deep breath and clasped his hands in front of him. "I disqualified you," he answered absentmindedly, like it was no big deal.

Like we both didn't know bailing wasn't an option. I didn't have his connections, power, or place in that society. There was no doubt I'd be punished for what I had witnessed and then ran from, no matter what his strange affinity with me was.

The butterflies in my stomach pawed at my insides and scratched at my skin. I was going to be sick.

"And what gave you that right? I don't even fucking know you," I forced out.

He scoffed. "Here we go with this again."

"You need to fix this," I demanded as I fully sat up and folded my knees under me. I ignored the shock wave of pain that traveled through my body and kept a steady glare on him.

"No. I gave you a way out. You bet on the wrong horse, and now you have a target on your back." Andrés ran a finger across his chin while he looked me up and down. "You don't get choices anymore. The wolves are after you now, baby. And I'm the only one who can save you. Should've taken my hand when you had the chance."

"I'd rather be eaten alive."

I didn't want what he was offering. I wanted to do it on my own if I was going to be subjected to the cruelty that came with being tied to the true rulers of the world.

My terms.

That was all I had left that truly belonged to me, and he took that away, too.

He tilted his head like he was deciding how to deal with me. But instead of a frown, his smile only grew, and his eyes were riddled with curiosity. "They will kill you, and then they will make it so the front page story on the *Post* is 'The Truth about Alejandra Garcia's Life, Mysterious Death, and Disturbing Secrets.' Then you really won't have a fucking say. You'll just be a dead bitch who gets all her flowers after she's six feet under. But eh, your cousin, team, and friends will accept them on your behalf. Then they'll sell your life story to movie execs, and some new actress who's six years younger than you were when you died will play you in some IMAX biopic. And she will get that Starlight Award you want so bad."

I gulped, and my blood turned cold. My heart sank to the pit of my stomach, and for only a second, that horror story felt real.

I was cornered, and my only saving grace at this point was him. "Fine. What—what do you want from me?"

"Good. Glad you got your priorities figured out." Andrés walked over to the bed and took a seat on the edge. "You're going to be my new wife."

I held back the tears that word never failed to pull out of me. "Why?"

"What? Scared you're gonna lose that sweet deal with Taurus Sawyer?"

"What do you know about him?" I caught myself leaning forward.

Thoughts of him had snuck up on me like a lion on the prowl, and I found myself wishing I was talking to him instead of a cruel stranger. Our differences were overwhelming, but even the sun and the moon came together to dance every once in a while.

"Everything," Andrés finally answered, but his gaze shifted to the view of the landscape outside.

I shook my head. "What—what does that mean? Is he a part of this or not?"

I watched him gulp hard. "No."

His shoulders tensed, and when he turned back to me, his expression was stone cold. "You're going to marry me. You're going to be as much a part of this as I am, and that's what's going to save your life and your friends."

I pushed Taurus out of my head and remembered what was at stake here.

My life.

"Don't look at me like that," he continued with an eye roll. "You asked for this, remember? Fame. To be immortalized . . . All of it."

I swallowed another lump of my fear. "I still don't get why you need me, and if you want me, then you're going to have to start being real fucking direct."

Andrés sighed. "In order to get rid of one leader, you need to replace them. There are requirements to be met before a replacement can take the chair. The council members set the tone for the Order. Unity is in everything that we do. It started with a union and will only continue in union."

"Who are you getting rid of?"

He hesitated but never broke eye contact. "Someone who shouldn't be where they are."

"Okay . . . So you are apparently chronically single and couldn't find anyone else to—union-ify?"

When he shot a squint in my direction, there was a hint of amusement in his glare. "You're the most intriguing woman I've known since—" His hand traveled to the tattoo of the woman on the side of his neck.

Andrés cleared his throat. "She was just as stubborn."

"Okay, I don't know who she is, but this isn't about me being stubborn. It's about you taking my free will." I leaned back against the headboard again, mostly because my knees were on fire. "I'm dead either way, right?"

"Right now, we're in a spot I didn't plan for. They will be after you. They have to be . . . It's protocol." He stood to his feet and casually paced around the room with his hands behind his back. "I can pull some strings to keep you as safe as possible until we're sworn in, but there's going to be some blowback."

"Wh-when is that going to be?"

"February."

My body drooped down, and all hope I had left faded within an instant. "Two months . . . I have to dodge them and hope they don't retaliate for two fucking months?"

Andrés shrugged. "Yes. You'll be staying here. Consider that house of yours done."

My face flushed, and I clenched my jaw. I could feel him shutting the door to my cage and throwing away the key. I was trading one imprisonment for another, and this time, it was all my fucking fault.

Too greedy. Too excited. Too much.

I once again proved that I was the girl willing to fly too close to the sun despite my wings already being reduced to ash.

Will she ever learn her lesson? was what the wine moms of the world would say as they clutched their pearls at my actions.

"How the hell am I supposed to just hide? I'm in the middle of a fucking album release. I-I need to go to my place," I protested.

"I can handle all of that."

"You're not my damn manager."

He smirked. "You have so much to learn."

"My Nila interview—"

"Can be rescheduled."

My nostrils flared. I ran out of things to say and opted to open the drawer next to me. To my surprise, he wasn't bluffing. My clothes, phone, and jewelry were all there, folded nicely with my sneakers lined up on the floor. "Get out."

Andrés, who had turned his attention to the beautiful and vibrant view out the window, whirled around to face me with another entertained look in his eyes. He didn't say a word. Instead, he let my command simmer and create a thickness in the air.

"What's the rush?" he finally said.

I scoffed and got up anyway.

Fuck. The balls of my feet were screaming for dear life with every step I took. I kept my brave face on and slipped on my underwear first to feel a sense of decency. I didn't care if he watched, either.

It hurt like a bitch to pull my jeans up over my burns, and it was even worse grabbing the fabric of my hoodie to slip it on. I grabbed my phone, and it lit up to showcase that I only had ten percent battery left and a million notifications. I shut it off to preserve the battery and stuffed it in my pocket.

"If I'm going to stay here, you need to take me to my place first."

"Why?" He was leaning against the wall now.

His eyes were studying me like some wild animal who had a habit of playing with their food. I had so many questions, but when he looked at me, it all went silent. I could only focus on his pupils and how nothing seemed to be behind them. He wasn't even blinking.

"Someone has to feed my cat."

He laughed. "Solo. You got her . . . less than a year ago?"

I stumbled back, and my already sore backside bumped against the edge of the dresser. "Wha—anyway. Yes."

"Mmm . . . I don't think that's it. Let me guess, is it Josefina?"

My heart stopped, and my breaths grew harsh. My gaze strayed from the man and to the door that was open. If he knew about her, then so did they.

I had to get to The Castle.

Without batting an eye, I made a move for the door, but I only made it a few steps before a merciless grip on my wrist and an equally aggressive yank caused my feet to give way. I let out a scream when my body banged against his chest. I wiggled out of his grip like a caged animal and tried to free my wrist from his hand. He only tightened his hold, and my whining grew in volume.

"I have been so nice to you . . ." Andrés whispered in my ear through gritted teeth. He used his free hand to push my hair out of my face. "I didn't even tell them about your sister, and withholding information would get me in a lot of trouble. *Pero sólo estoy protegiendo a mi esposa.*"

I'm only protecting my wife.

My blood turned hot, and when I looked up to see how the corners of his lips tipped at the sight of my eyes, I took all the spit in my mouth and launched it at his face. "Let me go."

In a swift movement, Andrés dropped me on the floor, and before I could look around for something to grab, heavy banging from the downstairs door startled us both.

The fear of a second person who could be equally as insane was causing my heart to beat so loud that I was sure both of us could see it. Andrés's snarl was quickly replaced by another sly smile.

"Our guest of honor is early." He stepped over my body like I was already dead. I stared at him as he walked down a hall I could only see now that I was on the floor.

"Open the fucking door, Andrés!" I heard from outside.

Taurus?

I quickly climbed to my feet and tried to ignore the series of emotions floating through my head.

When the prince of the Elite Order left the room, it was like he took the power that was keeping me alive with him. I felt drained as I held on to the door for stability. I managed to keep an eye on him as he casually walked down a few steps—then he looked back at me.

Adrenaline returned to my system, and I stood tall.

"You coming to see your boyfriend?" he teased.

I gulped hard. I wanted to follow, but I didn't want to confirm my suspicions that Taurus was a part of it all.

I needed to know, though.

Begrudgingly, I tiptoed down the steps, only making it halfway before the door swung open and Taurus came stomping in.

He pushed Andrés out of the way.

My breath halted, and I remained frozen in place.

Andrés stood there unfazed, like he couldn't care less— like everything that happened upstairs was a nonfactor.

"What did I do to deserve such an aggressive hello?"

I had never seen Taurus like he was standing in the luxurious foyer. Anger radiated off of him, and every move he made carried the lethality of a tsunami. He was chaos, and Andrés was a calm sea.

Both were capable of putting me through a painful, slow death.

"Where is she? Everyone's looking for her and I swore—" Taurus wiped his face and walked deeper into the charcoal-colored living room. "She asked me about that fucking symbol. And I thought, no, he wouldn't actually do it. But now I don't know where she is. What did you do?"

Andrés remained calm, cool, and collected. In fact, I was sure he was one more question away from laughing. He pointed in my direction, and I wished I had turned invisible.

With every possible second, my clenching heart was hardening once more toward Taurus. However, when he turned to face me, his wild and angry eyes quickly filled with sadness, and the way he dropped his shoulders in relief told a different story.

His pity only lasted a moment before he turned to my captor and shoved him once again, causing Andrés to barely stumble. "What the fuck did you do?"

Andrés didn't fight back or get angry like he did with me.

The way he allowed Taurus to dominate him showed me that there was more going on here than I was ever aware of. He looked at him like he missed the toxicity and kept his body open to receive more shoves and hits as long as the other man was willing to give them.

"I told you," he finally responded, "I was going to find somebody. What? You second-guessing that 'no' now?"

Taurus glared at him. "You're fucking sick." He walked over to me, and the intense worry overtaking his aura gave me a sense of safety, which I desperately needed to keep standing.

I released my grip on the banister, and I thought, for a moment at least, that I was happy to see him. Regardless of the distrust and the whirlwind of emotions that I was experiencing—I just wanted someone around who knew how to hold me.

He gave my body a once-over and hissed, "Who did this to you?"

"I-I just want to go back," I whispered as tears flooded my sockets.

Andrés followed closely behind, clasping his hands in front of him once he made it to the base of the steps.

Taurus analyzed the bandages on my hands, and his eyes welled with tears that, unlike me, he managed to blink away.

He whipped his head around to face Andrés and took one step down the stairs. Instinctively, I grabbed his arm, and he came to a quick halt. "You deserve your fucking ass beat, Dre."

"Whoa, hostility. Down boy." The other man laughed off the threat.

Taurus turned back to me. "I'll take you home."

"Aht, aht, aht. She's mine. She already agreed, and well . . . She got herself in a little situation, so . . . It's me, or you'll be attending her funeral. You're a little late to join this conversation, *mi amor*." He puckered his lips and made a kissing noise before chuckling to himself as he watched us.

Taurus didn't even turn around. "What'd you agree to?"

I shook my head. I didn't know who to trust anymore. "How do you two know each other?"

"I love this story." Andrés put his hands in his sweatpants pockets and walked up a few steps to stand next to Taurus. "Who's gonna tell it?"

Taurus took a few deep breaths and only looked at me. "We were together." My attention shifted to Andrés, who had a clear look of amusement on his face.

A knot grew in my chest, and if I didn't know any better, I'd say I was turning green.

The line between reality and fiction had been blurring with Taurus and me. I wasn't sure if I was the only one who had noticed it, but it didn't stop my brain from screaming "mine!"

Taurus cleared his throat to continue. "For like three years. This was, uh—our house."

Andrés rolled his eyes. "And it's now your safe house."

A scoff came from Taurus, who was looking anywhere but the both of us. "I can't believe this shit . . ."

Like he was fueled by Taurus's disappointment with him, Andrés leaned against the wall but kept his legs blocking my path further down the stairs. "Aw, mad it won't be you?"

Taurus turned his head to face him and damn near snapped his neck. "I said no for a fucking reason, and then you do this to someone I—"

Andrés's muscles tensed, and his smile dropped as he leaned forward. "Someone you what?"

"I—I don't give a fuck!" I interrupted after throwing my hands up in disbelief. It didn't matter that they dated or whatever the fuck this secret code they were talking in meant. I was stuck with Andrés and would possibly lose everything that I thought had become mine. Even if they were only mine to the public, like Taurus. Regardless, I'd have to mourn that another day.

The reality of the situation was that I was tired. I had been thrown, burned, and dumped on all within a matter of days. I was dizzy and in pain. For once, someone had to fucking do right by me, and I needed to get back to The Castle.

"We can talk about all of this when the child and pet in that house are with me and safe," I snapped. My attention went solely onto Taurus, who had let sadness and pity occupy his features once more. "You. I don't know if you were part of this or not. But let me be very clear when I say I trust you as much as I trust him right now. So, sit tight. I'm sure I'll have a lot to yell at you about later."

I whipped my attention over to the other one. "I am going back. I understand that I got myself into this mess where it's either you or them, but I am going to that house. And I will not be dragged back here without them and without my manager at least knowing where I am. Do you understand me?"

Andrés scowled and pulled his leg back, and Taurus followed suit. I then took the liberty of limping as best I could to climb down the rest of the stairs.

Once I reached the bottom, I spun around to face the two idiots who looked like they had just seen a ghost. Well, Taurus did.

Andrés stared at me like he had won the lottery.

With simple gestures and glances he had the ability to starve you and then be the only one who could satisfy the hunger. He was electrifying, and it very well could have been the amount of power I knew he wielded that caused my sudden pique of interest.

A fire in my stomach had brewed, and my chest roared.

Yet, when I looked at Taurus, the chaos was nowhere to be found. A warm blanket of serenity cast over me, and I knew if given the chance, my heart would be safe.

"Hello? Let's giddy up!" I waved them down and pulled the door open like I owned the place. "Animals," I muttered under my breath when I noticed them both finally walking down the steps.

The sun was high in the sky and damn near blinding. But as long as I could see it, I knew I'd be okay.

CHAPTER EIGHTEEN

Taurus ended up driving me to The Castle because Andrés received a call about something he, of course, couldn't disclose. He muttered some bullshit about being safe because no matter what connections he had, the looming threat of retaliation was something he invariably couldn't control.

I tortured Taurus with a silent ride. I was sure someone snapped a picture on the highway, but I stole his sunglasses so no one could tell I was distressed.

When I did arrive, I was ambushed by a frantic Yessenia, who had taken it upon herself to fill my living room with shopping bags galore. They were later explained away as gifts for Josefina. But the worst part about it was that my aunt and Nova were there too, and if I had known that, I wouldn't have let Taurus walk in with me.

We stood there and stared at each other like time had stopped.

When I looked at Nova, and she looked at me—and I looked at my aunt, and she had Josefina in her arms, the world stalled.

I didn't want Josefina with her.

No. Not anymore.

My aunt couldn't help her, she was only a clone of her sister.

"Um . . . Hey." Taurus broke the silence once he stepped from behind me.

Nova, who had her hair in a claw clip and a gray yoga set on, was staring at the both of us like we had gotten caught sneaking back in. "Where have you two been?" She paused to take me in. "Your hands?"

I shook my head and turned to face him. "Handle it. Tell them everything. I don't give a fuck about an NDA."

I couldn't.

I didn't have anything left in me. I walked away and ignored the shouts of concern as I trekked up the stairs, trying to ignore the pain shooting from the soles of my feet through the rest of my body.

I had a fucking target on my back and a psychopathic man telling me I needed to marry him. I didn't know what being his wife entailed, but I knew it couldn't be anything right or virtuous.

I locked my bedroom door and left the mayhem downstairs behind me.

No amount of yelling or chaos could get the echo of a familiar voice that I heard that night out of my head. I had to have been making it up. It repeated so much that it didn't even sound real anymore. It was only another bad dream.

Once I got to my bathroom, I locked that door, too, before letting the shower run and peeling off all my clothes.

The water beat aggressively against the tub and tiled walls. Flashes of my face hitting the ice came in waves, and my throat burned all over again. I blinked it away and stepped inside the warmth. I wasn't brave enough to take the bandages off yet, and maybe soon I would be.

As water beads slid down the locks still attached to my tender scalp, I pulled out clumps of hair by the handful. I tearfully watched them slide down the drain.

I was back at square one with the whispers occupying my thoughts from critics who ran blogs like the Navy with their assumptions.

She's not Latina enough. Can she even speak Spanish? She's just a fucking fame whore. She only got married for the fame, too. Talented? In what world? Her songs are soulless radio hits, I could name sixteen unsigned artists who could use her budget. She's a homewrecker too. God, someone tell her to eat a fucking burger. Those fillers in her face are going to backfire. Did she get buccal fat removal or is she skiing the slopes? Talentless slut. She acts like she's white! Maybe if she could carry a note and do choreo at the same time, her career wouldn't be in the toilet. Taurus is about to give her her career back, aw. Alejandra Garcia or . . . shall I say Aly, is a fucking vampire.

I carried the weight of all of those comments for fucking years.

They didn't know the true story or how I wore my losses like thick armor. They didn't know how impressive of a talent it was to keep going with your heart spilling out of your chest when all you had to work with were the ashes you were reborn from. No one gave a fuck. I had to stop cowering in corners and begging for acceptance.

Instead, I became everything they said I was, the fucking *Fame Vampire*.

It was a story about a girl who ripped herself apart, who was wronged by everyone she loved so deeply . . . so hopelessly.

For one album, sixteen tracks, I let Lilith speak. The girl my mother tried to drown away and whose fire I snuffed out long ago. The devil in me rose to the occasion, and she saved me.

In the face of Andrés, she gave me strength. Throughout that initiation, she forced me to keep going. Through all the heartbreak and my white feathered wings burning off while I fell to my death, she picked me up to rise like a Phoenix from the ashes. Lilith was capable of anything, and that was who I needed to get through this.

BY THE TIME I came out of the shower, it had to be early afternoon.

When I finally came downstairs, Taurus had managed to calm everyone enough to agree to leave us alone and go home. It didn't take much to convince my aunt to let me keep Josefina because she wasn't that stoked about it to begin with. On the other hand, it was almost Christmas Eve, and Nova couldn't deal with everything all at once. She had two daughters to take care of.

I was left to my own devices, and all I could think about as I paced around the godforsaken Castle was my biggest performance to date.

The unassuming Josefina fell asleep on the couch, and I tried to avoid Taurus's gaze as I crept by him. He was tasked with staying with me until I decided that I was packed and ready to go back to my new prison. Despite hating The Castle, I was in no rush to leave.

I gently pulled the sliding doors apart and ignored the shooting pain from my hands, but it was quickly relieved when the weight of the door shifted from my palm. I looked behind me to see Taurus standing over me, holding the door open.

I swallowed hard as I looked up at those somber eyes. "I wasn't going to run away."

He nodded toward the pool and spoke in a quiet whisper, not for me, but for Josefina's sake. "After you."

I wrapped my long cardigan around my body and let the wind brush past my fresh bandages and visible bruising. My skin was tender to the touch, and my head was filled with terror and disaster, but the warm sun calmed me for the moment.

I tiptoed over to the fire pit, which was surrounded by cushioned patio chairs and far enough from the pool not to suddenly strike fear into me. I plopped my body down into the chair and curled up by the fire that hadn't been started.

I didn't have the energy, but Taurus must have seen the way I was holding tightly onto my cardigan because he didn't hesitate to grab some firestarter sticks out of the bag that was sitting up against The Castle and proceed to ignite the flames. I watched as the fire went from tame to aggressive, crackling and burning everything it could touch.

When Taurus sat down next to me, not across, I was forced to lift my head from my folded elbow and acknowledge him.

"Can I help you?"

He laughed. "You're gonna be cranky until your last breath, aren't you?"

I squinted in his direction. "I don't know if you got the memo, but I don't fucking trust you. You don't get to play the hero this time, Taurus."

"I wouldn't dream of it." His words were laced with sincerity, but there was danger in the heat of his gaze and the weight of his words.

"What's that supposed to mean?" I scoffed.

He shrugged. "There's nothing heroic about me. If there was, I would have prevented this. Seen the signs."

"Maybe one day I'll believe you."

"Are you going to do it?" he asked after a long silence.

"Why didn't you?"

Taurus didn't shift in his seat or move his eyes away from me. Despite how invasive the question was (to me), he didn't flinch. "There was nothing they could offer me worth my soul. Plus, I think Dre was being naive. There was no way they'd let him pick a man," he answered effortlessly. "When I was a kid, all I wanted to do was make music, not be run by creepy cult people."

"You were making music as a kid," I interrupted with a snarl.

The large man nodded and scooched closer to the edge of the seat. "You know." His hands were clasped together, and his finger twisted one of his rings, but he didn't take his eyes off of me. "You say these things like they're insults or jabs, but I think . . ." The corners of his lips turned upward, and his pearly white teeth were borderline distracting. "I would say you're jealous."

I sucked my teeth and put my chin back on my folded arm. "You are insane."

"Then what is it that makes you hate me?" The question was positioned lightly, almost like a joke, but we both knew the question was overdue by three seasons.

"Besides the obvious? I hate you because I needed you to begin with." I sat up slowly and groaned as shock waves ran through my being. "I lost everything. I was starting from nothing and you know? I still had the wind in my sails and the air in my lungs, and I felt like . . . I still had room to move. Room to move forward and make everyone fucking feel me. Without help! So I signed with Locke and Key, and the first thing they did was tell me that you were gonna save me. You. Not some guy who would be a small stain on my record that no one would remember in ten years. You. The man who had been in the industry for over a decade, and I—I wanted to fucking kill you. Because I could never beat you."

"Well, that's nice to hear."

"I was—I am a big fucking fan. But now my golden comeback is touched by Midas himself, and I can't sleep at night knowing that I didn't do it all on my own. There's always someone's fucking name attached to mine, and I hated that yours came next. Because when the golden boy steps on the scene, all the credit goes to him, and I become the girlfriend."

It wouldn't be any different if I was Andrés's wife.

He leaned over the armrest on his chair to be closer to me. I could feel his breath, and if I listened beyond the crackles of the fire, I could hear his heartbeat, too. "You know what I said when I got that call?"

I pursed my lips together. "I'm sure you'll tell me."

"I thought . . . Fuck. I finally have a reason to talk to her and she's single now? Even better. Then my second thought was . . . Damn, now I have to tell her how amazed I am by her. How can I put it into words? She's talented, she's charismatic, and when I first saw you walk into that stuck-up-ass Fashion Week party in Paris, I noticed you were nervous to say what's up. But what you didn't know is that I was nervous also." He paused to playfully look up at the sky and then back to me. "Mostly because you were being chatted up by anyone within a five-mile vicinity. But, man. Your security guard was not budging."

"That fucking dickhead."

"Oh, you thought that too?" He laughed, and I joined him.

A deep sigh traveled from his belly and through her lungs, eventually escaping through plump lips. "You don't need any of what they're offering you. Him included. You're a powerhouse all on your own."

My gaze fell back to the fire. "It doesn't feel like that most days."

The larger man adjusted his blue crewneck and leaned back in the chair. His long legs spread out around the pit, and he stretched like he was home. "How come?"

"In every aspect of my life, I feel like people are waiting to replace me. Like they come in, and they see me, and I sparkle, and I shine . . . I'm a phenomenon put on a stage, but the stage is caged, and I can't get out. But hey, they can end the show whenever they fucking please." I swallowed the lump in my throat and fully sat up once again, but my vision stayed fixed on the fire.

"They see this value in me. I love that . . . I crave that. For a few moments it feels like magic. It always feels like I found my person, or hobby, or . . . goal, you know? Like this is going to be the one that satisfies me and it's . . .

always just another hyperfixation that ends in tragedy." I took a deep breath.

"Don't get me started on the people I've dated and the friends I've had. They always drift away, and I am left with my back broken and a bruised ego because I spent our last moments trying to carry us up a hill that they never even wanted to see the top of. I am twenty-five, and I am scared that, eventually, everyone and everything will just *drift*. One day I won't love music anymore, or the person I've settled down with, or the life I've made. I will have no bones left to carry. I don't know how many goodbyes I have left in me, but I am so fucking angry. I'm tired of loving things and ending up the only person performing CPR on dead relationships and situations. My old friends, team and bullshit exes . . . They all left me with no reasoning. There's never an apology. They're not living with the consequences of hurting me. I am dying inside every single day, and no one gives a shit. I'm pissed off! I am. I don't understand what prophecy I'm supposed to be out living, but all I'm gathering in this fucked life is that I'm not worth shit, and at the bare fucking minimum no one wants to be my friend. No one even wants to be my real boyfriend." I choked on my tears and aggressively wiped the ones dripping off my chin.

"That's supposed to make me feel good? That I'm good enough to be a trophy, great enough to take home, but never perfect enough to want forever? And just when I thought I was getting a little bit of color back, there's this kid in my house, and I can't even focus on that because she came with the news of Andrés's shit and my mom . . ." My voice cracked and forced me to take a breath. "She could be dead somewhere right now, and I wouldn't know. So no, I am not a powerhouse all on my own because I'm nothing but fragments. I'm done. But I can't be done, can I?" I finally looked up at him, wiping a stray tear with the back of my hand. "I think I lied before. The one thing I ever really wanted was love. I think that lie is ruining my life. Because there's this—there's this devil in me . . . Lying dormant for now, and I can feel her sleeping. I know—I know this sounds insane."

"It doesn't. You don't."

"There's a part of me that is so broken. Angry. She's fucking angry, and she's so close to becoming me, and I am so scared of her. I know with Andrés, he—I will wake her up. She's the one who wants the power, and I don't want to bury my desire for love just to survive." I wiped my cheeks aggressively once more and placed my hand on the armrest to pull myself up, but a warmer hand rested on top of mine.

"The longer I think about it, though. The longer I'm sure that agreeing to his terms is the only way I'll ever make someone stay."

"You don't have to—"

I ripped my hand away. "No, I'm sorry."

Taurus rose to his feet and didn't hesitate to bring himself to my side. He placed a hand on my waist, and my heart stilled. He whispered, "What are you sorry for?"

"Still being so angry about it all," I started. "They give you time limits on these things, you know? You write one song about it, it's okay. You make one post about it, you're human. But it's years later, and you're still crying. You've got to be some sick bitch who can't move on from anything. I'm not—I'm not human to them."

"Hey . . . Hey." He bent down and cupped my chin with his hand. "They—whoever they might be—aren't here right now. You have every fucking right to feel what you're feeling, and I do not blame you, do you hear me? You don't need to apologize for shit. You are bound to win, Alejandra, and I need you to understand that. The woman I'm looking at is stronger than anyone I've ever met in this industry. You came back stronger than you've ever been, and that's no thanks to me. You haven't lost your chance at love. Plus, with Dre . . . You have the power to tell him no."

"Hm." I turned in my chair to face the sky. Clouds were gathered in clusters, and the smell of firewood snuck up my nostrils, but it didn't stop me from sniffling. "I have to do Nila."

"I know."

I quickly looked back over at him just in time to catch that smug look on his face. "You know?"

"I've learned a lot about you being your fake boyfriend all these months."

"Hm." I averted my attention back to the sky because the butterflies in my stomach briefly returned. "I'm just tired of dreaming about rising above it. The only time I actually do is by doing the damn thing, right? So fuck it. Fuck this society for like—four seconds. I'm doing the Christmas Eve performance."

It didn't take much convincing before Taurus was following me to my studio to compose a medley that I never thought of. He found comfort at the computer and the keyboards. The songs were pulled up on the software, and he was fucking around with different settings and mixes.

By the end of the day, I'd call Nova to let her know the updated plan.

I found myself asking Taurus to stay the night. We watched movies and shared space on the living room floor, and I noticed how Josefina lit up whenever he told a joke—like she fully understood it.

I watched how he kept himself positioned closest to the door just in case he had to jump up in front of us.

In case it got that bad.

When I watched the moon replace the sun, I wondered if a guy like that was out there, specially made for me. It would be like catching lightning in a bottle, and I'd know God had written that we were fated mates in an envelope and sealed it shut.

Or would I be forced to live a tragic prophecy?

The woman who was sold to the highest bidder once again and doomed to spend the rest of her life howling at the moon with all the riches she could have ever dreamed of.

Who would I have to be to finally be dealt better cards?

First thing in the morning, my phone buzzed.

Unknown:

Where'd you go songbird?

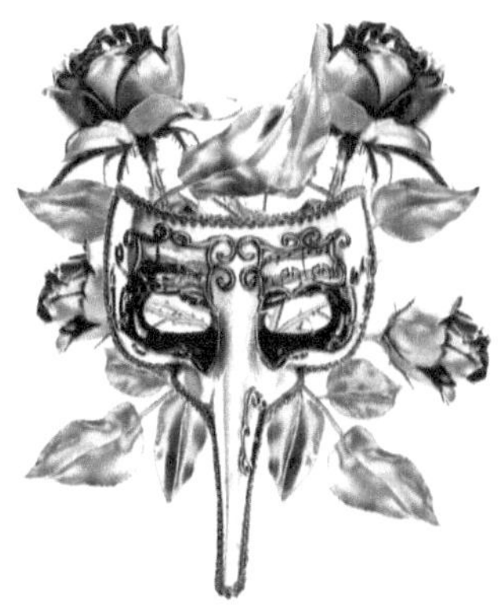

CHAPTER NINETEEN

"FIRST, YOU CONVINCE ME to let you perform a song that wasn't even rehearsed, and now you want to change your outfits?"

While sitting in the cramped dressing room, I once again explained to her that the new outfits appeared on my doorstep right before we left The Castle to come to the studio. I was convinced Andrés had forgotten about us, but Taurus kept checking his phone like he was anticipating a warning call before the Elite Order sent a flurry of bullets through my windows.

Then the gift showed up.

I brought the black box with silver ribbons inside and pulled out the card taped to the velvet wrapping paper. It read:

Let this be a reminder that I am letting you do this. I'll always be ten steps ahead.

—Andrés.

He was right. If he had wanted to drag me back yesterday, he would have within the hour.

It was safe to say the garments were gorgeous. Even though I had to scratch away that itch that screamed *it's fucking weird that he knows your size.* However, when I opened the obnoxiously large box, I pulled out several small jewelry boxes, two garment bags, and a shoe box.

He bought me a brand-new costume.

There were two pairs of gloves: one pair only covered the palms of my hands and was made of black lace. The ensemble, like the gloves, was fully lace with flared sleeves, and it resembled a dress from the 1800s, except it was chopped into a more modern pair of pants and top. My neck would be covered with a choker, but the open space for my chest would make it so people were too distracted to assume I was covering burns. The pants were cut out around my knees and thighs.

I was sure the ivy-patterned tights would cover the burns on my knees.

The boots tied the whole look together and allowed me to dance comfortably. Most importantly, the fabric made my heart skip a beat. The softness was unlike anything I had ever felt, and when I tried them on . . . it didn't irritate my injuries.

A silver-and-black trench coat acted as the main attraction. I would have accused Andrés of stealing it from some rejected pirate movie costume artist if it weren't trimmed with Swarovski crystals.

Heavy and expensive, I thought.

It only took a few twirls in the mirror for me to realize something else . . . I was dripping in diamonds, crystals, and silver. Branded like I belonged to Timeless . . . Like I belonged to him.

I brought it with me anyway.

"This song is better," I simply replied. "And the new outfit is stunning. If you would just take a look, then you'd get it."

"Was it from him?" Nova asked in a low tone.

"I think that's something we should be getting used to," I muttered.

"Like her." She pointed to Josefina, who had her face glued in a tablet Yessenia had bought her. "*Ay dios mio*, what are we going to do?"

I looked up from my phone and shrugged. "Perform."

"Where's that damn assistant of yours?" She looked around my dressing room, plucking a chocolate-covered strawberry off the nearby tray.

"I'm hungry," Josefina whined for maybe the first time ever. Without hesitation, Nova popped a strawberry in the child's mouth.

"You need more help around here than just me."

"No, I don't. I can't risk a damn leak before the Starlight Awards. We both know that," I protested.

Nova sighed and rubbed her orange pencil skirt before taking a seat on the couch, too. "Okay, I get that, *mija*. But the award we're trying to win isn't for Most Burnt Out."

"If it was, you'd win by a landslide."

"Haha, very funny . . ." Nova slapped her thigh and sent a playful glare in my direction. She was like the mother I never asked for—and maybe the one I needed. "I'd kill you, but apparently someone beat me to the punch."

I wanted to be annoyed, but instead, I found myself giggling. "Oh, that is low! It is too early to joke about that." I squinted at the woman. "Just look at the outfit."

Nova sighed and rose from her seat. "Okay. Let me see 'em."

I pointed to the clothing rack in the far corner. "Over there."

The older woman walked over to the hangers and unzipped the garment bags. She analyzed them in silence but eventually turned to face me. "Hair and makeup the same?"

I nodded.

"These are customs . . ." She sighed like a mother who was at a loss with their eldest child while she looked through the bags and fingered the fabrics. "I'll get hair and makeup in here."

"*Gracias.*"

She halted at the door. "Is Taurus still coming?"

I shrugged. "At some point, I'm sure."

"Good."

I pouted in my seat when the door shut, and the buzz of my phone sent my nerves through the ceiling.

Unknown:

> Last chance, songbird.

"And now . . . For her first performance in over two years . . . Aly." Nila, who was dressed head to toe in hot pink, moved from my stage back to hers, where the interview couches were.

One by one, purple and white lights illuminated the stage. The crowd's roaring halted, and the extended instrumental version of "No Tears" filled the silence.

Imitation grass, plastic flowers, Styrofoam rocks, and silk trees covered the stage as dancers slowly erupted from their positions. The fog machine cast the stage with clouds of gray, introducing the swelling music.

I lay in the center, lace covering my body and bone-straight hair sprawled onto the emerald blades of grass. The dancers circled me while the crowd gawked with eager eyes.

I felt at home.

I lifted the mic to my lips and formed a strong ninety-degree angle with my elbow while I waited for my cue. I gazed up at the wires and bulbs above me . . . Sparks erupted from one of the purple lights until it quickly blew out.

I rolled my eyes before slowly rising and hitting every note without hesitation. There was no way in hell I was going to let cheap stage equipment throw me off.

The words dripped from my lips like honey as I pulled oxygen from the depths of my diaphragm. By the time the chorus came around, I had been picked up and twirled around more than any normal person could take, but my voice remained steady.

The instrumental for "No Tears" faded, and clapping hands echoed throughout the studio before every light was shut off except for a single spotlight.

Before my dancers scattered away, they brought out my mic stand, took my wireless mic from my hand, and placed it in the stand holder.

It was time.

The mix Taurus and I came up with was cemented into my brain. I played it over and over and over again. So why were my knees quaking?

I gulped hard and waited several breaths for the music to start.

Then a couple more.

Where the fuck was my music?

I looked over to the sound guys, scrunching my face up and mouthing, "What the fuck?"

They shrugged and frantically pushed buttons until, finally, the instrumental began.

I stilled the beating of my heart and counted the seconds once again.

Except, as soon as a falsetto was loaded and ready to come out of my mouth, one of the beams hovering above came crashing down.

I swiftly jumped out of the way and to my left.

The entire audience gasped.

The cameras were still on me, and the instrumental continued despite the glass shards on the floor from the broken beam.

"I died my very first death, nine lives, but you've ruined me again."

A stage light dropped from the ceiling, and another directly after.

I was paralyzed as the fragments of glass and broken colors only missed me by an inch. I moved out of the way as crew members frantically crowded me and tried to pull me out of the way. Instinctively, I pushed them to the side and stayed under my spotlight as best I could.

The only thing I knew how to do while the world was burning around me was sing.

Pyrotechnics from the previous song began to misfire, a few sparks catching my arms and back. And even with security tugging at my arm, I kept going.

"Maybe I was carried away, blinded by a new boy who could make me stay. I-I . . . see it all now."

I wiggled out of everyone's grasp, looking around to see the chaos that the stage had erupted into. The broken lights and uncontained electricity set fire to the plastic-coated stage. Before I knew it, they had cut the music, forcing me to continue acapella.

I focused my attention on the crowd, jumping off the stage and walking over to them. "And I have tried to let go of the things that they said. Imprints and photographs, memories made. But I'm still holding on to the idea of you, and what could have been true. But what could I do? When the haunting was started by you."

I made eye contact and glided past their seats like the destruction was all a part of the plan. With every person I passed, the fear once held in their eyes was replaced by amusement.

The camera followed me. "If I'm in your orbit, only for a moment . . . At some party where the starlets are wounded and the conversations are morbid."

I kissed a kid on the forehead before making my way back down the steps. "Will I always be haunted by you?"

I could barely breathe, and Nila appeared next to me, finally cutting me off by announcing that we'd be back after the commercial break. But in the midst of my heavy breathing . . . I was smiling.

She had her arms around me, and every single person in that fucking room was clapping.

I basked in a glory that fueled my ego and cemented my star status all at once. They chanted my name over the chaos of the sprinklers going off overhead.

The cameras were off, and with every second that I stood there, water soaked my entire body, but I couldn't stop smiling.

Yet, when they were finally able to usher me back to my dressing room to be checked and dried off, I knew I didn't need to check my phone to know one thing . . .

I was in danger.

CHAPTER TWENTY

THE PAPARAZZI WOULD HAVE mowed me down if it wasn't for Taurus's body acting as a shield. He pushed them away with an effortless force that even I couldn't fathom. One hand kept them distant, the other wrapped around me.

Wearing Andrés's money and Taurus's arm conjured up a cocktail of emotions. But possible feelings for two men who had seen each other naked were the least of my concerns.

Nila agreed to make it seem like the set malfunction was planned after she apologized a million times and offered me more free promo than I could use as long as I didn't sue. Nova, on the other hand, was nowhere to be found.

I asked around for her, but the only person left in my dressing room was Josefina, who, thankfully, had no idea what was going on. Nova had to have been off somewhere using her magic eraser and spinning the stage collapse in my favor. I couldn't look any longer, though.

I had to go.

"Taurus! Over here!" A man in a baseball cap with a point-and-shoot blocked our way to the car. "What did you think about your girlfriend's performance?"

Taurus managed to push the man to the side and get the door open, ushering me into the car. "She did amazing. She's a natural talent, isn't she?"

"I see why you love her," I heard him reply.

"Today, tomorrow, and forever."

The door shut behind us softly, and the driver started the engine. I cleared my throat. "Around back, please. I need to pick someone up."

The driver said nothing as the SUV was revived with a quiet roar.

Taurus quickly raised the partition, and his body turned to face me. I kept my gaze forward in an attempt to ignore the icy silence.

"You know why this happened," he said once he realized that I wasn't budging.

My lips formed a thin line as I nervously tapped the back of my phone. "Thank you, Captain Obvious."

Taurus stared at me like he had more to say, but the vehicle came to a sudden halt. The force alone pushed me slightly forward, only to be stopped by my hand. I kept my mouth shut since I didn't have the energy to complain, pushing the door open to reveal Josefina standing there with a crew member and a ziplock bag of whatever chocolate-covered strawberries were left over.

"Where's Nova?" I asked in a whisper as I pulled her hand out of the stranger's.

"Not sure, miss. She was seen exiting the building, though," they quickly answered.

I took comfort in the fact that she was probably halfway home by now and slammed the door shut. I'd deal with her leaving Josefina later.

Since when do I care?

"You looked pretty," Josefina announced without even looking up from the tablet.

I hitched my breath and felt the weight of the compliment that fulfilled me more than anything else I had heard. "*Gracias.*"

When I noticed we were still in one spot, I looked over at Taurus, who was obviously steaming.

Another thing to deal with later.

I yanked the partition down. "Can we go?"

The driver removed his gloves and hat before locking eyes with me through the rearview mirror. "Oh, I'm sorry. I was waiting for everyone to get situated."

The eyes struck me before the accent.

I held on to Josefina tighter and saw Taurus sit up from the corner of my eye.

"What the fuck is going on?" he asked me.

Andrés traced the wheel with his pointer finger. "Taking her back before they finish the job. I'm sorry, were you also coming?"

"You've lost your fucking mind. You knew that they would pull that shit and you let her go anyway. Do you want her to get killed? Or is that something only I care about?"

"You didn't seem to care all that much when you were helping her hide," Andrés pointed out calmly, his words tearing through any semblance of sanity I had left like a round of bullets through my chest.

"How—"

Taurus turned to me and grabbed my hand. I yanked it back and watched as whatever hope he had left in his eyes flicked until they were completely dark like the lights on the stage. Yet he managed to force out, "Come on, I'll get us a car."

Guilt had to have been eating him alive. He wasn't strong enough to prevent me from taking the oath that sold my soul to the Elite Order. Taurus wanted to save me, but the fragments of what once was could no longer be restored.

"And go where?" I asked, my voice hoarse from my performance mere moments ago.

Andrés sat in silence.

"He's not a husband, and he's not your savior either, Alejandra."

"Oh, and you are?"

Josefina squirmed in her seat. The heightened tension had to have been triggering her. Instinctively, I grabbed her hand and laced her fingers in between mine. As if I had taken her anxiety and made it my own, fear tore through my rib cage and danced in my chest.

Taurus lowered his tone. "No. I'm not. But I don't think going with him and locking into this sh—" He paused. "Locking into this mess is going to help you. You don't know what you're signing up for, and if you go with him, you're doing just that. I know you think you want it all, but it is possible without his help, or his money, or his fucking family. They will take everything from you if you don't run, and I only want the best for you. Both of you. But you gotta trust me."

I had grown to respect him more than most people.

No.

I had grown to want him around more than most people.

But I had no fight left in me. I was one wrong step from being plummeted by stage equipment not too long ago, and the writing was already written on the wall. If I wanted to keep myself and everyone I loved safe, then I'd go anywhere Andrés told me to go. I'd do whatever he told me to do.

I'd give whatever he wanted me to give.

Taurus broke the silence with a scoff. "I can't watch you give your soul up to these people. I won't."

I swallowed the dread in my throat that was simply a reaction to how the words vibrated from his vocal cords and ripped through me. He didn't make it clear, but I knew it was an ultimatum.

Safety and fame, which came at the cost of my soul. Or I'd get to keep whatever decency I had left and spend an eternity hiding.

The worst was confirmed when I got a glimpse of Andrés's deadly eyes through the mirror. My muscles tensed, and somehow, I knew he wanted me to make the call.

My heart stammered, but I kept my chin up. "Then get out of the car."

The orange hue from the streetlights poured into the SUV as he swung the door open with a forceful push. My fingers flinched.

I wanted to grab his hand.

Instead, I leaned back instead and stroked Josefina's hand with my thumb. I couldn't look at him or let myself think for even a moment that I had royally fucked up. I had to be as cold as the Italian leather that kept me grounded while I counted four deep breaths.

Four breaths until the door slammed shut and rattled the vehicle.

Four breaths until I knew for sure he was gone.

He hesitated.

Andrés, on the other hand, didn't as he placed a heavy foot on the gas. We rode in silence until I asked about Solo, and he assured me she had already been relocated to his place, which placed breaking and entering at the top of his felonies. Then Josefina reminded me that she was hungry and out of strawberries to snack on, which led us to a drive-through where she and I ended up sharing an extra-large chocolate shake.

When we finally merged onto the highway, cars were smacked together like sardines in a can. We were motionless throughout the bumper-to-bumper traffic. So much so that Josefina managed to fall asleep in my arms.

And right when I was tired of playing with her hair and considering dozing off myself, raindrops began aggressively beating against the hood of the car. Impatient drivers brake-checked each other and honked their horns until the birds above us cawed in response.

"No one can drive in this damn city." Andrés spoke into the silence, his deep voice effortlessly combating the volume of the storm. "It starts raining, and everyone forgets green means go."

I stared out of the window as water splattered against the glass, making it almost impossible for me to see anything except blotches of color. We drove through puddles and splashed water every which way. I found myself wondering if California became Atlantis and I died with it, would anyone be able to say that they were truly loved by me?

My thoughts were interrupted by Josefina wiggling and whining in my arms. "Bed," she grumbled before turning in my arms to try to get comfortable again.

"I'm not sitting through this, and neither should she," I finally said.

"Well, what do you want me to do about that?"

"Do I have to spell it out for you, *pendejo*? Get us back or get me a place for her to sleep. Whichever is faster. I don't care at this point."

Andrés's eyes fixed on mine through the rearview mirror.

My breath stilled, and without warning, he swerved out of traffic and toward the closest exit like he had a beef with the asphalt.

It was only a few hours until Christmas, so it made sense for the roads to be congested, but there was no way we were getting back now.

"Where are we going?" I panted, my heart racing from the irresponsible driving.

"Need a place to sleep, right?" Andrés answered simply.

CHAPTER TWENTY-ONE

L *ET ME SEE HER!*
I was awoken by the vehicle coming to a very rough stop. The words echoed in my head every time I drifted off. There was never a time when the exact dream— or words—would repeat itself to me. Yet, for some reason, my brain couldn't let Saint's voice go.

It was a sick trick of the mind. Of course I would imagine one of my closest friends there. Anyone in some need of comfort would have done the same thing. But why did it play in my mind like a song on repeat? Why was I refusing to acknowledge it beyond an echo in my head?

By the time we arrived at the hotel, I couldn't tell what city we were in anymore. Andrés insisted on being the one to go in first, and I only let him because my arms had grown numb from holding onto Josefina like she'd be taken away. I still wasn't sure what I'd do with her, but there wasn't a person on earth other than me who could understand her story like I did.

When it was time to go in, unease crept over my body with every step. It had nothing to do with the eerily empty parking lot or the car alarms blaring in the distance. None of that could compare to the influx of panicked thoughts that occupied my mind when I stepped onto another hotel property.

With the enemy.

However, when the automatic doors slid open on command, the smell of burnt coffee and peppermint welcomed us with open arms. To our left, a tall Christmas tree was propped up by the fireplace. It was maybe ten steps from a small convenience shop they had set up for guests, complete with candies, refreshments, and travel-sized toiletries.

Josefina squinted through the blinding lights while Andrés walked swiftly ahead. He ushered us to a hall of silver elevators where one dinged open upon arrival.

The ride up was silent and uneasy. Andrés remained still at the other end of the metal box. He toyed with his nose ring once or twice, but his gaze was fixed on the ground, and his hands were clasped in front of him like whatever was on his mind was enough to paralyze him.

I wondered if he knew how triggering this would have been for me or if he even cared. For all I knew, bringing me to another hotel could be part of the master plan.

The elevator doors peeled open at the very top, and burgundy carpeting dressed the floors. Without a second of thought, Andrés headed for the door at the darkest part of the hall and pushed it open with ease. A small room trimmed with gold that provided a couch, TV, closet, bathroom, and only one bed was all I had to work with.

"Good to know that top floor didn't mean penthouse," I muttered to myself.

"They're all sold out. It's Christmas Eve," he answered nonchalantly despite me not directing my complaints to him. He spoke to me like a child he couldn't be bothered to explain anything to.

I focused on getting Josefina out of her coat and sneakers so she could be comfortable while she drifted off. It didn't take her long to curl up in the center of the bed and give in to her dream state, which left me in a two-by-four hotel room with a man who had already stepped out to take a call.

I plopped down on the hideous orange couch, forcing my breath to still while I had a spare moment to myself. The room wasn't as nice as the one that I had been hog-tied and thrown around in, but I could still hear their voices in the air.

It had all the same qualities—a door that was supposed to lock and a private space to torture me in. I fingered the fabric of my sweatpants to feel the burns on my knees underneath. I wiggled my ankles to test if they were still sore.

It was only a hotel room. There was nothing to be afraid of.

Except there was.

I focused on watching Josefina sleep. Her parted lips and already messy hair was far more entertaining than the anchor of anxiety that sat on top of my heart. When I watched her, I noticed the absence of my desire to leave. Perhaps it was possible for me to be someone who could take care of her. Maybe I had grown into someone who, hopefully, could be the person I needed when I was younger.

Maybe if I allowed myself, I could be there for her.

I shook the thoughts out of my head and swiped the spare room key off of the TV stand. I didn't know where I was going, but I needed air. When I swung open the door and entered the empty hall, I was greeted by a stone-cold Andrés. He looked behind me to see Josefina sleeping, and then his dark eyes met mine once again.

"You never struck me as the maternal type."

"That would make sense. I don't have kids," I snapped.

He only smirked and stepped back to give me room to fully close the door behind us and finish the conversation in the hallway. "Yet you're dragging her around. Why? You're in a life-or-death situation, and your plus-one is a child."

"You told me you'd protect us, so I shouldn't have anything to worry about, right?"

He gave me a once-over, but his dim eyes gave me nothing to work with. His entire demeanor was calm . . . or bored. It was as if he had dealt with someone like me a million times already and couldn't be bothered to entertain a million and one.

Then he simply said, "*Sí.*"

I rolled my eyes and leaned against the nearest wall with tacky red-and-white wallpaper that had begun to peel. I felt like Andrés had his hands around my throat, and there was nothing left to do but suffocate.

"Why me?" I forced out, turning my head to face the man who was standing there like he knew the question was coming. "I'm trading one prison for another . . . I should at least know why."

"My mom used to say that."

I stood up a little. "Your mom?"

"One prison for another."

I was looking at him from the side now. His face was sharp enough to cut glass, and his features were clearly carefully crafted. Whoever she was did a great fucking job.

My lips pursed, and I forced myself to stop staring at how his muscles bulged out of the fabric of his T-shirt.

"Who is she?"

"Was."

An apologetic sound escaped from my lips, but I swallowed whatever was left before it formed a full-blown apology. "What happened to her?"

"She was killed when Camila and I were younger." He went somewhere I couldn't reach him for moments in time, like he had gotten swept up in a memory. Yet he spoke as if he was reading off of a script. "She felt like the Order was a prison too." Andrés rocked back on his heels and cleared his throat. "Nothing to worry about, though. I know who killed her, and I'm going to make it right. All of it."

My heart sank, and everything I thought I knew disintegrated. I wasn't sad for his loss or concerned for his well-being. No, it wasn't that at all.

I had watched enough movies to know that if he was telling me this now . . . then Taurus was right and there was no way out. After all, he had spoken before about unions, but it sounded like insanity until I started to put the pieces together.

I was just one part of a revenge plan.

"You need me so you can . . . get promoted? And then what?"

He scoffed. "I need you because I'll be replacing my father." Andrés paused, as if he was debating on filling me in more. But by the way he shifted his weight onto his other foot, I could tell that he had decided to. "Everyone who needs to know what the plan is knows. He's the only one out of the loop, and so he's the only one looking for you. The rest of them just have to make it seem real enough to not tip him off. And when the timing is right . . . it'll be over. You'll know more when you need to. Stop asking me questions."

February.

"Why me?" I asked again in a clipped tone.

He tilted his head to the side but still didn't look at me. The older man remained focused on the door across from us like he was waiting for someone to jump out at any moment. I watched him take deep breaths and crack his knuckles leisurely.

"Even as a kid I remember this fire in her. I mean, she had to have it." He forced out a sarcastic laugh. "Only someone that fucking ballsy would try to leave. I thought that kind of arrogance was unique to her . . . until I came across you."

"Who recommended me?" I managed to finally ask.

I had been thinking about it since the day he mentioned recommendations . . . The entire process made it crystal clear that someone close to me had set my life alight.

It was asking this that made him finally turn to look at me. He had a smirk on his stupid face that showcased a single dimple.

My heart thumped against my chest, and for once, I recognized the raw and overwhelming power that I had mistakenly labeled as confidence before. It was much stronger than that. It was something I couldn't achieve on stage if I tried.

"The darling starlet wants to know who betrayed her," Andrés sang in a mocking tone.

I pursed my lips together. "Don't patronize me."

"Santiago Mendez."

I thought I didn't have enough disappointment left in me, but I was staring at him through blurry vision. I shook my head enough times that a tear managed to escape.

But I wasn't shocked.

I was so damn tired. Tired of another twist, another turn . . . Another obvious fucking answer. It made the most sense out of anyone else in my life. He was the networker of our group, and his unescapable career seemingly came out of nowhere. He was a poster boy for the Elite Order if I had ever seen one, and I was too fucking stupid to put the pieces together.

I should have known.

"Merry Christmas!" a woman sang as she walked by us, sending a shock through my system.

She was fully gray-haired and dressed in a long fur coat that was covered in raindrops. Her cheeks and nose were bright red from what had to be three pounds of department store blush.

"*Feliz Navidad*," Andrés replied with a genuine smile that I had never seen before. It wasn't sinister or the product of him laughing at someone . . . He was just smiling.

The woman stopped in front of the room across from us. "Got out of that storm, huh? I'm going to see my grandbabies not too far from here, but I'll finish up the drive in the morning. I got them all these beautiful gifts, and I can't wait to see their faces when they wake up and see I made it."

I swallowed hard at the crushing reality that Josefina needed something to wake up to, too. I had a chance to do better.

I had to be better.

"Yeah . . ." I wiped any remaining tears off of my face. "I'm sure they'll love it and appreciate seeing you."

She nodded. "Well, you two kids have a great holiday."

She didn't even recognize me. "Thank you."

I waited for her to enter her room and close the door before turning back to Andrés. "I need—I can't believe I didn't think to get her anything. Is anything open?"

"No," he deadpanned.

"Well—"

"I'll see what I can do."

"What?"

"Go get some damn sleep, Alejandra. The longer you're awake, the more questions you ask."

I wish I could say I objected, but I listened. My body felt like there was a thousand tons weighing on it, and I couldn't stand upright anymore.

Before falling asleep, I typed a "Feliz Navidad" text to Nova and a million drafts to Saint and Taurus—neither of which were sent.

I drifted off to sleep, accepting the reality that those words weren't a dream.

He was there.

When dawn came and Josefina stirred awake, I thought I could sleep through it. But when the bed shifted at a rapid motion and a blood-curdling shriek jolted me awake . . . that was absolutely impossible.

My eyes shot open in panic, only to be met with a glowing Josefina, jumping on the bed so carelessly she almost landed on my ankles a few times. I followed her focus and blinked several times before taking in the sight to my left.

A lit Christmas tree covered in candy canes and trinkets stood tall in the center of the room.

Did he steal that from the lobby?

Around it were several gifts wrapped, with Josefina's name on them, except one—an acoustic guitar with a silver bow on it.

I sat up slowly, squinting to see my name scribbled on one of the ribbons. I couldn't remember the last time I touched my guitar at The Castle. It was the only one I had—lilac, and given to me by the only neighbor who'd speak to me.

I poured my heart out whenever I touched the instrument . . . It was a cure.

But I could never lie to my guitar.

I could never gaslight myself into false truths whenever I picked it up. So, I hid behind computer screens and autotune because lying was easier that way. I could decorate time with deception while ignoring the truth that came with vulnerability.

By the time I finished processing, Josefina was already shaking boxes without hesitancy. She wasn't scared anymore.

Andrés stood in front of the bed with his arms across his chest.

We locked eyes, and I mouthed a silent thank-you. He nodded in return.

"Open it! Open it!" Josefina demanded through her toothy grin, slapping her small hands on my thighs.

A soft smile made its way onto my face, and I helped her with opening the gift. But as she moved onto the next one, and her voice faded . . . a daunting reality slammed into me like a wrecking ball.

I was accepting his gifts and following his lead.

Whatever happened within the Elite Order was enough to make his mother want to run. That was what I was headed into . . . A life she died trying to escape.

That was what Saint led me to.

But Andrés was sure that I was made for it. That I deserved to once again be the queen of another castle.

But all I could hear was a roaring voice in my head, screaming one phrase over and over.

You're fucked.

CHAPTER TWENTY-TWO

"I MEAN, THE RECENT PERFORMANCE where the stage malfunctioned was pure theatrical genius. Let me tell you, I went and bought vinyls for everyone I knew."

"On to other trending news in Los Angeles today, legendary rap artist Mike Michigan was stopped by Pop Mania reporters saying some very concerning things. Play the clip please."

The audio came clean through the speakers. "They can't control me. They can control all these pop singers, these athletes, these other rappers. But not me. I'll name them all—I don't take no disrespect from nobody. Nobody. I serve God now. Come on, man. They sacrificed my daughter. I can't get that back. I won't be one of those people who go missing in Hollywood. There's a lot of that going on, isn't there? Lots of missing people in Hollywood. But God protects me."

I should have turned it off. It was doing nothing to distract me from the fact that I had to see Saint and that Nova still was nowhere to be found.

I had to call it what it was the other night . . . An attempted assassination. That would be enough to scare anyone off. She also could have been on Christmas break like most people would be. I couldn't remember our conversations about her schedule, but I wouldn't interrupt what I was sure was time with her two daughters.

So, I stopped trying to text and call her. I'd surely hear back from her after the New Year when my appearances ramped back up.

The live stream continued blaring from my phone speakers. "Next we'll talk about how the people are betting on newcomer Bianca Veer sweeping the Starlight Music Awards. Including the award for Song of the Year."

Fear sat on my lungs and halted my breath. I was drowning all over again.

"Yeah, I heard that's a big one," said one of the podcast hosts.

"Bianca Veer is up against chart-topping and comeback queen Aly for the award this season. I don't know, though. It's looking like Bianca might be winning in the court of public opinion."

I hit the power button on my phone and took a few deep breaths to try to calm the butterflies in my chest.

The world never stopped moving.

I almost died, my whole team was off enjoying the holidays, and I was stuck with a kid, a psychopath, and a million unsent text messages. Regardless of all of that, people still demanded more of me.

The more I gave, the more they'd take. The oldest rule in the book when it came to the parasocial relationship between fan and rockstar.

And unlike Bianca, I wanted it forever. She wasn't going to be what killed me, and I had every tool in my arsenal to make sure of that . . . I just had to use it.

I leaned into the heated leather of the luxury car that acted as my horse and carriage. Even at my worst, I was a queen on her way to confront an ally.

I could only go and see Saint if I let Andrés's guard dogs drive me to his place and if he didn't have to stay with Josefina. We negotiated getting her a nanny he trusted, who just so happened to be the one who watched him as a child. I barely trusted her, but I needed help, and bringing more loved ones to his house wasn't smart.

At first, he didn't want me to go at all, claiming that it was too soon after the attack and he had yet to make sure the smoke had cleared. Regardless, I tried to convince him that I needed to see him for my own peace of mind.

He couldn't care less.

What did convince him was me saying I'd scream at the top of my lungs and point the gun at my own damn head if he didn't let me do it.

Upon arrival, I knocked on the door four or five times. My patience ran thin on the second knock.

The longer I stood out in the open, the more time I had to recall when my lungs filled with water and when smoke from collapsing stage lights filled my nostrils. I wished I was invisible as I stood in broad daylight in a fucking tracksuit standing outside of Saint's door. Andrés's security hadn't pulled off, but it wasn't their eyes I felt that were on me.

A chill ran down my spine, and I began to nervously tap my foot.

I peeked through the window nearest to the front door but couldn't see anything except a sliver of light. His electric-blue Porsche was parked inches away from where I stood—he was home.

"I swear to God if he doesn't answer the door right now I will fucking key it," I muttered to myself, never getting the chance to make right on my threat because the door swung open.

A messy-haired brunette greeted me in only designer boxer briefs and a Versace robe that was spilling off of him. Minuscule tattoos were peppered around various places on his arms, but you could easily miss them from a distance.

Wait.

Romeo Espósito?

"My goodness, you look like you've seen a ghost." His voice was slurred despite it not even being noon yet. He leaned lazily against the open door. "*Mi cielo*, you have a guest!"

Romeo gave me a once over while madness stirred in his pupils. His eyes widened like I had suddenly become Sunday dinner.

Unlike his brother, there was a twinkle still in his eye. In fact, everything about Romeo felt lighter—freer—but equally as traumatized. His tone lowered and his lips curled into a devilish smile. "And my, my she is a stunner up close."

"Ew," I said quickly before pushing him aside. "Santiago, bring your ass or I swear to God I will saw it off and feed it to Solo!" I looked at Romeo, and once I could get Andrés's fucking eyes out of my head I remembered someone else—Savannah.

Did she know?

If he was fucking an Espósito kid, then he was far deeper into this shit than someone I thought was a friend was very much a well-informed enemy.

Romeo slammed the door behind me, and when I spun around on my heels to give him a piece of my mind, he was already tripping over his own two feet.

Okay then.

The slam definitely wasn't on purpose . . . He was long gone. His eyes glazed over and the smile never left his lips while he stumbled over to the living room.

"Santiago!" I screamed at the bottom of the stairs. "*Pendejo!* Do not make me come up there!"

The crash of a broken lamp turned my attention to Romeo once again. He only stared at the glass shards for a moment before shrugging. I wondered what caused one of the princes of the Elite Order to be so . . . comfortable.

From photos, their inactivity on social media, and the way his older brother behaved, they all seemed like they had a stick up their ass. But behind Saint's closed door, that didn't seem like the case.

"I'm coming! I'm coming!" Saint finally shouted from upstairs.

I tapped my foot on the sparkling dark brown flooring as the traitor appeared at the top of the steps. He looked way more put together than his guest. Shocker.

That was sort of Saint's thing. At his worst he could bat those green eyes, and the world would crumble at his feet. But with the information I knew now—I couldn't tell if that was natural charisma or an image of him crafted by the Elite Order that I had fallen for.

"You know, I hate waking up to a messy living room—thank you, Romeo. Oh! And a broken lamp, wonderful. But I also hate waking up to fucking yelling!"

"What the fuck is the Elite Order?" I didn't wait for him to make it all the way down the stairs, and maybe I should have because he lost a few steps and damn near slid the rest of the way down.

"Told you!" Romeo's yell was muffled, and I could only assume he had his face in the couch cushions.

Saint gathered himself and adjusted his GUESS T-shirt and cotton knee-length shorts. He cleared his throat, and his brows knitted. "*Que?*"

I stepped closer to the man—pushing my pointer finger into his chest. "You have five seconds to explain why you're the reason I'm in this mess, or I will make sure that your house and every house within a five-mile radius of this bitch gets burned to the fucking ground. Then you will explain to me why I shouldn't take a photo of him in your damn house and send it to Savannah. Do you get what the fuck I'm saying now?"

Fear twinkled in his eyes and burned out as quickly as it came. Without warning, Saint's face turned stone cold. He pushed out his chest and backed away from my finger.

I never registered his height as daunting until the moment he looked down at me with hollowed eyes. He was always accompanied by a gentle aura, but it was no longer. For the first time since we met, his kind nature was replaced with something much more powerful.

"You were desperate."

"Excuse me?"

"He's saying you had no chance in hell without our help." Romeo was now lazily thrown against the back of the couch, watching us with wild and eager eyes like an instigating hyena.

"I can handle this, Romeo." Saint turned back to me and shrugged. "Do you not remember? You couldn't sleep for weeks, and when you did, you woke up screaming. Yessenia, Savannah, and I were taking turns staying with you for days at a time. You were begging and praying for it not to be the end. You wanted nothing more than to get your awards, praise, and recognition again. Then you ran off to Miami thinking it'd fix everything. You thought you couldn't get it all back without help from God himself. But I know God, and I brought you to him."

"How could you do this without even warning me? How could you do this *to* me?" My voice cracked, and it made me wince.

I hated that this hurt me. I hated that he knew the risks of what could happen to me.

"You were supposed to finish the initiation," he forced out in between hard swallows.

"Tsk . . . Tsk . . . Tsk. You can blame my brother for that one."

"Romeo!" Saint snapped, and even I jumped a bit.

"Fine. I'll go take a shower while you tell your friend she's gonna die if not by my dad's hands than Camila's if she doesn't listen." He peeled himself off of the couch and left his robe on the floor in his absence.

"What did you do?" I finally forced out in the midst of blinking back tears.

"I helped. Your Starlight nomination, the number one album . . . You're getting it all because they want you to."

"What?"

"If they wanted you dead, Alejandra . . . you'd be dead. They're all about strength and games. It's the way they do their rituals. I'm just trying to figure out what your big sacrifice is going to be at this point."

"No. No. No." I shook my head feverishly. There was no telling who I could believe anymore. Between him and Andrés, it still felt like I was missing the bigger picture. "I—that's not even the point! This is about me and you. This is about how you took the chance away from me to fucking try."

"You were blackballed!" Saint roared. His face turned a cherry red, and his veins began to bulge out of every visible place on his body. "I knew it. You knew it. There was no fucking way you were getting this far without them. Great comebacks don't just happen, Alejandra. Not after what happened to you. They control the media, the government, our technology—everything. It's not just the Espósitos and Timeless. It's not just California and your talent. It's the missing kids and dead mothers. It's the viruses and diseases. It's the right-on-time vaccines and suspicious deaths. And right now you need to figure out what side you want to be standing on. And because I love you and I would do anything for you, I let you get a glimpse of what your life could look like. A better life. The life you deserve."

I stood there in disbelief, and my hands trembled with rage.

"You didn't have a right to put my life up for auction." I shoulder-checked the bigger man and walked over to his bar where I quickly grabbed a bottle that had been left out from what I could only assume were Romeo's downstairs adventures.

"That would have hurt less than finding out you led me into this blind. Knowing there's a kid in my house who I—" I forced myself to pause. "Who deserves so much more than abuse and sadness. Yet here I am. Bringing it right to my front door." I popped the cap off of the bottle and chugged. "Oh wait! I can't even stay there anymore because I'm not allowed back there."

"I told them about you before she came. If I knew—"

"Right! Because they robbed me. That was my first test, right? I'm slowly learning a lot these days since no one is fucking talking!"

Saint walked over to me but still remained a few feet away. "You think any of us had it easy? Initiations, recruitment periods . . . Hell, memberships come with sacrifices. It all varies by person . . . by time. Some people have to pretend to be fucking insane to gain their membership. Humiliation rituals. Meaningless sex. Losing someone we love. We all had to give up parts of ourselves to gain what we have now. But it's worth it in the end."

His words drilled holes in my head and banged against my chest, but I couldn't let him faze me. Instead of screaming like I wanted to, I said, "How do you live that way? Knowing that nothing you have is earned?"

Saint considered that but quickly corrected, "The success you grew up to crave is child's play to what I actually earn. When you start seeing what you're really capable of . . . a Starlight Award is a fucking paperweight."

"You're sick."

He rolled his eyes. "Sure, let's call it that, but up until recently you were naive. Open your eyes. You're finally being introduced to the real world, Aly. That's not the least bit intriguing to you?"

I let the question cover me whole like a heavy blanket and said nothing in response.

"You had nothing to bargain with in this industry," Saint continued. "I just wanted to see you smile again. I wanted to see you create something you were proud of again. Because whether you liked it or not, in another world, Locke and Key would have taken your masters, sold them, and benched you for the rest of your career until you had no choice but to become a physical trainer or get a damn college degree." He took a step closer and moved my hair from off my shoulder. "You're better than that. You're better than them and their fucking objectives and KPIs. You're a fucking rockstar, *amor*. I'm not sorry for letting you in, I'm just sorry for how it's turning out."

I highly doubted he was sorry at all. He believed in the Elite Order undeniably. I could tell by the way his eyes filled with excitement and the way he couldn't stop the corners of his mouth from lifting up. It was sick.

I stepped out of his touch and put the bottle back down at the bar to distract my anxious hands. "You mentioned a sacrifice. What—what was yours?"

He toyed with the gold band on his finger, and his gaze dropped to the floor before he let out an empty laugh. "The puppet masters need to have full control of the puppet, right? A month after I moved here, I met them. I told them I'd give everything as long as I never had to go back to Portugal. They took me very fucking seriously."

"What did they do?"

"A few weeks later my family home was burned to the ground and I had nothing to return to even if I wanted to. Two days after that, my first album was number one. Twelve weeks later it still was. I skyrocketed. I got everything I asked for."

My soul felt heavy, and my heart felt undetectable. I could feel the blood rushing to my face while my limbs began to shake madly.

It was all out of my control.

My life, my soul, and the bliss that came with my ignorance. They were all replaced with a darkness that I hadn't scratched the surface of. And for the first time since the madness started . . . I knew for a fact that someone wasn't lying to me.

"Why is he here?" I spat out.

"He's my handler," he answered far too quickly.

"Excuse me?"

He chuckled lightly. "Whenever someone is made a member, they're assigned a handler. A trusted member or, in the Espósitos' case, a blood member."

"Oh." I considered it for a long moment. "So . . . Is fucking your handler a part of the gig?"

The redness in his cheeks returned. "No. That just sort of happened. He's good . . . Like, outside of being tied up in all of this. They all are."

I tried to digest the idea of them being "good," but the more I thought about it, the more I wanted to throw up. I walked over to the wall with the least amount of clutter around it and slid down until I hit the floor.

"He wants me to be his wife." I put air quotes around the last word and didn't even notice Saint sliding down next to me until his thigh hit mine.

I didn't want to punch him or call him names. I had barely anyone in my corner to begin with, and I couldn't lose another one. And if I really dug deep . . . I wasn't mad at all. I was intrigued.

I wanted to know what it felt like to really touch the stars. To be a real rockstar.

"Then his wife is what you'll be."

"He told me what he's trying to do to his father," I whispered, feeling some sense of relief that I could tell someone without fear of them coming up missing . . . or worse.

"*Si*. From what I know, Gianna, his mother, went missing when Andrés and Camila were toddlers, and Antonio started dating around almost immediately."

"Missing?"

"Yeah, actually now that I bring it up, I do remember one thing," Saint continued. "When Romeo got high like six months ago . . . We were in the South of France—beautiful by the way, you've got to add it to your list."

"Get on with it, Santiago."

"I am, I am. Romeo was . . . He was out of it, damn near sleepwalking the entire trip. He starts talking about his siblings. He wondered if Camila was the mastermind behind Andrés. The true psychopath while he was just the face. Because even though the siblings are close . . . Those two are closer—hence why they're called the twins. Now I can tell you why everyone is so scared of Camila. She works more with the cartel than the rest of them. Not because she has to but because she likes it. Julian told me once she's killed more men than the worst of 'em in the Elite Order. But then Romeo kept rambling and said that his grandma talked a lot about how when Andrés was like six or some shit he was seeing shrinks."

"Like psychiatrists?"

Saint nodded, and his vision darted back and forth from me to the stairs. "He used to say . . . Mommy was in the trunk. Drawing pictures of a car with blood pouring out of the back and shit. Got real violent at school. It all got cleaned up by his dad and no one really knows if . . ."

"He was a kid just making stuff up or if he knows what happened to his mom . . ."

"*Si.* Exactly."

I sat in the truth that Andrés was just another broken child. It was why he didn't hesitate to get gifts for Josefina and why he protected her from the Elite Order in the first place. She wasn't on any of their records, but he had known about her the entire time.

I could hear his deep nonchalant voice ringing in my head, telling me everything I needed to know in a code only he understood. I wrapped my arms around my middle and opened my mouth to speak. But before I could get any words out, my phone buzzed.

I fished the device out of my pocket and the text read:

Unknown:

Last chance to give yourself up.

If they were in on it except his father . . . how far would they really go?

"I have to go." I rushed up onto my feet.

"Wait, there was one more thing I wanted to tell you."

I turned my head to face him. "Okay."

"I heard they're recruiting Bianca too. If she gets in . . . it's hers. The Starlight Award, the spot you held for the last few years . . . It's all hers. If you let her take it? This would all have been for nothing. Plus, I can promise you're getting a better deal than she would. You can still win it all, Aly."

Fuck.

Throw up crept up my throat.

I forced it back down with a hard swallow and simply said, "I'm going to."

I was learning the rules of the game, and the only people playing fair in the industry were sheep led to slaughter.

The harsh truth of it all was that if I wanted to leave a legacy . . . I was going to have to say yes to Andrés when the time came. If a queen was what he wanted, then a queen was what he was going to get.

CHAPTER TWENTY-THREE

I DIDN'T REMEMBER GETTING BACK to the house.

Racing thoughts of failure consumed me the entire time. I learned about a society where children became killers, and all I wanted to do was beat Bianca Veer.

I had rewired my brain so that anger, hurt, and fear immediately became a cocktail that stirred a hunger for success in my belly.

It wasn't right, and it made me more animal than human. The lack of empathy, the desire to kill . . . My insecurities had manifested into a hardened heart.

If it were to ever thaw, I'd be sitting at the top by then.

At least I'd have everything I ever wanted.

I was awoken from my nap on the couch by the guard moving from his post and the front door swinging open. Andrés walked through the frame with a duffel bag in his hand.

I peeked over the back of the couch and quickly scrambled on my feet. "You weren't here when I got back."

"Didn't think I had to be." Andrés waved his hand at security, and he closed the door for him before standing back in place.

I picked at a loose thread of the silk shorts I had on in hopes it would soothe my looming anxiety. The longer I stood here, the more my feet felt nailed to the floor.

"Well." I rolled my eyes. "It'd help considering I'm still getting those creepy texts."

He pursed his lips and glared at me for a split second, then turned on his heels and started to fucking walk away from me.

Was he serious?

I scoffed. "Hello! I'm fucking talking to you."

He stopped in his tracks, and his shoulders stiffened.

Heat rushed to my cheeks, and it wasn't until I heard my knuckles crack that I realized I was clenching my fists. It was the slowest I had ever seen him move. Every vertebra of his body activated like an electric wave, but when he was finally facing me, it was clear the last thing he wanted was to hear me speak.

"Hello, Alejandra. How can I help you today?" Sarcasm dripped from his lips, and it enraged the ever living fuck out of me.

I'd had it up to here with his need to teeter on the line of possession and disinterest. I couldn't believe my own desires, but if he was going to fucking own me, then *own me*!

I wanted him to at least make the nightmare real. Force me to do unspeakable things because that's what the Elite Order was supposed to be about. Torture and despicable acts that lasted the length of a lifetime were supposed to be my new reality. That was what I gave Taurus up for.

I sat around and wished for Andrés to give me something that would hurt or be a man and put me out of my misery. Either way, I'd no longer be able to wait by the phone for calls that weren't coming.

Look, Mom. I'm alone again.

"You are such a dick!" I exclaimed, stepping up to him.

He looked down at me like I was a bug he could flick away at any moment. But I held my ground, pushing my hair over my shoulders and staring at him right back. "I am here in your house with my shit piled high in the master bedroom, my sister in your guest room, and my fucking cat sleeping on your furniture, and you can't even acknowledge me?"

"You're welcome."

"I need to know what my part will be in this, Andrés. I can't just sit here and watch as my life spins out of control and my fans accuse me of forgetting I just dropped an album. I don't have Taurus anymore, so that's in the toilet—"

"I thought you didn't need him."

I ignored the comment and continued, "My manager is probably spooked, because she won't answer my calls. You said you'd keep me safe, and physically you have done that, but mentally—my career is practically in your hands, and if you forgot about that, then I'm here to remind you. I need you to promise me that I am going to win."

He looked me up and down like he was contemplating if I was worth a response, and just as I was raising my hand to slap him back to earth, he spoke. "So what do you want exactly? A chore or a promise that that award is yours?"

"A reason not to blow my brains out."

"So both." He walked around me and headed toward the kitchen, and I didn't hesitate to follow.

I jumped on the island and sat my ass on the dark marble. That surely got his attention because he paused, glared, but ultimately went back to his unconcerned nature. "I admit I got myself in this fucked situation, but you also admitted you would have put me in it anyway. Which means I have a right to demand things. I demand a promise that Bianca won't be a fucking problem anymore. It's the least you can do."

It'd be a lie to say I didn't recognize the words that were coming out of my mouth. I was willing the power given to me and seeing how far it could go. I knew how dangerous a demand like that could be, despite me not being in any real position of power yet.

There wasn't a perfect bone in my body, and I had a habit of treating people like jewelry that I'd try on and throw out the second I no longer desired it.

I was sorry for that, but it wasn't my job to consider those who never considered me.

"That kind of thinking will kill you slowly."

My brows knitted. "What?"

He looked around, and a small smirk cracked the stone wall look I was getting before. "Nothing."

"Okay. Do we have a deal? I do what you want without complaining, and you make sure of that. I never want to hear her fucking name next to mine again."

"Hey, hey, hey." Andrés cracked the water bottle open and brought my attention to the words tattooed on his knuckles. Death. I looked for his other hand that was wrapped around the plastic.

Power.

"Don't get testy. You got a deal."

"Good. So, what, are you like my handler or something?"

His eyes narrowed. "Where'd you learn that phrase, Alejandra?"

"Answer me."

He stepped closer to me. "I don't handle anyone. The Order runs on a system. The oldest heir, so me, or any position higher don't handle members. We have more important shit to do."

I lifted my chin to try to hide the fact that my heart was racing with him that close. "Go on."

"Why?"

"Because getting information out of you is like pulling teeth," I admitted despite my heart banging against my chest like a bird in a cage.

"Fine. I'll show you something you might find interesting." Andrés inched even closer and put his bottle down next to my thigh. He then placed both hands on my scarred knees and peeled my legs apart, slipping inside with little to no effort.

I could smell the hints of lavender from his graphic T-shirt and looked up to meet the slashes in his eyebrows and the gold rings looped through his nose.

"Okay." I forced a wad of spit down.

"Okay?"

I nervously ran a hand through my hair. "You're being a parrot."

"Where'd all that eagerness from before go?" He reached for a strand of my hair and began to twirl it, something I assumed he preferred to do when he was getting under my skin.

"Oh, fuck off," I spat out in a much louder tone than the one he was currently using.

"Go get ready." He slid out from in between my legs, and finally I could catch my breath.

"For what?"

"A show."

"How long do I have to get ready?"

"Take your time. Nothing starts until we show up."

I WAS GREETED BY two things when I stepped out of the shower, one being the frail elderly woman who was once again watching Josefina, and the smell of chocolate chip cookies that were baking in the oven. At the very least, I was glad she could have some normalcy despite being stuck with me.

I tiptoed out of the bathroom to find another damn box resting on my bed.

Inside lay a red gown with a crystal-embroidered top. It fit me like a glove, and I paired it with the stack of diamond bracelets, necklace, and earrings that came in the box as well.

When I thought the box was empty, underneath crumpled ash-colored packing paper was a mask. I pulled it out slowly and let the face covering sit in my hands. It was made of black lace and didn't even have holes for my eyes.

The mask was different from the heavy metal ones that I saw during the initiation. Electricity manifested in my hands the longer I held it.

I walked over to the oval mirror, the train of the red gown flowing behind me. The mask continued to burn in my grasp like it was screaming for me to put it on.

Something about it felt so . . . familiar.

I lifted my hands and put the mask on over my head. It covered my face up to my nose.

My heart fluttered at the sight of myself for the first time in years. Everything was shifting.

"You look pretty." The soft voice caused me to quickly pull the mask off and spin around on my heels to locate the source.

"That's very nice of you to say," I whispered as I walked over to Josefina and kneeled down to meet her at eye level.

She placed a hand on my cheek and smiled. "I like that color."

I looked down at my bust. "Can I tell you a secret?"

She nodded.

"I like it too."

Josefina giggled. "Are you going to come get cookies?"

"I . . ." I cleared my throat. "Have an event. But you know what?" The lump in my throat bobbed up and down. "You are lucky because tonight you can have them all. Then when I get back, we can make all the chocolate flan you want, okay?"

Josefina nodded, and her hair that was in a messy bun, courtesy of my laziness this morning, slipped out of the hair tie. It fell down her face and past her shoulders like mine would, and all she did was wrinkle her nose and laugh.

I watched her with a fondness in my eyes.

Whether I wanted to realize it before or not . . . I did owe her something. I owed her the entire fucking world.

Marabella's hatred was bold behind closed doors, and I lost my mind trying to figure out if that was what being a mother meant.

Was I insane for screaming for her to stop hitting me at eight years old? Did all moms wake their children out of bed and strip them of their blankets because they got too wasted a few hours ago?

No one was there to answer my questions.

No one was there to hear the way I talked in my sleep and begged for a chance to live a life that she wasn't a part of. But I never sat down and stared in a mirror and said—

"I love you."

The words acted as rain washing away the pain of all the battles I lost. As I brushed Josefina's hair out of her face, I caught the sparkle in her eyes accompanied by a smile. She leaned forward and kissed my nose gently.

I tilted my head to the side, and our laughs joined in perfect harmony. "I'm not getting any more words out of you today, am I?"

A shadow cast over Josefina and me, causing me to look up at the figure before he even spoke. "Not unless you say please."

He was dressed in all black—typical. Earrings and necklaces dressed their respective body parts and a leather jacket was layered on top of a V-neck. There was a casual way that he didn't need to do too much but you could still smell the money on him. Or, that was the obnoxious amount of cologne he clearly sprayed before he walked out the door.

I rose to my feet again after kissing Josefina on the forehead and telling her to go find that nanny lady—whatever her name was. To my surprise, she hugged Andrés's leg before disappearing into the maze that was our safe house.

"Where are we going?" I said coldly.

He swirled the glass of white wine in his hand. "A place where you wouldn't want a tear streak on your face when we arrive."

I sucked my teeth and grabbed the beauty blender I left out on my way over to the mirror. After a few pats, I was good to go.

After forty-five minutes in a silent car ride with illegally tinted windows, the truck came to a smooth halt. The door slowly swung open, and Andrés leaned out first. He spoke in fluent Spanish quietly to the man holding the door. He leaned back into his seat, and the door slammed shut.

"What's going on?"

He slowly turned to face me but not before taking off his sunglasses. "We're getting ready to go."

"Okay—" Before I could object or ask more questions, the door on my side swung open this time. A strong grip on my arm yanked me out of the seat without a chance to even grab my phone or purse. A shriek left my lips, and before the door shut I caught a glimpse of Andrés calmly getting out on the other side.

"Relax." The deep voice spoke from behind me, and I knew from the old looming trees and gravel driveway that it was probably in my best interest to listen.

I stopped fighting and let my heels gently hit the ground. They yanked my mask out of my hand and put it on for me, allowing the strap to snap the back of my head.

Andrés appeared next to me, and I looked up to find that he had a mask on as well.

Tonight we weren't animals.

His mask was white and covered every bit of his face except his eyes. He put his elbow out. I looked at it for a moment but exhaled before looping my arm through.

I was guided through the large oak double doors with ease. The estate was completely different from the one we had entered before. Sure, it still looked straight out of a haunted episode of *Bridgerton* but much more fear inducing.

Intense bass met our ears when we walked through the foyer, and people walked around in gowns and tuxedos with drinks in their hands and masks on their faces. I kept my chin up and wondered if it was safe for me to even be out in the open yet. I almost asked, but as soon as I had mustered the courage, a figure stepped in front of us.

Her hair was ginger with blonde streaks. She wore a white vest with nothing else under it—showcasing her cleavage and the worlds of colors and drawings that covered her chest and arms. A few rings dressed her fingers, and she too had a white mask that covered her entire face. Her pants brought the whole milk-colored ensemble together, baggy and put together by a silver chain connected to her belt loops.

"Didn't know you were bringing a guest," she said in a raspy tone that I didn't hesitate to recognize.

Camila.

Something about her was scarier than Andrés himself. It could have been that I knew her history or that I was sure it was her who tied me up in that hotel room. If Andrés was the God of War in my supernatural story, she had to be the Goddess of Death.

Her eyes ran wild when she looked me up and down. I suddenly didn't feel safe anymore.

"I thought it'd be important for her to be a witness." He placed his hand on the one I had resting on his forearm like a signal to not say a word.

I pressed my lips together and shut the fuck up for once. *A witness?*

Camila rocked back on her heels as she stuffed her hands into her pockets. "You don't think—"

"No."

She let out a spine curdling snicker. "Well. As long as he doesn't see her—"

"He won't." Andrés cut her off again. It was obvious from the way her shoulders rose that she was growing impatient with him. I was standing in between two wolves who were acting like one common goal was the only reason they weren't ripping each other apart.

Camila leaned in closer. "If you screw this up for me." I felt her breath on the top of my head, the height of them both putting me at a clear disadvantage.

Andrés stepped back, and I went with him simply by the force of his hold on me. "You need to worry about what your role is, Camila. I got mine."

She didn't have a chance to react, and I damn sure didn't either because he turned and pulled me down the hall.

I continued to take in my environment. Smoke filled the halls, and the music swelled with every step we took. Normally, the simple rhythms would send a spark through my soul, but it wasn't enough to shake Camila's breath off of my body.

One thing was for sure . . . I had to watch my own back.

CHAPTER TWENTY-FOUR

MY WORLD BURST WITH color when we entered the ballroom.

There was nothing intimate about the opulent space occupied by columns and gilded mirrors. When the moonlight came through the partially opened drapes, a vision of reds, blues, and purples bounced off the lights. For the first time in my life, vibrancy consumed me.

Which was concerning because my first EP, *Life in Color*, was created around the topic of finally finding the light . . . But I had never felt so dark.

Purple hues from the lights danced around us, oranges from the candlelit chandeliers hovered above, and when Andrés squeezed my arm a little tighter, pink flushed my cheeks.

Masked figures parted for him like the red sea. The strangers stared through their face coverings, while some even whispered, "Who is she?"

"She must be here to see the show."

Andrés didn't even flinch as he guided me out of the crowded area and down a long corridor. The remnants of the pipe organ's haunting hymn remained in my mind despite the distance that grew between us and the ballroom.

My heartbeat quickened as Greek mythology–inspired art became the infrastructure around me. The vibe change acted as gasoline to my nervous system.

The ceiling and walls were covered from corner to corner with images of Ares, Hermes, Aphrodite, and Zeus. Lightning bolts and jewels held by Hera looked so real it made me uneasy.

Their eyes also followed me.

It started to feel like a dream that I couldn't wake myself up from, but as we entered an auditorium, I had a gnawing feeling that I was about to witness something sinister.

Andrés had me stand behind him on one of the red-carpeted aisles as other masked attendees started to flood the auditorium. I recognized the best gowns from the ballroom mere moments ago. The women were drowning in diamonds and stones while the men showcased their wealth with watches and cufflinks.

The stage below us was covered by a thick midnight-blue curtain, and as the lights began to dim, I almost lifted my hand to tug him to ask where the hell we were sitting, but before I got the chance, a man in a tuxedo ushered us up a few more stairs until we entered a box with only two seats. Andrés stepped to the side and allowed me to go first.

Without hesitation I entered the space, taking the furthest seat. It was cushioned and felt how I could only assume a throne would. I leaned forward and saw that there was an identical box on the other side of the auditorium. Two masked figures were seated like statues, and I swore to

God it was Romeo and Saint. I wanted to wave but from Andrés's straight-forward gaze and stonelike stature—I feared he'd knock my hand right off.

I looked diagonal to see one other box sectioned away from the crowd. From the hair and outfit from earlier I knew that was Camila, and the masked man sitting with her with a low cut that was freshly dyed blonde had to be Julian. He was the only sibling I hadn't seen head on (to my full knowledge anyway), but I could tell it was him from his broad shoulders and light brown skin.

"Stop looking around," Andrés demanded.

I immediately leaned back in my seat. "What is this?"

He leaned in to whisper, "A traditional ceremony."

I rolled my eyes, and my lashes fluttered against the fabric of my mask. "That feels obvious."

Andrés lifted his mask and let it rest on the top of his head. "Then why'd you ask?"

I slowly lifted mine as well once I noticed that the seats allowed us and his siblings the utmost comfort and discretion. We couldn't be seen but we could see everything.

"You should get a drink, and I hope it comes with an attitude check," I hissed and directed my attention forward as the crowd began to hush.

A creeping silence filled the theater, and the lights dimmed until I lost sight of the color of my nails. But from the corner of my eye, I swore he was pulling that cocky smirk that made me want to vomit.

"Good idea." Andrés's snaps forced me to look at him once again, and a suited man appeared next to him. "Just scotch. And . . . you?"

I scoffed. "I'm not drinking in front of you."

He ignored me and turned back to the man waiting for the order. "She'll have a coconut rum and Coke."

He knew my bar order.

"Stalker," I whispered as the waiter walked away to retrieve our orders.

"Not this time."

"But you are."

"Nah, Taurus told me that one."

The sound of his name made my heart flutter, and if I could tear the wings off of every butterfly in my stomach, I would. He still hadn't texted, called, or even talked about me publicly. I wondered what he thought about me.

I wondered if it was the reality of me choosing the Andrés route that made him disgusted by me. Or was it that him being his ex hurt too much?

There were a million questions that I feared I'd never get the answers to.

We spent the next few minutes in silence while I tried to act like my palms weren't sweating. And with perfect timing, our drinks were placed in our hands as the theater went black.

The curtains slowly parted and revealed an empty chair at center stage. A single spotlight appeared that replicated one of my many nightmares.

My train of thought was interrupted by a woman being escorted under the light. She was naked and blindfolded. Her body was clean and oiled to the point where she was practically glistening. Her hair was an ashy blonde, and I knew exactly who it was.

Bianca.

We were the same age, but I often remembered her breakout year as if I was her elder. I suppose that was because it was also the year where everyone was in search of a new me after kicking me off my throne and ripping off my crown.

Everything she ever accomplished was in spite of me. The awards, the features, the guest appearances in blockbusters where the directors would see me out and let me know I was their first choice.

She kept her head held high despite being blinded and her ankles and wrists being tied together by thick pieces of rope.

A theater of people were staring at her naked body. She couldn't have known.

Did she feel us staring?

My question was immediately answered when the escort took the cotton off that was covering her eyes.

She didn't look shocked or confused. She remained frozen, but I swore I could see her light brown eyes go dark.

The person behind her was the only one wearing one of those blood-red robes from my initiation. When they pulled a pair of scissors out of the pocket, my lips parted to ask Andrés what was going on, but I couldn't.

Shock left me paralyzed.

As they cut pieces of her hair and clouds of blonde fell onto the stage, I couldn't bring myself to look away. Fire swirled in my eyes.

After several swipes at her long locks, she was left with a pixie cut. I gripped onto my armrests so tightly that my palms and fingertips had turned red.

Another assistant entered the stage with a hair clipper in hand. When they turned it on, the buzzing echoed throughout the theater. They replaced the original person, who silently exited stage left with the pair of scissors.

In one quick swipe, shorter strands of light curly hair fell onto her exposed skin before joining the longer strands on the floor.

"You will be new now." The person who was shaving her head finally spoke, and it echoed throughout the speakers surrounding me.

"Yes," Bianca tried to say proudly, but the crack in her voice spoke for itself.

"Your mind, body, and soul belong to us. And in order to elevate . . . you must first transform."

"Yes." She did better that time.

"And in this new era, Bianca Veer will be seen by fans as refreshing, new, and elite."

They weren't only shaving her head for the humiliation of it. This was a ritual that anyone who was a part of the Elite Order could watch. She was being rebranded, shaped into a more profitable item right before the biggest award show of both of our careers so far.

They were preparing her to win.

I sat back and thought about all the celebrity rebrands I had experienced—including my own. Sure, there were those who had shaved their heads, gotten a million tattoos, plastic surgery, or walked around in embarrassing fashions. There were even some who had gone from clean and proper to rock 'n' roll or, like Saint, being a nobody from another country to America's heartthrob.

Humiliation rituals. Meaningless sex. Losing someone we love. We all had to give up parts of ourselves to gain what we have now. But it's worth it in the end.

"Yes."

The commands and agreements kept on until there wasn't any hair left on her head and a tear rolled down her perfect skin. I jumped slightly as a knuckle brushed against my own cheek, wiping an escaped tear that I hadn't even registered.

I was trembling.

Fame and recognition was my dream. Once innocent, now violently tainted.

It fueled me throughout my entire life, and I chased it.

I wanted it all without a second thought about what people were sacrificing behind closed doors.

Was I just as despicable for craving it in the first place? Was I already too far gone from birth like my mother said? If only I had seen behind the curtain before but . . . I couldn't confidently say that it would have changed my mind.

Maybe that was the flaw in my code.

The lights flickered, and Bianca was gone, only to be replaced by an older man with salt-and-pepper hair and a perfectly tailored suit. His mask wasn't like the others. He wore the metal eagle mask I had become accustomed to since my initiation.

The audience gasped.

Andrés only flinched, but his siblings began to squirm in their seats around us.

A bitter taste formed on my tongue, and my muscles clenched as I tried to fight the urge to run. His appearance wasn't a part of the plan, and that was clear from the way everyone leaned toward the stage with anticipation.

"Well . . . That was just beautiful, wasn't it?" He commanded the space with little to no effort, and a pit formed in my stomach. "It's always refreshing to see a new member come into our space. To watch them purify themselves and fully commit to excellence. I mean, that's what we're about right?"

His accent.

It was thick and Puerto Rican like Camila and her older brother. He wasn't trying to mask it, and from the way Andrés and his siblings were foaming at the mouth around me, I knew who it was.

I had never seen Antonio Espósito in person, and even behind the mask he was a haunting presence.

"We respect those who commit. Which is why you're all here tonight. It doesn't make me happy to punish those who come into our space . . . our home and our community. Only to make a mockery of our practices. That doesn't sound right to me. Does it sound right to you?"

The audience murmured their "noes" while others shook their heads nervously.

"Recently, someone has been making a fool of us. Ignoring our warnings and prancing around on stage like we're nothing to fear. Well. That just won't do, and I have had to make the terrible decision to retaliate. Let that be a lesson for you all. Whenever you bring us a possible recruit . . ." He sighed deeply. "Don't waste our time with those who won't commit."

A tightness revealed itself in my chest. I turned the rings on my fingers until my skin turned tender.

"Because if we can't get to them, we'll get to someone. Anyone. Whether it be a friend, a family member or . . . a manager."

Nova.

My flames of fear had turned into embers of panic and confusion. I scrambled to my feet and pushed through the guards who surprisingly let me slip by them without any attempt at restraining me.

I ran down the empty halls and only made it a few feet before I heard heavy boots swiftly catching up to me.

I looked up through blurry vision to find myself at a dead end. There were two doors on each side of me.

Fuck.

My lungs filled with glue that felt impossible to swallow. I had no choice but to spin around, only for my face to smack directly into Andrés's chest. His chains bounced from my face back to his chest. I blinked away the static before wiping the tears that I knew had surely fucked up my makeup from the eyeliner smudged all over my hands.

"Calm down," he commanded. "You cannot draw attention to the fact that you're here. Do you hear me?"

He didn't know.

I shook my head and rubbed my aching face. "I— where is she?"

He avoided my eye contact and instead focused on frantically looking behind us. For someone who was always in control of everything, sweat beads on his forehead and the quickness of his breath only made matters worse.

"I need to get you out of here," he finally said.

"Where is she?" I screamed at the top of my lungs, only to be met by a firm palm clapping over my mouth.

"Shut up."

I bit down hard on his hand and stomped on his foot with all my might.

"Fuck," he groaned, but managed to keep his tone low as he backed a few steps away from me.

The metallic taste of the liquid that I had drawn filled my mouth. My lips tightened and my nostrils flared as

I watched him shake his hand—his eyes focused on the blood that had dripped onto the floor.

"You are going to get me out of here and take me to her," I demanded. "I am tired and I am scared but I am not weak. And you will take me to her, now!"

"I don't know where she is." He didn't raise his voice, but I still heard him loud and clear.

"Then find her." My words hung in the air while my face flamed with anger.

I wanted to sob uncontrollably and drop to my knees right then and there. The walls felt like they were closing in around me, and my head throbbed from the consistent rising of my blood pressure.

But nothing would measure up to the shattered pieces that would be left of me if something happened to her.

If I didn't do something, fast, then one of the only people I loved would be in danger because of me.

Everyone who loved her wouldn't have her anymore because of me.

CHAPTER TWENTY-FIVE

I DEMANDED MY PHONE BACK and somehow was met with very little resistance when exiting the estate. When I turned it on, it was as if everything was working in Antonio's perfectly orchestrated timing. Nova, who I had assumed was with her daughters, had been somewhere else for days, and no one knew . . . No one but Antonio Espósito.

His speech, the texts and calls from Nova's daughters that I had been fishing through in the backseat—how effortlessly I was let out of the ritual . . . Clockwork.

Celeste:

I thought mom was busy working with you but then we got a call that she was at the hospital and ran straight there. Where are you???

Sofia:

Hi, I know my sister texted you but mom's really not doing well. You're busy, we get it. But please come. The nurses are saying they're doing everything they can. We were told she ingested something and they can't figure out what it is.

The texts came after a string of missed calls, and with each text that populated, Nova's daughters gave up on the idea of me coming. From the timing, they must have gotten the call the minute I stepped out of the car and entered the property.

I spent the entirety of the car ride to the hospital trying to calm the panic by steadying my breath. I performed the million techniques I had learned from therapists in the past, but nothing provided relief.

To lose someone you love is to lose a little bit of yourself.

"Make sure the cameras get shut off and watch every fucking door. He can't find out she came here," I heard as I jumped out of the car and through the automatic sliding glass doors.

I didn't have the time or energy to protest that that was useless. Antonio had proven to be one step ahead of us every damn time.

Andrés knew not to protest taking me to the hospital. There was one condition, though. I would change into something that made it hard to recognize me. If not, then I'd be next.

Sunglasses and a hoodie had to do. It hid how much color had drained from my face, and I wasn't suffocated by the confines of a gown.

It was borderline inhumane how I wasn't allowed to kick or scream without going through a process to ensure my identity was masked first. She could have been dead already, and I had to change first.

I had always been used to being a loose cannon and acting on instinct, but Andrés forced me to think. He forced me to slow down.

"It'll save both of our asses," I remembered him saying as I pulled the hoodie over my head.

I skipped the front desk and ran straight to the staircase to get to the floor that Celeste and Sofia had texted me. The heavy door slammed behind me and echoed through the vacant stairway. It smelled of rubbing alcohol, and the halls were painted a dreadful gray. I charged up the stairway and flew through the entrance . . . Only to be met with both girls holding each other in the center of the hall.

Celeste, Nova's eldest, spotted me first. She slowly raised her head to reveal bloodshot eyes and a messy ponytail that was one nod away from completely coming undone. She parted from Sofia, who was weeping uncontrollably in her palms.

I took a few steps closer, finding myself paralyzed by Celeste's glare.

"Where were you?" She kept her tone low. The taller woman blocked my way so that I couldn't get any closer to Sofia than I already had.

"What—what happened?" I stuttered.

She couldn't have been gone. There was no way.

Celeste shook her head. "She asked for you over and over and over again." The woman spoke sourly, her eyes no longer looking at me with admiration from the few times we had met before. "She barely noticed us by her side because she was too busy looking for you. You weren't even in the room."

"Celeste. What—"

"She's gone." Sofia spoke up in between gasping breaths.

No.

"I—can I see her?" I forced out despite it feeling like my lungs were being crushed, and a searing pain had occupied my chest.

She scoffed. "No. For once someone has to tell you fucking no. Our lives for the last few years revolved around you and your wants. Aly! The one she knew would make her proud. Hey! Maybe that's what she wanted . . . A better daughter. One that had the same interests as her. But you couldn't even bother to answer the phone when she died."

I wanted to grab her and let her know that they were all Nova talked about. At the end of every day, it was about getting back to her daughters, and when they were off at college, calling to make sure they were okay. I wanted to tell her that Nova's life revolved around us all, but the guilt that filled my heart like an overflowing bottle only allowed me to stand there with a pitiful fucking look on my face.

Sofia's wailing sent shockwaves through my system. Celeste left me to crumble while she ran to grab her younger sister, who was pawing at the gurney that several nurses were transporting out of the room. My hand covered my mouth to stop the blood-curdling scream that tried to force its way out.

Agony had slithered its way in my body and sucked the air out of my lungs.

The low hospital lights followed what I knew was her body. I stared from a distance, knowing that the girls wouldn't let me close. Why would they? It was all my fault.

Without thinking, I spun around on my heels and darted out the same way I came. I ran until I was standing in the stairway on the first floor and my lungs were on fire. My heart was pounding in my eardrums, and everything felt foggy . . . like a dream I had yet to wake up from.

I placed a hand on the cold gray wall and bent over to try to contain my shaking body. I tried to stand up straight again once . . . three times, but lost my balance each attempt.

I knew the truth. I knew that she'd still be here if I had made different choices.

Suddenly, I felt violently sick. My knees seemed to hit the ground slowly. However, from the way I winced from the pain, I knew it happened faster than that. A sick noise erupted from my throat, but there was no stopping it. A thick wave of liquid erupted from my mouth and splashed onto the concrete floors.

I gagged over and over again until my body had no choice but to focus on how empty it had become.

"I'm so sorry . . ." I finally cried as I threw myself against the wall while the tears streamed down my cheeks. I allowed myself to feel the sorrow and revel in it for as long as I needed until I came to one decision.

Antonio Espósito had to pay.

I gripped onto the wall again to pull myself up and wiped my mouth with my sweater sleeve.

Two doors presented themselves to me. One had a glowing red exit sign above it, and the other led me to the lobby where Andrés and his goons were waiting for me. There was no one left. No one I could truly trust . . . Except—

I pushed open the emergency exit door and ran through the parking lot until I couldn't hear the sirens going off anymore. Energy from unknown sources coursed through my veins as I sped through the different properties and parking lots. I needed to get as far away as possible.

I ran through mud and tripped over broken tree branches, avoiding any cars that zipped by on the other side of the road. I stopped at the back of a gas station and quickly clicked on the contact that glowed on my phone like a Bat-Signal.

One ring.

Two.

"Hello?"

"Please . . . Come get me," I panted.

CHAPTER TWENTY-SIX

I DIDN'T BREATHE THE ENTIRE car ride.

My world felt significantly smaller, and there was no longer a difference between grief and rage.

I checked my phone a few times, staring at her last text message and hoping she'd call and say it was all to mess with me.

Please let it all be a sick joke.

I would rather her be involved. I would rather hate her than know I'd never hear her voice again.

Nova would have gone to war for me without me asking. I never told her that I considered her the only real mother I ever had . . .

But I should have.

I should have brought it up at some point, when she came banging on my door in Miami and told me to get my ass to work . . . That I cried all night while looking up at the stars because someone actually cared enough to find me.

She always found me.

Yet I didn't even notice she needed me. She could have been clinging on for days, and I was too busy focused on my shit to notice.

Always too busy focused on me.

Grieving felt selfish and borderline disrespectful. She was the one gone, yet I was the one missing something.

"Can you tell me what's going on?" The weight of Taurus's words knocked me out of my train of thought.

When did we get inside his house?

I rubbed my cold hands in hopes of finding some warmth in between my fingers. "He killed Nova."

The words caused my heart to get stuck in my throat despite how low I had whispered them. I hoped that at the very least, if I couldn't hear myself, then it wouldn't make it real.

"I—I mean," I continued, not needing to look up from the ground to know he was staring at me like a deer in headlights. "I don't know how. The girls said she ingested something, but I know that can't be true. All I know is why. I know who, and I know it's because of me. I am the reason Antonio did that because I didn't listen to you, I listened to *him*."

The last word burned my mouth like venom. A way out didn't exist anymore.

"Alejandra, I'm—"

I put my hand up in protest and stepped deeper into the living room, leaning against one of the couch arms. "No. Please." I swallowed the tar that bubbled in my throat. "Look, I know you hate me."

"I could never hate you. I just can't be around you," he quickly interrupted.

I stalled.

Everything fucking stalled.

"I know that I have been selfish and scared and . . . basically a fucking child that has been hard to work with since we met. I am so, so sorry that I didn't realize it until now." My voice turned raspy as tears dropped onto his carpet. "I can't fix it. Everything I thought I wanted is muddy now, and it's all a fucking mess. It's never been about the awards, Taurus. It's been about the admiration and the love and filling a fucking hole in my heart that I think I was born with. If I just looked up and listened for five seconds . . . I would have realized—"

"I'm sorry," he interrupted again. His soft voice gently commanded my attention. I looked up and removed my sunglasses, allowing him to see me in my puffy, inflamed state.

His kind gaze overrode any looks of judgment or disgust that I expected. His pupils were decorated with waves of understanding, and for once, I felt the ground underneath my feet.

I shook my head and sniffled until the snot in my nostrils smacked the back of my throat. "I need to do something about it. I can't keep wondering if Josefina is safe, and I can't protect her or myself. If something happens—" My voice heightened until it cracked at the top.

A firm grip on my shoulder sent an air of calm over me. Without hesitation, I placed my hand on top of his.

Warmth.

"Come," he whispered over my head.

One foot was put in front of the other until we reached his bedroom. The low lights illuminated our way through the home, highlighting specs of dust on furniture that I hadn't noticed before.

The monument of a man walked past me, and I didn't move a muscle. I focused on his flooring and the way one board creaked when he opened his closet door. I remained in the doorway, clutching onto my hoodie sleeves and praying that if I kept my nails embedded into my palms, I'd wake myself up from the nightmare.

Taurus turned slowly after shutting his closet door, shielding whatever was in his right hand with his body. After several steps, my line of sight was aligned with his chest. He took my shaky hand and placed the black gun in my palm.

It felt heavier than I ever imagined that a handgun would—like he had placed a ton of gold in my hand. I stared at the weapon like it glowed, and my heart banged against my rib cage. My hands may not have held my way out, but it held my way to revenge. I could avenge Nova and protect myself if anything went left.

I parted my lips to say thank you, but Taurus's finger brushed against my velvet skin before I had a chance.

"I can't watch you marry him," he started. "I don't want any part of this shit. I'm gonna be real with you. But I couldn't live with myself if it had been you instead of her so . . . don't miss."

"I won't."

I WENT BACK TO Andrés's house without a fight. I needed to see Josefina, and at the very least . . . watch her sleep.

It didn't take them long to find me. In fact, his men showed up at the door with him in the backseat five minutes after I stuffed the gun in between my jeans and panties. I balled up my hoodie in front of my crotch and slid into the car.

"I had them watching every door. Stop thinking you can run, because the time will come when I stop letting you," Andrés notified me.

CHAPTER TWENTY-SEVEN

A GUST OF WIND PUSHED the windows open, and each LED light that lined the ceiling had blown out bulb by bulb. Sparks erupted above me and sprinkled onto my bare skin.

It was only then that I could tell that the blanket had been ripped off of me.

With my mind's eye, I could see the black bra and panty set I had fallen asleep in. I was staring at myself from a bird's eye view.

My hair was sprawled against the silk pillow cases, and my legs were parted while each arm was spread out next to me. I watched myself struggle to move, but an invisible grip kept me glued to the sheets.

Then it all went black.

I moaned and squirmed out of fear. I wanted to ask someone to help or get up and run, but I couldn't even open my eyes or peel my lips apart.

Two hands wrapped around my ankles, and my breath hitched. "Don't scream," I heard from the wind that had been aggressively traveling throughout the space.

The whispers were chilling hisses that crawled against my ears and distracted me from the hands that were now traveling up my exposed thighs. The curtains blew sporadically, and the dresser drawers began to shake. Shudders traveled down my spine as a figure straddled my small waist, but I felt nothing except cold brushes against my skin.

"Hush, little baby, don't you cry . . . Mama's gonna wipe every tear from your eye." The tune was followed by a sinister snicker that echoed throughout the space. The butterflies in my stomach began to rattle in their cage. They slammed against my skin, scratching at the lining to find a way out.

Long fingernails tiptoed along my palms and . . .

The creature on top of me placed a kiss on both of my hands. Then my inner elbow and both my shoulder blades. Its butter-soft lips moved to my neck, placing another delicate kiss on my chin and both cheeks.

I didn't shudder or flinch.

Every kiss felt like hot iron against my skin but . . . something about it felt like home.

When the lips moved to my eyelids, its exhale breathing life into my eyelashes, it whispered, "See me, little star."

My eyes fluttered open.

Then I saw her.

I was first introduced to a figure hidden behind a golden raven mask. I reached up to brush my fingers against it and feel its mass.

It beckoned to me like a hypnotic song, like I needed to wear it too.

With a quick swipe, I ripped the face covering off, and it turned to dust in my hands. Her eyes absorbed any light left in the room until the white had been replaced with two perfectly circular obsidian crystals. Black face paint was brushed around her eyes, and her lips were plump and rejuvenated. She held a crown on her head with enough jewels and diamonds to illuminate her large vessel.

The worst part about her, though . . . the strangest thing, I suppose, was that she was me.

Her lips crashed against mine, and it didn't take long for the burning to subside and for me to kiss her back. Flashes of storms and burning buildings filled my mind. I couldn't see anything other than pain and suffering. I could only hear screaming and crying from helpless children and terrified adults.

Every time I fought for a breath and tried to pull away from the kiss, the yells became louder and the storms destroyed villages. As long as I stayed entangled with her, the sun would come out. I'd see myself smiling. I'd see Josefina smiling.

My back arched as I yearned for her, pulling her in for more until she forced me away and back onto the pillows. I kept my eyes on the mirror image as I lay there breathless with red lipstick smeared all over my face.

She smiled and tilted her head slowly, caressing my face and staring at me like she was honoring the mess she made. "Without me. There is no you. Without us . . . no one wins."

Every word landed like a sweet song. She was the side of me that I held dormant for so long. The side of me who could take on anything and anyone.

Lilith. The part of me I tried so desperately to hide because she was created out of hate and ill intent. I saw her as a stain on who I was but . . .

No.

She wasn't the worst part of me, she was the most powerful part of me. The capable part of me. The side of me that could swallow pain and abuse and birth out something beautiful. She was a god.

"You need me," were the last words I heard before her fingers forced my lips apart and she shrunk herself down and climbed inside.

I swallowed with ease.

CHAPTER TWENTY-EIGHT

I WOKE UP EVERY DAY with rage running through my blood and grief hovering over me like a gray cloud.

I only turned on my phone to watch the news report and tell my fans I was "fine" once a week and bless them with a story-posted selfie every so often. I had become quite the fucking liar.

January flew by, and I could count the amount of times I left my bed, every single one being because of Josefina. Oftentimes she'd turn the TV on and lie with me, but most days she'd sit next to me scribbling on sheets of paper. I didn't know who was giving her the materials. I never asked.

The Elite Order covered everything up flawlessly. My label let me know that Nova had resigned, and I sat on that call and swallowed the truth with a hard gulp. I couldn't be sure what they told Celeste and Sofia, but I hadn't received a text or a call from them since that night. The news had nothing to say, and when I finally uttered a few words to

Andrés to ask about it, he said his father was most likely holding the news until he could leverage it against me.

If he lived that long.

I still didn't trust Andrés, but I was smart enough to know that I was stuck.

I kept the gun in a shoe box under the bed and moved it around the room whenever I left . . . even for a second.

When the clock struck February, I had no choice but to get a grip and pretend like everything was okay in person. There were fittings, calls, and obligations that secured my seat at the Starlight Awards. One of those calls let Taurus and me know we had a contract to oblige by and appearing together was mandatory.

The day of the Starlight Awards felt particularly heavy. On the day I had been waiting for, I was nothing more than hollow.

There were times I thought I had met my limits, but I had been pushed beyond comprehension. And in a few hours, I was going to accept an award I already knew was mine. After all, it was the only way Antonio could draw me out.

"It's how we're going to do this," Andrés explained to me only a few nights before. "He wants you. You're gonna let him think he has you. You've been off his radar for almost two months now. He knows that show is where he'll find you. He'll probably taunt you, scare you . . . But you'll be fine. You just need to wait for me, got it? I'll take care of the rest."

Award day didn't feel as surreal or magical as I thought it would have. The car ride went exactly how I imagined, though. It was excruciating as I left the hills and isolation of the estate and reentered the buzzing California freeways.

Although my heart wasn't filled with anxiety like I had originally anticipated, only a red-hot swirling fury. And in the thick of it, I found space to mourn the version of me that died so many weeks ago. The version who was excited for that award, who thought she'd be talking her head off while getting glammed up with the knowledge that her friends and team were down the hall. While that reality would have been a blessing, it no longer existed.

But God, I would have preferred it.

I wish I would have fucking recognized that before I fell into the trap door the Elite Order had led me to.

My phone buzzed.

Unknown:

| Come out, come out wherever you are.

Time to be a big girl.

I held my phone tight to my chest and let the security guards waiting in front of the hotel escort me upstairs and away from the flashing cameras.

My first step was to sit with the nail artist who I trusted to bring my vampiric era to life for the final time. I sat silently and thought of the life that lay ahead of me. It was everything I had wished for. But I was here and she wasn't.

"Is everything okay?" the man asked as he glued the clear tips onto my freshly buffed nails.

"Mm-hmm."

"You just seem . . . away," he said softly as he moved my hand to place it under the nail curator. A bright purple light cast a glow onto my hands, and for a moment I became lost in that too.

I shook myself out of thought. "I'm okay," I said softly. "Just nerves. And—" A faint knock on my hotel room door stopped me from even attempting to spill my guts. "Mind if I?"

He pulled my hand out of the machine and made some room for me to get up. "No, go ahead."

I lifted myself out of my seat and started to head toward the door. "Please not now," I whispered to myself as I swallowed my fear and continued to put one foot in front of the other.

"Wait!" I heard behind me. Before I could ask what was going on, he scurried in front of me and pulled the door handle open without a warning. I wanted to scream, and my heart thumped against my chest without restraint.

I tried to figure out how to explain that that was not okay. We didn't know who was on the other end of that door and—

"Happy Starlight day!" Saint, Yessenia, and Savannah stood proudly with chocolates, wine, and balloons in their hands.

It wasn't a henchman coming to take me away hours ahead of schedule. It wasn't something out of my nightmares . . . It was the only bit of family I had left.

"*Ay dios mio . . .*" I whispered into my hand placed on my mouth to mask my audible gasps. "What the hell is going on here?"

Yessenia kissed my forehead as she passed me and let the balloons release into the room. A swarm of silver and gold expanded on the ceiling, some with the actual award printed on it and others with . . . my face on it. Except it wasn't me now—it was me as a kid.

The chubby cheeks, the long black hair, and a string of pearls laced around my neck that I had stolen from Yessenia's mom. My aunt was the only one who really had pictures of me left, and the lump in my throat only grew when I realized I hadn't seen me like that in ages. So much so that I never noticed how much like Josefina I really looked.

Once I sat back down at the edge of the bed, Saint came and presented me with a gift. "I'll open it for you," he said softly as he kneeled down. I could tell he was dragged out of his room from the eye patches that were still on and the clips keeping his curls from falling in front of his forehead. But when our eyes met and he pulled open the little black box—I froze.

My heart was on fucking fire while the diamond ring sparkled under the chandeliers in the hotel room.

"For me?" I tried not to sound surprised, but I knew from that moment that he wasn't the one who bought this.

He was the messenger.

All Saint did was nod and place the box next to me on the bed before kissing my forehead. I was so distracted by the square blue diamond that had to be seven . . . maybe eight carats.

I quickly shut the box and damn near sat on it while he moved to the side to make room for the blonde doll holding the wine and chocolates. Her hair was held up by rollers, and her robe was tied tightly around her waist. I felt bad for my distance the last few weeks and wanted to tell her all about what I had been experiencing but I couldn't . . . So I smiled. I watched as her eyes darted between Saint and me.

God, she was so smitten by him that even when it was about me, she couldn't keep her eyes away.

"Where's baby boy?" I asked in a somber tone while taking the flowers and bottles and placing them on top of the ring that I did not need any questions about.

"With his father," Savannah replied sweetly as she took a seat on the other side of me.

The trio spread out around my room despite having to finish getting ready themselves. Yessenia lay on top of the bed, her hair still wrapped in a doobie like how the ladies used to do it in the Dominican salons when we were younger. "She didn't tell you? He took him on a private yacht cruise in the Caribbean. Real fancy."

I raised a brow and turned to Savannah, trying not to move too much since my poor nail artist had to move his station over to the bed since I was too busy running my mouth to go back to my chair.

"Oh *wow*," I started. "You let that man take your precious baby boy for more than three days, *and* out of the country? My goodness, where did my overbearing mother Savannah go?"

She rolled her eyes and nudged me with her elbow. "I needed a break, okay!"

"That she did," Saint chimed in with his Casanova tone that we had all become so accustomed to. Maybe if he just told her about it all . . . they could work it out.

"And what about you, though?" Yessenia interrupted, poking my back with her toe.

Saint rose to his feet and shook his head, but the smile on his face never wavered. "We all need to be focused on the carpet right now." He walked past me and stepped in front of Savannah, putting his hand out, and she took it without hesitation.

He knew.

He then leaned down to give me a kiss on the cheek. "Good luck, mi amor. We'll all be rooting for you."

When they cleared out after random mentions of after parties and "I love yous," they were quickly replaced with the rest of my glam team. And all I could think about was the giant diamond burning a hole in the mattress that matched the one in my heart.

Buzz.

Taurus:

> See you soon.

CHAPTER TWENTY-NINE

"O FF THE SHOULDER! OFF the shoulder!"

"Aly you look so beautiful in the white gown!"

"Taurus, grab her waist!"

They shouted from a million directions, and we posed for so many photos that the flashes had caused a kaleidoscope that clouded my vision.

We had cut wispy bangs, and the rest of my hair was curled and tucked behind my ears to complement my off-the-shoulder cream gown. It had a deep slit to showcase the ivory lace tights that went over my closed-toed stilettos and stopped mid-thigh. The satin material was thick and layered, perfect to conceal the gun tucked between my leg that wasn't visible and the tights.

The ring lay on my left hand.

Taurus kept a strong grip on my waist despite claiming he wanted to be as far away as possible. So I returned the favor and kept myself as close to him as he'd allow. For once, I was the only one not acting.

As we walked off the carpet, I held his hand, and the ring Andrés bought burned a hole through both of our skin. Reporters pointed at it, and it was glaringly obvious that the ring would be a hot topic tomorrow.

Little did they know they'd have the story completely wrong.

"You look beautiful, darling." A random actress from a sitcom I couldn't remember grabbed my free hand briefly and smiled. I nodded and said a silent thank-you before continuing to follow Taurus through the venue.

"You two are a gorgeous couple!" TV show host.

"I'm literally gagging?" I think . . . That was someone's publicist.

"Congratulations, you guys!" And that was Ansley May—one of the best songwriters of our generation and a pioneer for LGBTQ+ rights in the industry. I should have stopped for a picture.

The nerves finally kicked in. I tried to focus on hating Bianca Veer in her silver dress, but I only pitied her.

My gaze shifted to Randy Coleman and his big-ass top hat, and every other celebrity who was either competition or worth admiration. But in every corner of the space, by the large pillars and exit signs, were security guards who all had their eyes on me.

It took Taurus squeezing my hand for me to realize that I was holding on to him until my knuckles went white. I looked up at him, looking gorgeous as ever with his freshly braided hair—dyed a deep red for the occasion—and plain black tux. His facial hair was cut into a trimmed mustache and a disconnected goatee. He looked as mature as he acted, yet as artistic as he was, and even though my heart was rattling within the confines of my chest, I still made time to admire him.

"You okay?" he whispered in my ear, and I realized that we were standing in the middle of the first floor of the lobby and everyone was gone. "You've been staring into blank space for a while, and my hand is sort of starting to bruise, I think," he said lightly, and normally I would have laughed at the joke, but the anxiety ripping through me made that nearly impossible.

"I'm just—"

Four guards closed in. "Come with us."

I was boxed in, and they had pushed Taurus out of my grip without me even noticing. The gun started to feel hot against my thigh. Our eyes found each other between the two men who stood between us, and I found some relief.

Taurus pressed his lips together and balled his fists. The realization that there was nothing he could do from this point forward was eating him alive. That was why he couldn't be around me. It wasn't jealousy. It wasn't because he thought I was fucking stupid . . . Maybe I thought so, but that was beside the point. It was because there was nothing he could do to stop it anymore.

"It's okay," I mouthed in hopes to calm the outrage stirring in his eyes.

"Come on." One of the men ushered me toward the closest exit sign, and I stumbled over my heels to keep up with the sudden movement. No one was around to notice that I was gone. Everyone was grabbing their seats and preparing for a show without the knowledge that they were missing the greatest one of all time.

"Be careful, Alejandra. I need you to be okay."

"What?" I forced out as I continued to be pushed halfway out the door, the cold air brushing against my exposed upper back.

"I do. I did then, I do today, I will tomorrow, and I damn sure will forever."

"If forever will have me," I managed to get out.

The door slammed in between us when the last suited man walked through.

Every inhale from that moment forward was painstaking, and my stomach dropped and lifted in a rhythm that I couldn't put my finger on.

Unsettling.

Like a dark symphony ripped straight out of a horror movie.

I looked up at the swelling skies that had gone completely gray and hiked up my dress so the light fabric didn't drag against the concrete as we walked to the vehicle. My heels echoed with every step faintly. The only stragglers left outside were staff members and people whose press passes didn't clear them to go any further than the carpet outside.

Heavy winds smacked me in the face, and I became breathless when a black SUV hastily pulled up in front of us with windows so tinted it couldn't have been legal. The guards surrounding me finally gave me my space— like I was being allowed one last choice. But every time I considered running, the rage that stirred inside of me gained momentum.

I dropped my dress and let it hit the mud, pulling the car door open and climbing inside. Before I could even close the door fully, the car peeled off and I was thrown to the other side. I kept my mouth shut just in case but called them a million names in my head. In a panic, I mentally checked in on my body to ensure the gun had stayed in place.

Thank goodness.

I breathed a sigh of relief and jumped at the sound of the doors locking. The partition was up and . . . sealed shut? I couldn't see who was driving even if I wanted to.

I was doomed to sit alone with my fear and uncertainty. Except I didn't have a pool to scream into, a child to distract me, or bottles of tequila to drown myself in.

I tried calling everyone, anyone, about fourteen times before the car came to an aggressive stop. By the fifteenth time, though, I realized my phone didn't have service. I swallowed the horror that filled my lungs when the doors on each side of me clicked. I waited a few moments, but no one came to open my door.

"Oh-fucking-kay, then . . ." I said in a low tone before reaching over to try the door on the right, and it swung open with ease.

Before me was the same house I had gone to before for the initiation. Except it felt . . . emptier.

Yet the hairs on my arms spiked like there were a million eyes on me from the moment my lace-covered heels sank into the muddy terrain. Rain pounded on my head, causing my bangs to mold to my forehead and the thick fabric of my dress to stick to my skin. I pushed through it anyway, trekking up to the front door where, to my surprise, no one was standing.

With one deep breath, I knocked on the door, and before the sound could even attempt to compete with the roaring thunder, it swung open. No one was on the other side.

The home was illuminated far more than the first night, and as puddles formed at my feet from my soaked dress, a voice caused me to look up.

"You made it."

There weren't many pictures of Antonio Espósito on the internet anymore. At least, not recent ones. There was an arsenal that came up from his earlier years, but he had successfully stayed low-key for at least the last decade or so.

I squinted as the older man leaned against the railing. I got a glimpse of his silhouette and any unmasked features at the event but . . . While standing on the glistening floor, I had a rare opportunity to look him in the eye.

He stared down at me with a hardened yet amused gaze. Like I was some plaything he had taken the enjoyment of toying with while I stood there shivering in my custom Betsy Johnson gown. The gun called for my attention.

Not now.

"What now?" I mustered up the confidence to ask.

He snickered and stood up straight while his hands remained planted on the railing. He looked scarier that way. "Bring her up."

Two masked men came from out of fucking nowhere and grabbed me by each arm. I knew better than to kick or cry no matter how bad I wanted to. If they knew what was in my dress they'd use it on me, I had no doubt about that.

My attention dropped to the ring that hadn't been taken from me yet. I quickly turned it so that the stones were facing my palm instead. The men carried me with ease, causing my feet to hover over the stairs rather than walk up them on my own. I had never been to the part of the mansion they were dragging me through.

Every new corner I laid my eyes on looked recently built. It had more turns and pathways than a damn corn maze, and the dark abstract paintings only made it worse. One of them detailed a face painted only using shades of black and white. The distressed swipes and aggressive strokes along the canvas looked as if they painted with their hands. Yet the eyes held the only pop of color, red.

They dropped me at the top of the stairs and vanished down one of the many twists and turns.

After a few breaths, the echoes of their footsteps had faded, and I was left on the second floor on my own. I looked down at the freshly buffed wood flooring and back up to the long corridor. It expanded out into two directions, and I was once again faced with a choice. Droplets of rainwater dripped from my hair and splashed onto the floor with every step I took. If I listened close enough, I could hear that too.

They took everything from me but presented it as if they were giving me the world.

There were three ways it could all play out. Andrés's plan, their plan, or mine.

My plan was better.

I straightened my stance and puffed out my chest. My hands ran through my soaked hair in an attempt to look less distraught. I stood in the middle of both separation points only to see that I was standing on another balcony. No matter which side I chose—I'd end up in the same place, at the bottom of those steps that led to . . .

I looked at the space that was laid out below me and gripped onto the banister so that my nerves didn't send me plummeting to the floor. It was another ballroom, but smaller and unlike the one from my initiation.

It wasn't golden, no.

It was caked in shades of black and gray. The only shimmer came from the accents of silver that lined the windows, curtains, and framed paintings. Like before, there was a raised platform with five thrones painted midnight black. Only four were empty.

Antonio sat patiently with his legs crossed and a smug look on his face. He wasn't looking up at me, but I could tell he knew exactly where I was.

I was Alice in Wonderland except Wonderland was a freak show and Alice was being hunted. I pushed the wet strands off my shoulder and gripped onto the railing. My eyes found him once again. He looked so . . . small.

I turned to head down the stairs, triggering the curtains to peel open, and four cloaked figures slowly made their way beside him. They stood proudly with their masks tightly wrapped around their faces and their cloaks perfectly tailored. They stood strong, and from the way Antonio's chin lifted, I could tell he felt safe.

That was the funny thing about feeling safe in numbers, it only worked if the people with you hadn't turned their backs on you. But for once, I was in on the joke. I knew the big secret.

But I also knew that doing it Andrés's way had gone out the window the moment they rolled Nova's body away from me. The moment I knew that the only woman in my life who had ever been nothing but kind to me was dead . . . It was all off the table.

I wasn't going to roll over for anyone or play anymore games. Initiations, sacrifices, rituals—it was all bullshit mind games used to divide them from us. It would always be, no matter how far I climbed that ladder. Them versus us. And I had a chance to become one of them and destroy it all from the inside out.

I was a madwoman.

A woman consumed with rage that bubbled up and bounced around within me like neon lights—begging for a target.

"Come forward," Antonio roared from the stage once I made it to the base of the steps. I wiggled in my damp gown and made my way to the center of the ballroom. "They didn't get you an umbrella?" he asked with a smirk while the other council members stood quietly with their hands clasped together in front of them.

I cleared my throat. "No. Kind of rude of them, if you ask me. I have an event tonight."

Antonio chuckled and hooked a hand behind his back, pacing back and forth on the stage. His diamond cufflinks reflected in the light with every muscle he moved, and his shoes were shined to the point of sparkling. The man who had a nasty habit of taking women out was already dressed for his own funeral and he didn't even know it.

"I'm sorry your travels weren't more—comfortable." His thick accent echoed through the large space without a microphone. "But yes, your event. The Starlight Awards . . . You're up for—"

"Song of the Year."

"Ah-ha." The slimy old man dug in his suit jacket pocket and pulled out two envelopes. "There's still time to decide." He licked his lips and held one envelope in his left hand and one in his right. "You told us during your first initiation that there wasn't anyone in the world that you loved. That you would do anything to win this award. A paperweight to those who came before you, but you . . .

you were willing to give up everything for it. Tell me, is that still true? Or have you lost enough people by now?"

"It's funny you say that." I took another step forward before crossing my ankle over the other.

"Is it?"

"Death and loneliness aren't losses I'm unfamiliar with, and thinking that was the case is where you're very wrong." I shrugged. "So let me guess. One envelope is my win and . . . If you're being predictable, then the other envelope is Bianca's name. Am I getting warmer?"

Antonio chuckled and dropped his hand before turning to the four cloaked figures behind him. "So much for theatrics, right? I know, I know. You told me she wouldn't find it funny." He turned back to me now, leaning as far forward as he could without falling off the stage. "Everything you want comes with a price. A price that you've paid by now. Which, you should be grateful I let you make the payment even though you were in the wind. So, I'll ask you a question you've been asked before. Who in this world do you love the most? What makes you feel less alone?"

I could have pulled the gun out at that very moment, but my aim wasn't good enough and he was still too far from me despite how his words felt like they were dancing across my shoulder blades. I was still the vulnerable one, and if I missed . . .

"I feel like I've loved to my limit since the last time I was asked that." I glanced over at the masked figures. I couldn't tell which one was her, the one who imprinted on my body and made herself unforgettable. "My answer is different." I stepped closer to the stage, and no one stopped me.

"My mom raised me Catholic, and I was shamed for desiring anything too loudly or too proudly. I carried that shame with me along with promises I was too young to make and baptisms that only felt like drowning. I was told that all of that pain and shame I was experiencing was only God's love. And every time I tried to experience that love in a different way . . . it was too much to carry. But then I was told that only God could help me carry that weight too. So, I prayed. I hated God and religion because nothing came out of it but punishment. And when I was first asked that question, I had run through enough hearts—given each of them a small piece of mine . . . I had nothing left but hurt, and religion wasn't there to save me. It was a fucking catch 22. So I loved nothing. That was true. But it didn't stop people from loving me, touching me, wanting me, comforting me. And maybe, I don't know. Maybe that's God. Maybe what you're offering me is better than anything He could do, I don't know." I took a few more steps until my palms were touching the edge of the center stage.

"I know I have people who love me, and I love them too. I have people who need me, and I need them too. And that is good and invaluable, so my answer is I have so much that I love now . . . that I don't even know where to begin. But when I was first asked that I barely knew what the word meant. I just knew it was something I was supposed to get from Him." My brown eyes locked with his as he looked down at me. His feet were only a few centimeters from my fingers, and it was time. My only chance was now.

I couldn't move.

"Well, that was beautiful." He crouched down to meet my line of sight. "But what about the love you've lost?

Nova, was it? Sorry, the story hasn't broken yet, and I'm horrible with details."

He was testing me.

But I had to play the game until I could muster the courage to pull out the gun that was stuck against the back of my thigh. "If you expect me to act like you did me a favor, I won't," I spat out.

He raised a brow. "Sacrifices are what gets you through our doors. A willingness to accept loss . . . It shows strength and eternal dedication. A life for a life." He pretended to sigh. "If it makes you feel any better, she didn't even see it coming."

"She had two daughters." I choked.

"The ones she kept pictures of in her wallet right next to yours? Well, yes, she did."

My hands began to shake, and my lip quivered, but I couldn't reach behind me.

"What's wrong?" he asked with a smile.

"Father." The thick accent commanded the room, and Antonio immediately stood up straight to look behind me. I didn't need to turn around to know who it was.

Instead I shook myself free of the grip his aura had me in and reached for the gun. There wasn't enough time between me backing up to aim it and the shocked screams I heard around me from the first pop. I didn't dare close my eyes. I watched as the first one hit his shoulder. My ears rang with an echo of the second gunshot, and soon enough I couldn't hear anyone. Everyone around me became a panicked blur, and when I aimed higher and a bullet found itself lodged in between his eyebrows—blood splattered across my face and chest.

I was determined to be worse than my demons, consumed by the vile energy implemented in me by my mother's preventative hate. I was determined to be bigger than he ever thought of me, and I didn't stop pulling the trigger until his body had fallen to the ground with a loud thud. I dropped the gun on the floor and took one step back—my dress was splattered with blood and so was every visible part of my body. Yet that wasn't what was the most concerning. I didn't feel sad or scared. I felt relieved.

A life for a life.

"Come." I hadn't noticed one of the masked figures getting down from the stage or even wrapping their arms around me, but I recognized the grip.

As she ushered me away, my eyes remained fixated on the stage. The other members circled around Andrés, who was completely still. Blood began to drip off the edge of the stage while they left his father's body to rot.

The further from the stage I was, the more I wanted to call out and ask if Andrés was okay. But I couldn't speak, and eventually the double doors closed behind us.

The woman didn't say a word as she gently escorted me down another flight of stairs. The labyrinth of an estate that I had been to multiple times was a real castle. It was equipped with secret passageways, numerous ballrooms, diamond chandeliers, and endless staircases. The paintings had to be older than me, and the statues in the corners never had a speck of dust on them. It was fit for a real queen—the one I was becoming.

After a few flights of stairs, I knew I was underground. The lighting was dimmed, and the walls were painted black. We walked past silver door after silver door until she chose one with no rhyme or reason to my knowledge.

When the door opened, I was welcomed into a dressing room that was so eerily normal.

There was nothing creepy or culty about it, actually. I took a seat at the marble vanity without being told, and for once I acknowledged the person in the mirror. With tearstained cheeks and mascara trails that I smeared while trying to peel the damp strands of hair off my face. Blood was splattered everywhere—my chin, my neck, my chest, and it had absolutely ruined my once cream gown. The longer I stared at myself, the more splatters I noticed, and my heart began to race as the weight of all that had happened fell onto my shoulders.

It became hard to breathe while the memory of blood pooling onto the stage was all I could see. Moisture gathered in my eyes, and I placed a hand on my chest to try to catch the little bit of air that no longer filled my lungs.

I sobbed. Like a baby without a sanctuary, I fucking sobbed. Closing my eyes didn't stop me from seeing the horrors that I had just experienced. It didn't stop me from realizing that none of it brought Nova back.

Violently, my fist met with the center of the mirror, and shards of glass shattered onto the vanity and sliced through my skin. My hand stung as I pulled it close and watched as blood pooled around my knuckles and seeped in between the webs of my fingers.

The woman snaked her arms around my body, pulling me in close without a care.

"My first one was hard too," she whispered in her actual voice and not the fake accent I had heard before. My eyes shot open when I recognized that tone, and when I looked in the mirror to see that she had removed her mask and gloves . . . I was right.

Nila Arora.

"What you're feeling right now? All of it is temporary," she whispered as if immune to my shock. I was frozen, and it wasn't because of the gown that was plastered to me like it was made of clay. "My little bird . . . Just watch what I do for you," she whispered as she combed her hands through my wet hair.

Her golden skin shimmered under the low lights, and even though I could only see pieces of her through the broken glass . . . I still felt the same warmth. The same sick comfort from the initiation.

I remained speechless as she called more individuals in to fix my hair, wrap my hand, clean up, and undress me. There were no more gloves, masks, or secrecy. I wasn't going anywhere now, and everyone knew it.

As they blow-dried and fixed my hair, my eyes fell to the ring on my left finger that had a spec of blood in the center of the diamond. I wiped it off and focused my attention on my broken reflection.

They wiped my body down with warm washcloths and stripped me of the blood-splattered gown. My small pearl earrings were replaced with diamond chandelier ones that were so heavy I was sure my ears were going to rip right off. The redness on my chest from me rubbing my skin until it was tender was covered by a diamond cross that sat perfectly in between my cleavage. They dressed my right fingers in four statement rings of various designs to hide where the bandages lay and cut bangs in my hair before redoing my makeup with dark blush and heavy contour. My lips were lined with a deep brown, and the corners of my eyes were accentuated with midnight black.

Two people gently grabbed my hands to help me stand as if I was made of porcelain and they were scared of my inevitable shatter. They ushered me into leather platform boots that no one would even see once I slipped on the beast of a gown they presented to me. The lace corset caught my eye first and then the lace sleeves attached to it. The Cinderella poofy black gown was all too familiar.

I had seen it before. But it wasn't until the corset was tied tight and they spun me around to look in the full-body mirror that I realized I had become her.

I was Lilith.

CHAPTER THIRTY

THAT AWARD WAS MINE.

I was escorted back to the car with several umbrellas surrounding me and one bodyguard carrying me so that my dress wasn't soiled by the mud like the previous one was. When I arrived, I was able to see the time on the dashboard, and only two hours had passed—there was still enough time to collect my award . . .

They planned it this way.

When the car doors swung open to let me out in front of the venue, Taurus was waiting at the door like someone had told him to be there, and by the look on his face I could tell he wasn't sure what version of me came back. Without hesitation, he grabbed my arm and escorted me back through the lobby and into the auditorium.

Cameras and a single spotlight followed our every step as we walked down the aisle. Everyone turned their attention from the host telling shitty jokes on stage.

"Well, if it isn't the royal couple! And is that . . . an outfit change?" It echoed through the microphone as

Taurus stepped to the side to let me sink into one of the seats three rows from the front. I blew a kiss to the host whose name I couldn't bother to remember and took a seat down. There were two other empty seats next to me, and when Taurus sat in one, I knew the other was for Nova.

In another reality she was sitting with us, wearing that horrible red lipstick that she insisted was her best color. I never agreed, and we fought over it all the time. There was only one event where she compromised with me and lined her lips for the first time. I actually did it for her.

If she was in that chair, in that horrible red shade, she'd be squeezing my hand the whole time. So much so that I probably wouldn't have looked up at Taurus like I did and pleaded for his leg to at least brush against the ruffles of my dress because that small spark was better than focusing on the emptiness that had consumed me.

I also knew that in the reality where she sat in that third seat, it would also be the one where I lost.

A life for a life for a life.

Antonio took hers, which cost him his, and I had been reborn.

"For our last award tonight, the one that everyone has been waiting for—well, I know I have. Song of the Year. Now this category has been causing a frenzy online, innit?" The crowd chuckled, but anyone too close to me or Bianca's seat in the other aisle were mute. I squeezed Taurus's thigh like my life depended on it—and in a way it did.

He looked at me with eyes that wanted so desperately to ask how far I went.

I burned down my entire world for this award.

But instead of saying it, I just gave him a quick kiss on the cheek.

He flinched.

"Well, in my hand I have the winner of this award, but first . . . the nominees." The host stepped to the side, and the room darkened while the giant screen behind him illuminated. Bianca's name ran across the screen in bold white letters while a sizzle reel of her fairly short career played over year-long hit song "Somethin' About You Now." I had ears like everyone else, and it was clear why the song became a smash hit. That wasn't what pissed me off, no.

It was never her. It was the articles and reviews raving about Bianca and how the pint-sized star was on track to pop supremacy. She came into my house with her shoes on and rubbed mud all over my hardwood floors whether she knew it or not, and because of that I did whatever it took to beat her.

Another three videos started, one for NF1, a one-hit-wonder boy band that no one would remember in a year. The second was for Jessie Mendes, who Saint notoriously hated and felt stole his name despite the spelling being slightly different. I always assumed it was his version of ignoring he had a crush on the six-three guitar player with dark hair, but he had enough people on his roster for me not to push the topic.

Then came Wishbone, a country singer who a lot of people cared about because he was one of the most accomplished black artists in the space. It would have been an honor to lose to him.

My reel came last, and those big three letters appeared on the screen one by one. The crowd cheered a little louder, some people clapped a little heavier. Taurus rubbed my thigh, and I couldn't help but wonder if he was looking to see if the gun was still somehow attached to me. My heartbeat accelerated, and I couldn't tell if it was the accumulation of everything that had happened or nerves. Thoughts of losing despite what I had gone through crept into my mind and refused to leave.

Then unlike the others, the instrumental to "No Tears" completely stopped, and the auditorium was quiet. The screen turned grainy, and a video of me as a kid materialized. I was maybe five or six, with my shoes off and my toes deep in the dirt while I stood behind my grandparents' house in Mexico City. My mom only let us visit once, and I always thought it was so she could prove to them she was doing something with her life in America. My hair was everywhere, black strands blowing in the wind as I squinted up at the camera.

"*Que quieres ser cuando seas grande?*" *What do you want to be when you grow up?* It echoed throughout the stadium with small white captions printed at the bottom.

"Mmm . . ." the smaller version of me started, pressing my lips together until the dimple on my right cheek showed. "*Cantar y bailar como Selena.*" *Sing and dance like Selena.* The crowd laughed, but I couldn't move as I watched a girl who looked exactly like Josefina shimmy in place. "*Seré una gran estrella y te ayudaré a ti, a mi abuela y a todos en el mundo!*" I was going to be a big star, and I was going to help my grandparents and—the whole world. The audience loved that by the way they muttered their aws and ohs. Someone reached over to touch my shoulder, but I remained as still as a statue.

The lights came back on, and the video faded. "Now that's a kid who could predict the future." The host introduced himself back to center stage, but this time he wasn't alone. "Presenting this award with me is a showstopper and icon herself, Nila Arora. And if you haven't caught on already . . . the winner for Song of the Year is— Aly."

"Come get your award, songbird!" Nila screamed as she held the golden star in her hand.

I released every grip I had of Taurus and rose to my feet with a quickness. The crowd roared, and their claps felt like thunder.

Even though I was smiling and blowing kisses to people whose faces were only blurs, my sights were set on that award. I hiked my dress up and walked past Bianca and her team to head up the small four steps onto the stage. The orchestra several feet away from me began to play a crescendo so beautiful that it made my heart beat a million miles a minute. Violins fit for an opera performance ushered me to center stage where the host and Nila stood.

Her eyes sparkled as she smiled at me like a proud mother, a reaction I only had space in my heart for from Nova. I swallowed hard and reached for the award. When it rested in my hands, it was nothing like I ever imagined. The gold on the star was still cold to the touch, and the black base had my name printed onto a golden plaque. I could only bask in it for a moment before stepping to the microphone and staring at the hundreds of people who were seated below me and envisioning the millions who were watching.

My eyes avoided Bianca's poker face. She was clapping, but I could tell that behind her eyes was a regret that I'd never know.

I held the award close to my chest, letting the gold cool the heat of my overactive heart. "This . . . I can't believe this," I stuttered into the mic. "I know I have a million people to thank . . ." My voice trailed off as my eyes landed on the empty seat next to mine. "I want to take a moment to thank my manager, Nova, who—couldn't be here tonight, but I know if she was up to it she would have. It was all we talked about since the beginning of time. Well, that and her telling me to get my act together." The crowd laughed but I couldn't. "So, this award is for her and everyone who has been with me during this roller coaster of an experience. In a little over a year I went from terrified to—more terrified—to knowing that I could do it and doing the damn thing." The crowd laughed.

"I wouldn't have had half of the confidence I have now if it wasn't for her, Taurus, Saint, Yessenia, Savannah, my little sister, Josefina, and of course my fans. There's just truly nothing good in life if you aren't going through it with a heart in overdrive, so thank you for helping me conquer the greatest fear I ever fucking had—love. Because without love I wouldn't be standing here, so thank you because of your love—my fans' love—I'm no longer afraid of anything. I'm a fucking rockstar, baby!"

EXCLUSIVE:
SUPERSTAR ALY'S MANAGER PRONOUNCED DEAD DUE TO PNEUMONIA COMPLICATIONS

12:20 PM PT - Only a few days shy of Aly's big Starlight Awards win, her manager Nova Valdez was noticeably absent from any pre-award events and appearances. It was later revealed that she had come down with pneumonia, and three days later, the Hollywood mogul had been pronounced dead due to complications.

We have yet to receive comments from Nova's family, Aly, or her team.

Comments

mimilopez3: this is so heartbreaking for aly :((((

angellovesmusic: i smell a setup lol

crybaby707: maybe the fame vampire was her trying to tell us something because why does death follow her wherever she goes

colorsreneww: replied to @angellovesmusic if she has to sacrifice people to keep getting these number ones, taurus better be next, #1 world tour, lead in a blockbuster hit, songwriter hall of fame here we come!

THE LAST ACT

THE FIRST TIME I got married it was a shitty Vegas wedding that we got annulled a few weeks later. I never had the heart to tell anyone, though. Plus, we stayed together long after and loved the attention . . . It became a secret between us and our accountants.

Here I was, yet again proving that I wasn't the woman deserving of a public ceremony with doves that's sponsored by designers and magazine publications. Instead, I was peeling myself off the bathroom floor because I had to face a mistake that I couldn't undo.

Over the last few weeks, the heaviness of what I had become crashed into me like a wrecking ball. I was fighting to keep vomit down some days and dizzy and stumbling through the night. Nova, Antonio, my mother, Nova's daughters, Josefina, Taurus keeping his distance, taking an award that Bianca went as far as she could for . . . The beauty I was promised under the grief and shame was yet to be found.

I was so fucking desperate to catch my own breath. But Andrés only gave me fourteen days before it was time to take my title. The title that Nila had wasted no time coming over every day to prepare me for. No one had said it, but I knew that she was grooming me for the throne.

It was happening no matter how many hours I spent in bed staring at the award that was put in a glass case on the other side of the room.

Was it all worth it?

At dawn, the entire house was emptied and only a driver and Josefina's nanny waited for me at the front door. I held my breath and grabbed her hand softly. Feeling her soft palm against mine and the warm energy between us reminded me—even for a moment—that I had my reasons. It wasn't only about me anymore.

I made it halfway out the door before looking back once more to make sure that Taurus wasn't trailing behind me. He wasn't there, and I couldn't blame him, yet I waited. I waited for what felt like an eternity until the driver spoke a subtle, "Ma'am?"

I dragged my feet to the car while Josefina skipped, her unassuming spirit causing the knife in my heart to twist forty-five more degrees. She deserved so much more than what I was willing to give, and maybe one day she'd understand why I made the choices that I did.

It was never the fear of fading to nothing that lit the match in my body that so many tried to blow out time and time again. It was the fear of being trapped again.

Whether it was under the knowing that my mother was always right or between the teeth of critics who could one day get so close to me that their punches became headshots.

I was always scared of one thing and one thing only—being someone else's fucking victim.

When we entered the Elite Order's castle, several women met us at the door. Their hair was tied in the same low ponytail, and they wore matching black satin slips. A few of them took Josefina and reassured me that she would be fine. I trusted them, knowing that I was already in a position of power far greater than what I could even understand.

Three of the remaining women escorted me back down to the basement where Nila had revealed herself, except when they opened the door at the very end of the hallway, I was introduced to a room truly made for a queen.

A bed that could fit me and everyone I knew was the first piece of furniture I noticed. It had sheer cream drapes hanging from the bedframe and ten or so pillows wrapped in satin oak-and-espresso-colored pillowcases. There was also a mini bar and fridge, which forced my gaze to the long coffee table that had a fruit-and-cheese spread laid out. A full-body mirror was placed next to the open closet that had several garments, but the black sleeveless gown that was placed in the center kept my attention.

The 808s thumping in my chest didn't calm when the mindless version of myself was poked, prodded, and stuffed into the gown. They slipped lace gloves that reached my elbows on my hands and arms. I found it hard to move through the storm cloud I called my sadness, so the women tag-teamed my hair and makeup as I sat at the edge of the bed. When it was all said and done, a coal-colored veil was placed over my slick bun and covered my face just enough to hide the shame that was written all over my features.

"You look stunning." Saint spoke from behind me as he closed the door behind him. I hadn't heard him enter or any of the girls leave—but I was so glad that they did.

"I feel like a fucking nightmare," I said honestly as I stared at myself in the mermaid gown.

Saint threw himself on the bed in spite of his freshly pressed tux and propped his body up on his elbow. I watched his green eyes through the mirror reflection—distracting me from rubbing against the embroidered leaves around my bust and waist and snagging my gloves.

Saint smirked. "Best damn nightmare I've ever seen. I believe they call those . . . dreams?"

I pouted in the mirror. "Must be your dream because it's not mine."

"Come on, give the people a smile!" He cupped his hands around his mouth and roared like a crowd. "We're cheering for you!"

I lifted my dress slightly so that I could turn and face him. "There's nothing to smile about, Saint. Knock it out."

Saint sighed and sat up on the bed. "None of us knew Antonio would pull that . . . You couldn't have predicted it. Andrés couldn't have either."

"But he did. And now, like my almost-new husband's mother—she's gone. Buried, six feet fucking under and everyone—her children are going to live the rest of their lives thinking she was sick. Now that—that's a joke." I scoffed and inhaled deeply so that whatever tears that even thought about showing themselves would second-guess that decision.

He nodded, and I could see him biting the inside of his cheek. Like everyone else, he was tiptoeing around the topic with me, and like I did with everyone else—I bottled it back up.

"Are you ready?" He finally spoke.

"Fuck if I know," I said in a defeated shrug. "Damned if I do, damned if I don't. I could get over it all, you know? I always do. But I can't shake this feeling of being so—"

"Selfish?" He completed my sentence for me and scoffed. The male rose from the bed and made his way over to me. "There are worse people to be in this world, *mi amor*. I don't believe you're one of those people. No, there are awful people with far more power. On the other hand . . . There are millions of others all over the world who would kill to be right where you're standing—you're just the only one who has."

I stared at my reflection in the mirror, and the woman I had become stared back. "Does that make me a shitty person? That I wanted to be a part of something so sick and twisted up until they took something from me? I didn't care when it was Bianca—I . . . I still wanted to take everything from her. But it was all so much more beautiful before all those monsters finally found me."

His gaze went blank before looking back up at me. "I think I'm the wrong person to ask. But if you want my opinion . . . no. It makes you someone willing to take an opportunity. That's always been who you are, and he knows that . . . That's why he chose you. Life is fucking hard, Alejandra. We do what we need to do because we have to, not because we want to. What you did is not who you are. What you've been through is not who you are. Who you choose to be right now is who you are." He placed his hands on my shoulders and spun me back to the mirror.

"So who are you? Because we've all lost things, we've all messed up . . . But who do you want to be?"

The question danced around my head for longer than I intended. But when I looked at myself again, I saw her.

I saw dark eyes that hid not only a boatload of trauma, but also a lot of fucking power that she was only just now learning how to wield. I saw heartbreak and new possibilities all at once—I saw a beautiful mixture of all three of us. Aly, Lilith, and Alejandra.

All together we were the only love and acceptance we ever needed.

We embraced never being Eve, expressing our emotions as violently as we pleased. We were sin incarnate and burned brighter than the fires that attempted to engulf us. Together I saw an ability to mourn every mother I had ever known while taking care of the innocent and giving her the experiences we never had.

I didn't see a woman forced into marriage. I saw a man so consumed by such a complex woman that he used every tool in his power to give her all he had to offer. And for the years that came after, he'd learn to follow her lead and leave her with enough breathing room to feel real love. Because she was going to have Taurus if it was the last thing she did.

"I want to be Alejandra." I finally said.

Saint's green eyes lit up like a firework show. "I like that. The most beautiful thing a person can do for themselves is to let their ghosts in instead of giving them up."

"You sound familiar with the process."

"I know enough," he said with a sly smile before the door swung open again.

Camila entered dressed in an oversized suit. Her dress shirt alone looked like it was ripped straight out of Andrés's closet and placed on her smaller frame. That was the first time I had seen her under normal light. She didn't look as terrifying as she was described.

Still, Saint parted from me.

"Camila," Saint said, but the heat in his voice had dissipated.

The copper-haired woman smiled and leaned against the dresser, her eyes devouring me with a single look. "Just getting a look at who my brother chose."

I pivoted on my heels to fully face her. "Oh?"

Camila nodded. "You killed my father. I mean, I was thinking . . . Wow. She has to be backing out now because she has done effortlessly what I had to convince Andrés to. That has to fuck you up, right? Do something crazy to that fragile psyche of yours and yet . . . here you are. Ready to spill blood."

I swallowed my insecurity and learned fear of her. "Careful, Camila, if you stare any harder I'd think you would prefer I was vowing myself to you instead."

The woman's lips flinched, and I swore she was about to smile. "If that was the case my brother would be dead already." She stepped closer to me, and I felt Saint stop breathing.

I kept my cool and watched as her manicured nails brushed along the lace of my veil. "A true black-veiled bride," she whispered, and this time she actually did smile. "Lucky for you both, him in that seat is exactly what I want." The woman paused, and her breath steadied—I wondered if she could hear my heart beating against my chest. "We've only just gotten started. You are where it all begins."

Camila's words ran circles in my head as I waited alone for someone to collect me from the room in the basement. I hated the part of me that watched the door in case Taurus would show.

I would be lying if I said there wasn't a gnawing at my core that whispered, "Protect him."

If it was truly only the beginning, no one was safe until I wielded the power. But they already knew it was no longer fun when the rabbit got the gun.

My only visitors after Camila were the women who were sent to fetch me. They presented me with two roses, and I held them close as I walked through the castle.

Unlike the flowers in my hands, the backyard was decorated with a blanket of white and black ones. There were chairs for the few guests and additional members who would be joining us. Josefina sat happily in one. The knife in my chest turned once again when I realized the gravity of what I could be exposing her to.

It was better that way.

I would rather her be as close as possible than out of my sight for another moment longer. Andrés stood tall at the other end of the garden in a black suit surrounded by a circle of lit candles where the only opening was where I was being led to. Eagle-masked figures hovered outside of the circle—specifically behind him. He warned me that this was as equally his inauguration as it was a wedding—and he was right.

Instead of a council of four, there were nine who wore ceremonial blue robes with red rubies embroidered along the sleeves and neckline. The woman in particular, whose slender frame I recognized by now to be Nila, was holding a glass of . . .

Wine?

They whispered long sentences in Andrés's ear. My escort abruptly stopped, leaving me in the center of the garden . . . Only a few steps off of the path that led to him.

"Come on," Julian whispered in lieu of a proper greeting. I hadn't noticed him getting up from where he was seated with his siblings or that his hand was out to grab mine. I nodded at the quiet brother, and my heart calmed as his soft brown eyes made me feel safe again. He didn't say a word the entire time he walked me to the entrance of the circle, but a pure warmth radiated from him that I only ever recognized from Josefina and Nova.

Andrés's face remained unmoved, but his hand reached out for mine. Despite how utterly fucking creepy all of this was—it had promise.

I had to believe that, and whether it was a delusion or not, it was the only truth that helped me put my hand out to meet his. For the first time in my life . . . I could be fulfilled. Or it could kill me—but at least I tried.

And I had come too fucking far to quit now.

The group dispersed from behind him and began to slowly surround us, standing behind one candle each. Nila handed the glass of red liquid to him, and he released my hand to put the glass to his lips and chug until it was gone. That was when I noticed that the liquid was thick and from the look on his face—utterly disgusting.

"You have consumed the one before you." The masked man spoke softly before waving over to Camila, who had another ceremonial robe in her hand. Romeo quickly got up to grab the glass out of Andrés's hand while Camila slid the robe onto his shoulders, and all I could do was blink as the remainder of the liquid spilled from his lips and onto the black roses by his feet. The robe created a silhouette of his body that was so strong that a fire in my head had been set just from the sight of him. I was disturbed, terrified, and utterly exhausted. But in the midst of it all, there were sparks of excitement that I was too embarrassed to acknowledge.

You have consumed . . . Was that his fucking father's blood?

I was going to be fucking sick.

With every passing second I was at war with myself. And as the sun rose to the highest point in the sky, it felt like someone had pressed a blade against my throat, and the one person whose eyes brought me back down the earth wasn't here.

So instead I choked.

I let color infuse my cheeks when Andrés's hungry orbs met mine for a mere second. *Thank God for the veil.*

"*Ay dios mio . . .*" I whispered to myself but kept my composure.

"Now for the union," Nila said loudly, no longer using the false accent that disguised her identity.

The siblings, who were still standing, took calm steps back to their seats. Camila led the group with Romeo keeping closely behind while Julian trailed pretty far behind them both. I watched as Nila separated herself from her post and entered the circle of red embers and melted wax that we were trapped in. My skin crawled, but I didn't flinch despite my feet wanting to move as far away from her as humanly possible.

She leaned in, her breath causing the hairs on my neck to rise. "Welcome." Before I could break myself out of the trance, she had grabbed my flowers, pulled one of my gloves off, and met the palm of my hands with a blade so sharp I was sure that simply looking at it would draw blood. I didn't flinch or pull my limbs back—there were so many eyes on me that it no longer felt like something sacred—it was merely another performance.

She maintained a straight line as she pressed down and sliced my palm open until the bright red liquid started to spill. I blocked out the onlookers and hoped that Saint was distracting Josefina. She closed my fist, and I watched as the blood dripped into a small silver dish she balanced in between her fingers along with the rose stems. Not a single drop escaped onto the grass or even the side of the dish—nothing was wasted.

Within a few blinks, she had left me, and my hand was quickly bandaged before my glove was reapplied delicately. It was only when her shadow left my aura that I noticed another one of them had been draining Andrés as well. I could tell we both knew what was coming next, but I was the only one with worry in my eyes.

The leader standing directly behind my almost-husband poured both blood mixtures into a single glass with such ease and experience.

I couldn't focus on that when every time my gaze fell on Andrés . . . he didn't seem real. He was stoic as he stared beyond me. All I could look at was him in front of me, but his gaze was fixed like there was a movie playing behind me that only he could see.

I swore I caught his coffee-colored eyes sparkling with hints of green before they were filled with darkness once again. With a chin held high and his hands clasped together at his groin, I knew he had been waiting for this his entire life. To avenge his mother, get rid of his father, and be the one who took care of his siblings despite how chaotic they might have been.

Did he care that I took the chance away from him to do it himself?

"Join hands," one of the leaders announced.

He reached for my hands before I could even contemplate handing mine over first. Despite the way my heart ached, I felt it flutter when we touched.

Hell no.

Well . . . Could he really be that awful? Maybe I could learn . . . Or we both could—to tolerate each other.

It couldn't be that hard if I could crack his shell and make my way to the center.

Andrés was a quiet storm with the ability to knock my walls down and rip my home off of its foundation if I allowed it. But I could never think about him without thinking about Taurus, the man who could build a house from a broken home with his bare hands.

If only I kept him.

Another name to add to the graveyard of people I once knew. I would swallow it, like I always did, but I'd dream about him until he no longer consumed my ever-waking days.

Time and time again I ripped myself apart for the sake of entertainment, before anyone else could even think about it, until there was nothing left but hollow bones and stories that could only be found woven in songs.

I was a time bomb, and Andrés was too. Together we were a national fucking disaster.

"Repeat after me. I offer my soul and being."

"I offer my soul and being."

"To the shadows and the blood of those who have sacrificed before me. I vow to only serve my society, for my soul belongs to it and the secret schools of wisdom." The leader paused, swirling the blood in the glass with the knife. He cupped Andrés's chin so that we didn't have to let go and poured a few drops of it down his throat. But when his gloved hand touched my veil and revealed my face for the first time—a shiver ran down my spine. He cupped my chin, and I opened my glossed lips to allow the metallic taste to snake past my teeth and down my throat.

"Repeat. And with this blood I drink, I bind myself to my partner. Never to stray. Never to put another in their place. Never to show disloyalty, and to stand by our leader with undoubting faith."

". . . With undoubting faith," we said in unison. And when we did, every member slowly removed their masks, dropping them onto the floor and causing a gasp to release from my lips when I realized who they all were.

"Come tomorrow, neither of you will ever feel pain again. You have paid the price with your most precious gift—your lives. To show our gratitude and usher in our new council member, Andrés Espósito, and his counterpart Alejandra Espósito, the Order will not only reward you but mold you both into untouchable figures. You'll no longer be picked like the roses that surround you; instead, you'll live like gods and glow brighter and longer than the lights in Times Square, under one condition—you never mishandle your power. With that, we welcome you with the utmost glory to the Elite Order."

No one seemed to mind my desire to stay in the garden after Josefina was confirmed to be put to bed in one of the rooms and the candles had been blown out. I let the quiet moment on the hill settle in and wash over me. The darkness became real once the garden had been emptied and only I was left in the silence.

In a way, I had what I wanted.

I had the castle on the hill, the award, and the admiration. For fuck's sake, I was the queen no matter what room I stood in now.

No. From this high up I was an eternal being.

The religion I grew up to know only made me feel shame and despair—but I grew into a position where taking what you wanted only made you look stronger. And if I looked down long enough I could see a little girl who wanted nothing more than to be up here too—like I once did.

But Camila was right, this wasn't the end of anything for me. I wasn't back where I started. I didn't feel the weight of isolation that drove me to drink, and I wasn't filling empty spaces with people who meant nothing to me.

No.

Because despite everything that I had lost . . . and everyone, I still had the option to pick up my phone and within an hour be surrounded by love of every kind.

Sexual, platonic, manic, familial . . . self.

That was what made me the most powerful woman in the fucking world. So why was I still scared?

"Don't tell me you're sitting out here frowning." Taurus's voice echoed throughout the estate, and it caused my muscles to tense.

Was I imagining it? Had I gone insane?

I tore the veil off and held it tightly in my hands, slightly wincing at the tender flesh that hadn't stopped throbbing. My head turned over my shoulder before I could stop myself, and there he was.

I scrambled to my feet. As if he teleported, he was suddenly close enough to hold on to my arm and help me up.

"How—why—who let you in?" I hid the relief in my eyes by focusing my vision on the arm that he held, but my somber tone was telling.

He shrugged and released his grip. "Turns out your new husband thought you could use a friendly face."

I rolled my eyes and stumbled back a step or two. "Josefina and Saint were here. Plus, I can go pet my cat whenever I'm ready. I'm just fine."

"Oh!" He pointed his thumb toward the door behind us. "I can see myself right out, then. I'm a very busy man."

"Oh yeah? Doing what?" My lips curved into a smile, and my eyelashes fluttered against my lids.

A dimple appeared next to his lip as he showcased an award-winning toothy grin. "Watering my plants."

"You've taken up gardening?"

He snickered. "My parents are farmers, you know."

My smile faltered and my brows furrowed. "No. I didn't know. I guess I didn't know much of anything. I never asked."

Taurus's kind eyes were filled with forgiveness, and behind them I could see a flicker of desire that still lingered.

He stuffed his hands in his oversized jean pockets and took another step closer. I allowed it because if he wasn't completely over me, then I hadn't been destroyed as much as I thought.

I was a loaded gun, and he knew it—but he wanted it. No matter how moral he tried to be, he stayed with Andrés until he had no other choice. No matter how angry he had to be, he still wanted to comfort me.

"What made you want to come?" I finally uttered to distract myself from the electrical pull that was occurring between us.

"You are an epiphany, Alejandra. And while I won't always understand what makes you tick or why you do the shit you do . . . I know you're far more than your shortcomings and the sides of you that you're ashamed of. You're a woman worth standing on the frontlines for. And I only have you to thank for helping me realize that there's a fight worth fighting. You're beautiful, talented, fiery, and true to yourself whether it's wrong or right. I wanna live where all your favorite things are in your head. The songs, the melodies, and the poetry. That's where I want to be. You hear me?"

The man who would die a superstar looked down on me with an openness that I had never experienced before. My eyes traveled from his lips to his exposed biceps (thanks to the wife-beater he was wearing), and returned to his eyes. I felt like the stars were finally aligning in my favor for once, and even though in his grasp I felt perfectly at center—a looming gray cloud that came with an itch that desperately needed to be scratched. The birds sang in the background, and the squirrels rustled through the hedges and trees while bugs buzzed past our ears. There wasn't a single soul out to stop us.

"Shut up and kiss me, for Christ's sake."

And he did. Not tenderly or with hesitation, but with control and domination. And once I had a taste, it proved not to be enough. Our breath mingled, and the smoke that had consumed my lungs was replaced with fresh air for the first time in months. My lips chased his like I was born to bleed out for my entire life and someone had finally come along and put pressure on the wound. It was equally terrifying as it was exhilarating. Even with my eyes closed, I was staring at the tip of his blade and forcing it into my chest like it was the only way to bring me back to life.

I was reeling him in as my gloved hands traveled from his waist to the back of his head, and he did the same—stealing the fear that consumed me and replacing it with adrenaline as his strong body pressed against mine. I craved it, and I was no longer wading at the deep end, I was drowning.

The kiss. The moment. It was the only thing that mattered. It was the only thing capable of quieting my wrenching heart.

We held each other so tightly that our body heat created a shield over us for the future that someone else had already mapped out for us.

Because whatever it was . . . it was coming soon.

EPILOGUE
Andrés

"WHAT HAPPENED NEXT?" JOSEFINA asked eagerly, tugging at the pages of the book that I was cursed with the task of reading her during soundcheck.

Alejandra had come into my life and derailed my plans without mercy. She was taking me for a joyride, and hell no, I didn't mind it. There wasn't a woman I had met before who matched my mind the way she did, and maybe even surpassed it.

There was a time when she was a means to an end, but the more time I had with her, the more I was forced to respect everything about her.

What she didn't know was I watched that girl enter the industry and turn the world on its head with a halo over her own. But as time went on, the halo had broken and formed horns—horns that I had put the finishing touches on.

"Well," I started plainly, looking up at the crew members who were running back and forth to make sure Alejandra was happy with the strobe lights or fog machine or whatever she was being so particular with that they were dripping in sweat and tripping over untied laces. "They lived happily ever after."

A fucking lie.

I remembered watching her mull over every part of this show. I didn't care to pay attention in the beginning, but I underestimated the way she would pull me in anyway. There were nights I came trekking in, and she was nursing a migraine over the coffee table with scattered pages of a story she had written that she wanted so desperately to convey.

She trusted that I didn't care enough to worry about what she was up to—especially since the man she confided in was my ex. So, she often left the pages around the house when she was frustrated enough to give up and head to bed. It took about seven nights of me walking past them before I finally got curious to look. I'd never let her catch me, so I took photos of the story instead.

Josefina tugged my sleeve. "Boring!" she sang in a teasing tone.

I couldn't even think about a reply before the stage went black, and Alejandra strutted past us without even turning her head. She was focused on the crowd that was already going wild before even seeing her.

She wore a black cloak (a little on the nose if you ask me) and charcoal eyeshadow that stood out from the makeup-free face that I had grown accustomed to over the last few weeks.

I grabbed Josefina's hand and took her to the balcony that had been closed off from guests to keep the show as intimate as possible.

It was a small venue that held maybe a thousand people, and she wanted to give them a show fit for Madison

Square Garden. Her new manager agreed with me, and a compromise was reached—if she wanted to do a show in Carson City for the sake of nostalgia, it would be broadcast.

The stage turned red, and fog rose as she appeared in center stage. Her silhouette was small but commanding. The crowd's roaring only ignited with every step she took. Violins swelled and crescendos bubbled. I was starting to remember who the superstar was that I made mine.

Before any lights came on, the screen behind her illuminated, and a darker silhouette appeared that had to be about ten feet tall. The face was blacked out, but the wings and horns were clear as day.

Josefina clung to my leg out of fear, and I begrudgingly placed a hand on her shoulder.

The piano joined the violin and played a daunting theme that counted in every step forward that Alejandra took. A single spotlight finally appeared, and she ripped off the cloak and revealed a short black corset and tights.

"The castle's crumbling soft and slow, the bones I buried they'll never know. I'm the God they worship . . ." Alejandra began to sing.

The choir behind her sang softly, "Soft and slow."

"They've all bought tickets to see the show."

And then silence.

She commanded the stage with ease, and the crowd immediately burst out with claps and cheers as she stood there—taking it in and making being five feet tall look massive.

I couldn't take my eyes off the figure on the screen behind her whose face was now illuminated. At some point she recorded herself in a gown with dark makeup and bleached eyebrows. Someone had put the horns on her and attached the wings to play the part of this demon looming over her.

I didn't have to ask where it came from, though. All I had to do was pull out my phone and finish the story.

After many years, Lilith managed to rebuild the kingdom in her image. The great massacre was an event only she could remember. Her subjects worshiped her and never knew that she was capable of monstrous acts such as ending the life of another.

Yet every time Lilith looked in the mirror, she saw a girl who could have been her, but she was more sinister and demonic. Black ash was smudged along her face, and her eyes held the heat of a thousand volcanoes. Oftentimes she'd whisper that if Lilith let her out again, she'd consume her new kingdom like a bear would a honeycomb. But the queen never listened. She'd learned her lesson the first time.

Then one day the demon in the mirror came with another proposition, eternal life. What were a few sacrifices to immortality?

Greed was one of the deadly sins, and Lilith embodied them all. She wasn't happy with knowing she'd eventually meet the same fate as her enemies and knew that the demon who she had let in all those years ago would give her everything she ever dreamed of and more. "I deserve to live forever!" she'd scream into the black for years, only to be met with no response.

So, Lilith let the demon have whatever she desired so that she'd be granted one more wish. Within days she witnessed enough bloodshed to fill the Nile River and cried enough tears to turn it from red back to clear. Furthermore, she crossed paths with a prince she couldn't have and was instead forced to a man who was as hard as the statues they made for him in order to remain at peace with the neighboring kingdom.

That was the price she paid to be immortal.

Once again, she had gotten what she wanted . . . Everything down to the riches, the title that came with the tainted crown, and the moat that protected the castle. She had the stoic king by her side and an orphan girl whom she'd raise to be the fairest in the land.

However, they all began to die. One by one everyone she had come to adore had passed on. From the animals to the aging townsfolk. Even the king and the prince from another land who had only been able to hold her in the dark through ink-filled letters.

Lilith was granted eternal life! Just as she asked!

Over time her heart hardened, and she refused to let anyone else in. And without fail, she visited their graves every day and would return to her bedroom where she'd stop at the mirror and visit the only company she had left.

And no one lived happily ever after.

My phone buzzed, and a notification dropped down that forced me to close out the story and open a new tab.

Camila:

> **You know what we need to do next.**

Want to stay in the Hollywood loop?

goddessabrouette.com

Find out what they're saying about your favorite stars.

www.ingramcontent.com/pod-product-compliance
Lightning Source LLC
Chambersburg PA
CBHW032151190726
48290CB00005BB/1515